I0637695

The Jilted Lovers Club

Lahoma Springs
Book 1

Crissi Langwell

Cover & Interior Design: Crissi Langwell
Cover Image: Igor Borodin
Inside Images: Canva (SmmrDesign, thipftisland, anawill)

First line of Epilogue (page 335) credited to
Charlotte Brontë in her novel Jane Eyre.

ISBN: 978-1-961240-07-0

Publisher: North Coast Stories
This book is also available in ebook.
Please visit the author's website to find out where to purchase this book.

www.crissilangwell.com

NORTH COAST
STORIES

And the day came when the risk to remain tight in a
bud was more painful than the risk it took to blossom."
~ Anaïs Nin

Books by Crissi Langwell

ROMANCE

The Jilted Lovers Club ~ Lahoma Springs 1

Masquerade Mistake ~ Sunset Bay 1

Naked Coffee Guy ~ Sunset Bay 2

Savior Complex ~ Sunset Bay 3

For the Birds

Numbered

OTHER BOOKS BY CRISSI LANGWELL

Loving the Wind: The Story of Tiger Lily & Peter Pan

The Road to Hope ~ Hope Series 1

Hope at the Crossroads ~ Hope Series 2

Hope for the Broken Girl ~ Hope Series 3

A Symphony of Cicadas ~ Forever After 1

Forever Thirteen ~ Forever After 2

www.crissilangwell.com

Sign up for Crissi Langwell's romance newsletter:
crissilangwell.com/subscribe

For every woman who made herself smaller
to fit into someone else's story—
may you take up all the space you were born to own.

The Jilted Playlist

Ghosts That We Knew ~ Mumford & Sons
rain ~ mxmtoon
Redemption ~ Nathaniel Rateliff
Wake Up, Breathe In ~ Laura Lucas
Born & Raised ~ John Mayer
This Feeling ~ Alabama Shakes
28 ~ Zach Bryan
Re: Stacks ~ Bon Iver
Feels Like ~ Gracie Abrams
River ~ Leon Bridges
Everywhere, Everything ~ Noah Kahan
Angel By The Wings ~ Sia
Phonetically ~ Hailaker, Lowsimmer, Jemima Coulter
Stubborn Love ~ The Lumineers
Open ~ Hunter Metts
Starting Over ~ Chris Stapleton
Ends of the Earth ~ Lord Huron

View full playlist at
crissilangwell.com/lahoma-springs/the-jilted-lovers-club

Chapters

Trigger Warning:

While *The Jilted Lovers Club* is full of steamy romance, small-town charm, and second chances, it also touches on some deeper topics—including conversations about pregnancy loss and complicated, toxic family dynamics. If those are tender spots for you, please take care as you read.

A Note for Readers

This isn't the first time I've written about the main characters in *The Jilted Lovers Club*. Jordy Gallo made her debut in *Savior Complex* (Book 3 of the *Sunset Bay* series), and Ashton Elliot was first introduced in *Hope for the Broken Girl* (Book 3 of the *Hope* series).

You absolutely don't need to read those books to enjoy this one, but if you're curious about where Jordy and Ashton got their start, those earlier stories are where their journeys began.

To avoid spoilers, a complete Lahoma Springs character list (so far) is located at the back of the book.

Lahoma Aroma

Jordy

The moment I pass the Lahoma Springs city limits sign, the air hits me—rotten, putrid, like the stench of decaying animal or a festering festival outhouse. It's strong enough to make me think there's something wrong with the car, and I'm afraid to find out what. I mean, did the rental company leave something in the trunk? We'd done the standard inspection. I'd checked every inch of this Lexus, scanning for scratches and dings and taking pictures of anything suspicious. But apparently in my fastidious scrutiny of this SUV, I failed to notice whatever was emanating from the vents, the floorboards, or the leather seats, which is getting stronger by the moment as I approach my exit for downtown Lahoma Springs.

The town is everything my New York neighborhood is not. Craftsman houses with river rock chimneys, cobblestone pathways, and white picket fences. A green copper drawbridge over a lazy river, and kayakers drifting downstream. Trees that make up the center divider and bike paths on every goddamn road. Drivers slowing to allow other cars to merge in or to just wave at someone on the street. And a banner over the main street, inviting the town to a gazebo dedication in the town square.

My god, this place is basic.

Alexander Winslow, my boss, had described the building I'm driving toward as a huge, historic bank, originally called The Till. The place sold seeds of all kinds, which seems like a strange use of such a large space.

The Till isn't the only historic building, I realize as I approach the downtown area. New York has its fair share of historic districts, but apparently Lahoma Springs does too. Lining the downtown streets are looming stone buildings in earthy-toned colors, each with long, arched windows, decorative framing, and ornate cornices crowning the top of the structure. The details are intricate and impressive, almost like they're telling the story of what the town used to be. For a moment, I forget my earlier thought at how basic this town is as I take in the beauty of the architecture.

Maybe I have the heart of a small-town girl, after all. Maybe there are some added benefits to this design job.

I glance at the GPS, but the map disappears in favor of my cousin's face. Nina calls me at least once a week. She's always the one who calls and doesn't seem to notice that I don't. Don't get me wrong, I love my cousin—but in small doses. This might have to do with the fact that she's married to Brayden, my ex-fiancé.

Long story. Someone should write a book about it.

Honestly, though, that isn't the reason. The real reason is because all Nina wants to talk about is their daughter, and I'm just not into babies—especially ones with Brayden's eyes. But if I don't answer, she'll just call again in an hour. And an hour after that. And keep calling until I finally cave.

Sighing, I answer the phone.

"You'll never believe what Juniper did," Nina squeals, not even waiting for me to say hello. "Watch this."

My phone starts pinging, requesting to accept her Facetime Call.

"I'm driving," I mutter, but I pull into a parking spot near the sidewalk and press *accept* anyway. Immediately the video screen in the car is filled with my niece, who, by the way, is probably the cutest baby I've ever seen. Still not a fan, but cute.

"Juniper," Nina calls off screen. But June is fascinated with the phone, her little hands covering the camera as she tries to grab it. "Juniper, look at Mommy. Juniper."

"Nina, I'm on the job right now. Can we talk later?" I actually have no concrete schedule for today. All I have to do is scope out the bank location and check into my hotel, maybe get acquainted with my surroundings. But honestly, this call is giving me a headache.

"Just a few minutes, please. She did it just a moment ago. She's probably just shy."

No, she is probably just bored, like I am.

"What did she do, exactly?"

Nina turns the phone to herself, her hair a bright purple with white-blonde streaks, and her face a painting of disappointment. "She turns when I say her name. She knows her name!"

"Are you sure she doesn't just know your voice? Nice hair, by the way. Purple suits you."

She grins, flipping her hair. "I was getting tired of the pink and thought I'd switch it up." Nina had been sporting pink hair ever since the baby was born, as she'd held off on dyeing it while she was pregnant. It was the longest I'd seen her with natural hair, which is a pretty blonde color. But I can't help thinking the purple is a nice touch. "I swear to you, Juniper is really smart. Oh! See?" Nina switches the phone back to the baby, who is now looking at me through the screen.

"Hi baby," I say as Nina continues to coax her in the background. Juniper blows bubbles before smacking her lips.

"She's probably just tired from all this cleverness, aren't you Juney Joo," Nina coos.

"No, she's probably distracted by your bright, shiny phone. I believe you, though."

Nina turns the camera back to her, her mouth twisted into a pout. "I really wanted you to see it. Where are you anyway?"

I shrug, not wanting to admit I'm in California. Nina lives on a ranch about eight hours south of Lahoma in a beach town called Sunset Bay. It's where I was going to live when… Well, in a past life when I was supposed to marry you-know-who. Living in New York is a relief in so many ways, including the fact that there's an entire country between us. If Nina knows I'm in Lahoma Springs, even if I'm almost five hundred miles north of her, she'll find a way to visit me.

"Nowhere special," I say, looking out the window.

"God, I'm so jealous," she sighs. "You're out there designing all these shops and offices, and I'm here smelling like sour milk, manure, and hay."

If I were paying attention, I'd probably have laughed, correcting her about her ideas of my success. Then I would have told her about this shitty smelling car I'm in. But I'm distracted, realizing I've reached my destination. The Till stands tall on the corner of the street, a majestic building that, with its pillars and arched windows, resembles the classic details of structures in the Italian Renaissance. Its beauty and grandeur takes my breath away.

And so does the crowd picketing outside.

"Hey, I need to go," I say to Nina, then hang up before she can say anything else.

How I missed the protest just across the street is beyond me, but now the sounds of shouting ring through my closed windows.

"Fucking hell," I mutter, then open the car door. I'm immediately met by a warm blast of shit.

No, not literal shit. The smell of shit. And it's everywhere.

The smell I'd noticed before, it wasn't coming from the floorboards. No, this is definitely not a car issue. It's a town issue.

"Oh, my god." I start to close the door, getting ready to drive off again. But I can't. Despite the smell, and despite the modest crowd marching with signs outside of it, I have to get inside that building. This has little to do with my job, and everything to do with needing to see if the inside of that building is as gorgeous as the outside.

Covering my nose, I get out of the car. But my stilettos are not meant for the cobblestone road. I frantically grasp for the car door, but catch air as I pitch forward. That is, until two strong hands grip me under my arms, then hoist me to standing before I can catch my breath.

"Easy there," a deep voice says, and I turn to see my rescuer, all while still covering my nose.

"Thank you." My voice is muffled under my hand. But when I look up, what I really mean is, *thank you, Universe.* Does the Universe even make men this beautiful? Because the man standing in front of me is easily the most magnificent thing I've ever seen. I mean, there's a Neo-Renaissance building across the street—dripping with history, secrets, and who knows what other treasures—and yet this man, with skin the color of burnished bronze, eyes like dark espresso, and a smile so disarming I forget how to speak ... *he's* the architectural masterpiece. Not to mention that I can see the shape of his chiseled chest through his flannel shirt, the thickness of his thighs under his faded blue jeans, and that worn out baseball cap on his head, the brim curved over his brow. The whole look seems to be the standard uniform of well-built cowboys, not to mention my absolute kryptonite. Fuck, I'm a sucker for this look, as much as I hate to admit it. I'd escaped to New York to immerse myself in high fashion and culture. But goddamn, those men in fitted suits have nothing on this country boy.

"I see you've discovered Lahoma Aroma," he says, nodding at me with an amused look on his face as he guides me toward the sidewalk, his hand at my back.

"Lahoma … what?" I grimace. I'm having a hard time looking at him. He's that attractive.

With my hand covering my nose, I'm aware that I look like a fool. Not that it matters, I'm here on business only, not to meet someone—even guys like this one.

"Lahoma Aroma," he repeats, then gestures all around us. "The fields were recently fertilized, and it can get pretty fragrant around here."

I pull my hand away, then wrinkle my nose. "Fragrant? More like rancid. How do you stand it? Your town smells like a giant bathroom."

His smile widens, catching the corners of my heart with it. "When you live in a farming community, you get used to it."

I look him over, partly to get another look, but also as I realize he is probably one of those farmers. "I take it you live on one of the farms here?"

He nods. "Just on the cusp of city limits, all two hundred acres of it blessed with the holy juice to prepare it for the next planting season."

I nod, though I can't hide my disgust. My face has always been a billboard for my thoughts, and judging by the way his eyes dance as he looks me over, he is reading me loud and clear.

"You must be new around here. Or maybe visiting? I'm Ashton." He holds out his hand, and I instinctively take it, then do what I can to hide my reaction at the warmth of his calloused palm curving over my much smaller hand. But I can't keep my mouth from betraying me, breaking into a smile before I can stop it by biting my lower lip. Damn, I like my hand in his. It's like an invitation to see what else fit against him, around him, all over him. There is something about him that feels like home to me, which is so weird and cliché I can't stand it. I've never had this reaction to any guy. I didn't even feel this way about Brayden. But here I am, ogling this familiar stranger

"I'm Jordy, Jordy Gallo. And yeah, I guess you can say that I'm new." I slip my hand from his and nod at the building across the street. "Winslow & Associates, the owners of that building over there, hired me to work on the interior design, but I didn't realize there would be a protest today. Do you know when it will be over so I can go inside?"

Ashton's smile evaporates, and the warmth in his eyes cool to an icy, narrow focus. But then it's gone, and he shakes his head.

"They're there every day," he says, then shrugs. "I imagine when they see progress being made on whatever's going in that spot, the protest will get worse."

"Seriously?"

I look over at the protest, but this time I note the signs they're holding.

"GO HOME BIG BUSINESS."

"KEEP LAHOMA SMALL."

"THIS IS OUR TOWN."

And the funniest one of all: "OUR TOWN SMELLS LIKE POO, BUT YOU STINK MORE."

"Wow, they're a passionate bunch." I turn to Ashton. "I didn't realize this was an issue. Alexander didn't tell me."

Ashton takes a deep breath, stuffing his hands in his pockets. "Yeah, I imagine he's not aware, or even concerned about Lahoma Springs. But why would he be? This is just business." He nods at the building. "As for crossing that picket line? I don't recommend it, not if you want to make friends in this town."

This time, it's my turn to narrow my eyes. I give a short laugh, then smooth my skirt. "I'm not here to make friends, I'm here to do the job I'm being paid to do."

He glances my way again, and this time when he looks me over, I feel his eyes all over my body. I know he's just sizing me up—the enemy, apparently—but damn if I don't feel completely naked under his gaze.

"Got it," he says. Then he touches the brim of his hat and gives a quick nod. "Good luck, Ms. Gallo."

And then Ashton walks away, leaving me to figure out the mess I'm in on my own.

2

Crossing the Picket Line

Jordy

I watch Ashton's retreating back and feel the smallest amount of hesitation as he disappears around the corner. This isn't my fight. I'm not even sure I'd have taken this job if I knew there'd be protests. Did Alexander know about this?

I pull out my phone and tap his number on the screen, then wait for him to answer.

"Hey troublemaker, did you have any issues finding the building?"

I roll my eyes at his nickname. Alexander had invited me along to a few fundraising events and one ritzy date before I started working for him, and while he was a nice guy and had more money than I'd seen in a lifetime, I realized quickly that the chemistry wasn't there. It was entirely apparent that a romantic connection with him would mean he'd be center stage while I served as arm candy, standing by without an opinion while he discussed his art collection, his latest golf game, or how the stock market was doing.

No, thank you.

If my mother knew I'd turned him down, she'd disown me. Growing up, she often told me I could fall in love with a rich man just as easily as a poor one, but I can't pay the bills with a warm heart. I always felt like this was a dig at my father, even though our family was not poor. But she was the one who came into the family with money, not him. We'd had a comfortable lifestyle growing up, but my father and I both knew she wanted more. Which is why I never told her I'd dated a guy like Alexander, and definitely kept it a secret that I'd turned him down.

That said, I know Alexander is still interested, even if he mostly keeps things professional. I want to believe he hired me for my design skill, which I'm quite proud of. He's a businessman first, so I'm sure that was part of his decision to bring me on board as their corporate designer.

But when he calls me nicknames like *troublemaker*, *darling*, *sweetie*, or the like, it's this little reminder of our brief romance, and a hint that he's open to explore it again.

"Alex, we talked about this," I say, biting back a grin. He hates when anyone shortens his name. Sure as shit, he sighs heavily on the other end.

"It's Alexander," he growls.

"And it's Jordy, or it's Ms. Gallo."

"Fine. Ms. Gallo, did you find the establishment, and was it to your liking?"

I can't help laughing at his formal tone, and he gives in with a low chuckle. But then I glance at the protesters, sobering with the dread of dealing with this headache.

"Listen, there are a bunch of townspeople with picket signs in front of the store. What's going on? Did you take this place by force or something? Did you know this was happening?"

"That's odd. No, it was an easy sale, actually. I primarily collaborated with Mr. Elliot, the store manager. But Mr. Felix, the owner, was the one who approached me and signed the documents in the end. There was very little discussion other than they needed to sell quickly." He pauses, then says, "What are they protesting?"

"Something about leaving their small town alone."

He huffs a low laugh. "Small towns are notorious for hating change. I wouldn't put much stock in it. By next week, they'll be onto something new."

It's hardly a comfort. I'm supposed to be here for almost a month, and I need to get to work immediately.

"What do I do in the meantime? I can't just wait them out."

"You'll think of something. You're a smart woman."

This is not the reassurance I need.

"Listen, this is not the job I signed up for. I thought I was going to be focusing on lighting and textiles, not..." I glance at the people circling out front again, narrowing my eyes as they continue their little circle in front of the building. "...focusing on a bunch of country bumpkins passing the time with a protest. I mean, maybe they could put some of their energy into making this town smell better. Did you know this place smells like—"

"Shit, Cooper. I told you to wait."

"Excuse me?"

"Sorry, I have to go. Look, you can handle this, okay? I believe in you. Just flash that Jordy charm, and they won't know what hit them."

The line goes dead. I stare at my phone for a moment, then lean heavily on the car. The circling group across the street appears to have gained momentum, and I'm getting the impression this will be an all-day event.

This, apparently, is not going to be the fun, lighthearted gig I thought it would be.

I study the members of the protest, assessing what could happen if I cross the picket line. In all, there are only about ten people, and two of them are kids who are having more fun swinging the signs at each other than holding them up for the nonexistent traffic. Leading them is a woman I take to be their mother, wearing a large yellow garden hat and the loudest paisley dress that my fashion-eclectic cousin Nina would probably die over. There are three older ladies, all wearing overalls over t-shirts, as if they've just finished farming. By the vibe of this town, I don't doubt it. There's a young couple and their three-legged dog, an elderly man who appears to go at a snail's pace holding a sign resting on his shoulder while he leans on his cane, and a bored looking man wearing a fitted button up shirt with slim pants and loafers—probably the most stylish person in this town. As I'm watching, he hands his sign to the paisley mom before disappearing into the shop next door, leaving the crowd to nine.

I can take all of them, I realize. I mean, not that I'm looking for a fight. These stilettos cost me a damn fortune, and I'm not about to ruin them on a bunch of simpletons.

But I also have work to do, and if not now, when exactly am I going to find my way into that building? It's a sure bet they'll be back tomorrow, and the next day, and the day after that. I can wait until they leave before I walk in … but why? What would that solve?

"Fuck it." I grab my purse from inside the car, along with my bag full of design plans, then march across the street. I don't break my stride as I approach the circling picketers, walking right through their little protest to make it to the door. Their chants grow silent. I can feel their eyes on me as I pull out the key Alexander gave me before I left New York, then let myself inside. When I turn to lock the glass doors, a few phones point in my direction as they take photos of me, the enemy.

I offer a huge, toothy grin, then wave for good measure, then I turn back around and ignore them.

What I see in front of me takes my breath away.

I may have been impressed with the architecture of the outside of this building, but I'm severely unprepared for the inside. It's incredible. A huge, expansive room with twenty-foot ceilings, roman pillars, and large windows that lets the sunshine spill into the room in dramatic rays. The floors are pure marble, grey with a kind of crystal sparkling from the sun shining through the windows.

It's a blank slate, albeit a beautiful one, completely ready for me to work my magic.

I cannot wait to get started.

For the next few hours, I lose myself in amending the designs I've already drawn up, working from my tablet to find the right kind of textiles that will enhance the history of this building. All of these are rough sketches at best, but I feel like I have a better handle on what the interior needs now that I'm inside.

Before I know it, the natural light turns to a dusky pink with the setting sun. I flip the light switch and note the dim glow from unimpressive hanging lamps. Yup, the lighting is going to need an overhaul as well.

The rumbling in my stomach reminds me that I haven't eaten anything since this morning.

I glance out the front door window and note that the picketers have left their post sometime during my design work. I'd been so engrossed, I hadn't even noticed their departure, but now I'm relieved to not have to face anyone on my way out. I'd had the element of surprise on my side when I first faced these yahoos, and if they come at me now, I have ways to make them sorry. I was raised by a woman who had a barbed response to everything, and I've learned the art of taking down my opponent without lifting a finger. But I also know I have weeks of work ahead of me, and if I make enemies too early, it will make my life a living hell.

But making friends is not my forte, especially with people who obviously want me gone. So I'm very relieved to be free of the picketers—at least for now. Still, I feel cautious as I open the door and peer outside, half expecting someone to jump out and ambush me. But other than a few curious looks from people walking by, no one seems to pay me special attention.

Relieved, I lock the door, then head across the street to gather my luggage from my car.

I'd booked a room at the Lahoma Hotel weeks ago, mostly because of its convenient location right across the street from the shop I'd be working on, but also because it's literally the only hotel in Lahoma Springs. And at this moment, I cannot wait to check into my room, order up some room service with a bottle of wine, and settle into bed with some trash TV.

Pushing through the double doors, I'm greeted by a disaster of a lobby. The bones of the place are there, with red Spanish tile floors, ample windows, sparkling chandeliers, and rustic beamed ceilings that would make Joanna Gaines drool. It has that same century-old architecture The Till has, which makes my heart ache a little.

Because the decor? It's awful.

This is the plight of being an interior designer—my critical thinking cap never comes off. But in this case, I don't need a degree to see how this place is all bad. Judging by the tired 1970s striped couches and shag carpets, it's been in need of a makeover for at least fifty years. It's not even retro in an ironic way. It's like someone went into their grandmother's attic and made use of the plastic covered couches. I mean, there are even doilies on some of them. Whoever chose the color palate must have been really into purple and orange, because both colors are vomited all over the place, clashing with the natural palate of the building.

"Can I help you?"

I tear myself away from mentally redesigning this whole hotel and turn to the woman calling to me from the front desk. She's older, wearing a brown uniform with her silver hair piled into a tight twist. Her age has settled into her face, with deep lines and overdrawn eyebrows. But her red painted smile is turned up bright, and I can't help smiling back as I approach the desk. Her eyes take on a look of surprise as I stop in front of her, and her smile freezes.

"Yes, Jordan Gallo checking in."

"Uh, yes. Hold a moment."

She picks up her phone and glances at the screen and back at me, which is odd because I'm standing right here, a whole paying customer. I glance at the nametag—Bernice—taking a mental note in case I need to speak with management about her. The brightness in her face has completely disappeared, and her eyebrows furrow as she places the phone on the desk, face down. Then she starts typing fast. She pauses and looks at me with narrowed eyes.

"I'm sorry, we don't have a Jordan Gallo staying here."

And then, with her long French manicured nails, she turns her phone back over just long enough to see a photo of MY FACE staring back at me before she flips it again. I recognize it immediately, especially the indignation in my expression as I glare at the photographing protester.

Those fucking trespassers. My photo is probably being passed around like a trading card in this backwards town. If I wasn't afraid of losing my business connection with Winslow & Associates, I'd walk my ass out of this hotel and book the next flight home. But I need this job, and I'm not leaving this hotel without a fight.

"I made this reservation weeks ago," I hiss. The gloves are off, especially as I see the slight tilt in her mouth. She actually finds this funny! I pull my own phone out so I can find the confirmation in my email, but she just shakes her head.

"I'm afraid I can't help you," she says.

Fuck. This. Place.

"Can't?" I ask, "Or won't?"

She says nothing, only turning her back to me to do some invisible work on the counter behind her. "I am not leaving this spot until you give me the keys to my room." I bang my hand on the countertop, trying to get her attention. "Are you listening to me? I reserved the suite, and if you don't want a huge lawsuit on your hands, you'll make sure I get what I reserved. Do I make myself clear?"

Bernice turns, peering at me over her glasses, and she shakes her head. "Ma'am, there is nothing I can do for you. Your name is not in our system. Furthermore, we have no rooms available for the night, let alone the month. If this is going to be a problem, you are free to sit your ass on those chairs over there and wait to tell your story to the police for loitering. Is that clear enough for you?"

I glare, though I'm panicking internally. What do I do if she really doesn't let me stay here? I don't know anyone around here, and the nearest hotel is at least an hour away. I could get an Airbnb, but the last time I stayed in one, I ended up in the room of a hoarder house that looked nothing like the photos on the website. It was so traumatizing, I swore I'd never do it again.

I have no choice but to pull out the big guns.

"I would like to speak to your manager," I say, narrowing my eyes as I enunciate each word. Bernice smiles, almost sweetly.

"How about the owner?" She hands me one of the business cards from the stack on the desk. I look at it, and my stomach drops. Bernice Lahoma, Owner of Lahoma Hotel.

Fuck me. With a last name like Lahoma, she probably owns this whole fucking town—and I've just made an enemy of her.

"Now, if you'll excuse me, I have to get ready to welcome our registered guests." She glances pointedly at the door. "I suggest you move along." She smiles, then tilts her head, "Or maybe you really do want to talk to the cops."

"You won't call, I've done nothing wrong."

Bernice picks up her phone, then dials. I stay where I am, arms folded in front of me. What exactly are the cops going to do?

"Ted?" Bernice says, then relaxes into a laugh. "Yeah, it's Bernie... Oh for sure. You tell Emily that's an old family recipe, I'll bring it over the next time I come for dinner. Hey, I hate to bother you, but there's a disturbance happening at the hotel, and I was hoping you could send one of your cars over."

Right. Bernice's town, not mine.

"Forget it," I say, grabbing my luggage.

"Oh, you know what? Never mind, it looks like the situation is seeing itself out. All right now, you all take care over there. Don't work too hard." Bernice hangs up, then turns to give me her back as she prepares for ... no one? There isn't a soul in this lobby except me and her, and whatever died on this god-awful furniture.

There's also no point in arguing. By this point I'm famished, and I need something to eat before I figure out my next move. So I roll the suitcase behind me, banging my way through the double doors as I head out into the evening.

The fun didn't stop at the hotel. When I get back to my car, there's a ticket on it for being an inch into the red painted on the curb. I crumple up the accusing paper and throw it on my passenger seat before jamming the luggage into the trunk.

Finding food proves to be a disaster as well. I come upon a French bistro a half block down the street, and even though the place is only half full, the hostess insists they have no more tables left. The next place, an Italian restaurant, tells me they're closing in twenty minutes and aren't seating anyone else. A place that serves Peruvian food locks the doors before I can open them.

I want to cry, but I won't. This is personal. I hate this town, and yet, I hate the feeling of rejection even more. It's not even my fault. I'm not the one who bought this building. I'm not even the real intruder of their small town. I'm just a person trying to do her job, and they're vilifying me for it.

I'm fucking hungry, tired, and I have no place to go.

I try one more door. Charred Steakhouse. As soon as I open the door, the scent of seared steak overwhelms me. My stomach rumbles, and I know there is no going anywhere else, even if they try to kick me out.

"We're full for the night," a guy says, cleaning a glass behind the bar. I look around, noting that every table is indeed taken. But there's room at the bar, and I nab a seat immediately.

"Looks like I'll be sitting here, then," I say, offering a curt smile and hanging my purse on the hook at my knees. "I'll take a menu and your house chardonnay."

"Get her the Manhattan, Griff."

I turn to my right, and even though this day has gone to shit, my heart does a little leap at the familiarity of Ashton's face. In a town full of strangers, just looking at him as he stands and makes his way over to me helps me feel less alone. Like I have a friend in this angry, unfriendly town.

Then I recall the way he abandoned me just beforehand, how his face turned stony once he knew who I was. Even though I'm desperate for an ally, I force my heart to ice as I direct my gaze in front of me.

"You haven't had a Manhattan until you've had one of Griffin's," he says, and I feel his presence as he slides onto the bar stool next to me.

"I live near Manhattan," I say, unable to keep from looking at him. God, he's beautiful. "I doubt anyone in California knows how to make a decent one."

Ashton just laughs, offering a *we'll see* raise of his eyebrows. "I see you survived the protest."

Clenching my hand on my thigh, I'm tempted to say, *no thanks to you.* But immediately bite back the words. Just because he saved me from falling doesn't mean he owes me loyalty. I'm the outsider here, and it's apparent I won't be making any friends.

Not the goal, I remind myself.

"Survived, yes. Welcomed, hardly."

Before I can go into detail, Griffin places a Manhattan on the bar, along with the tab, but I wave that off.

"A menu, please?" I remind him, pushing the tab back in his direction.

"The kitchen's backed up," the bartender says, pushing the tab back towards me.

"And I can wait," I say, pushing it back again.

"Come on, Griff. Just take her order, and then get her another Manhattan while you're at it."

"I haven't even touched this one," I point out, as Griffin finally takes the tab and heads off—hopefully—in search of a menu. Ashton nods at the drink.

"Trust me, that one won't last long once you try a sip."

I give him side eye. Then, just to prove him wrong, I lift the glass to my lips and taste the goddamn drink. And maybe it's because I haven't consumed anything since the flight, but holy hell, it's delicious. Smoky and sweet, the perfect splash of vermouth, a hint of spice, and two shiny black cherries, of which I take one in my mouth and enjoy a small burst of brightness. It's a bit stronger than I'm used to, but Ashton's right. Within ten minutes, the glass is empty.

Two Manhattans later and a third one in front of me, I still haven't seen a menu. But I cannot stop laughing as Ashton recalls last weekend's beer fest to everyone around us, including the moment when the town mayor disrobed and fell in the river.

"Seems he started a trend, because soon the entire festival became a sort of nudist revival, everyone drinking beer and splashing their bits in the river."

"I was there," one of the guys calls out.

"I thought that was you. I didn't recognize you with your clothes on." Ashton shoots me a side grin as the room erupts in laughter.

And me? I'm seeing double, but happy about it. For the first time today, I don't feel the weight of the town's wary eyes on me. I feel included, and that's a good feeling. I mean, not that I care what this town thinks of me, not like they even matter. But this is a whole hell of a lot better than being rejected.

"Another Manhattan?" Ashton asks, pushing my glass at me. I shake my head.

"I'm a two-drink minimum girl. One more, and I'm bound to be dancing on this bar top, and maybe even recreating last week's beer fest."

To this, Ashton throws his head back and laughs. It's deep and rumbly, and goes straight through me in delicious ways. I distract myself by taking another sip, then flag down Griffin, who actually smiles as he approached me.

"Griff, darling. Could you *pleeeease* get me that menu. I'm starving, and these damn cherries are delicious, but they don't make a meal."

"Sure thing, sweetheart."

The pet name sounds strange coming from a man who wouldn't serve me just a half hour ago, but I overlook it as he finally places a menu, plus a fourth Manhattan, in front of me. The words seem to wave like a flag, but I finally make out a cheeseburger with fries. I don't eat bread, and I definitely don't eat fried potatoes, but both sounded absolutely divine. And maybe the carbs can sop up some of this alcohol so that the room will stop spinning.

"They're good, right? Maybe the best you've ever had?" Ashton said as he nods at the Manhattan.

"They're all right," I lie, picking it up to give it another sip. I'm not about to give him the satisfaction of knowing they're at least on par with the OG Manhattans. Even as a native Californian, my loyalty feels tied to my New York home. This Manhattan could be a hundred times better than the ones in the City, but I'd never tell him.

"So, do you have a shift on the picket line?" I ask, then lift my chin to eat another one of the cherries. But when I tilt my head back, I lose my balance and nearly fall off my stool. Ashton grabs me by the elbow, and I try to right myself, but the whole room is swirling and I end up leaning my full body weight against him. When I look up, I see the humor has left his expression, a look of concern replacing it. Or at least, I think that's what I see. It's hard to focus with all this noise, my intense hunger, and the fuzziness in my brain.

"I don't picket. I have too much work on the farm to do," he says, once I'm seated again. "Hey, let's get you some water, all right?" He waves down Griffin. "Water, bro?"

"I'm out of glasses," the bartender says. "I'll just go in the back and—"

"Here, take this one." Ashton shoves his drink at Griffin, the beer splashing over the rim onto the bar.

"Whoa dude, relax. I'm teasing." Griffin pulls a glass from below countertop and fills it with water before placing it in front of me.

"Is that food almost up?" Ashton asks.

"I'll check," he says, staring at Ashton for a moment before disappearing.

I sip more of my Manhattan, but Ashton takes it out of my hands before I can finish.

"Hey, I wasn't done with that!"

He places it on the other side of him, then pushes the water to me. "You also can't stay in your seat. Drink some water, and eat, and then if you still want it, you can have it."

"God, you sound like you're my boss or something." I pout, but I drink my water. I have to admit, I'm suddenly super thirsty. It's not as good as the Manhattan, but at the same time, it feels like the best thing I've consumed all day—which isn't much. I finish it off, then push the empty glass aside. "My boss made me come all the way down here to start planning the designs for the new store that's going in there. You know what's going in?"

He shakes his head, and keeps glancing at the kitchen. "No, what?"

"A luxury watch shop. Because what this town needs is some time to move into the future. You know what was there before?"

"A seed shop," he murmurs.

"A seed shop. A brilliant space full of archteshur… Architcher…"

"Architecture?"

"Yeah, Italian Renaissance arcisher, and it was filled with boring old seeds. No wonder the place went under."

"Here's the burger," Griffin says, then places it in front of me. I'm pretty sure it's burnt, judging by the black brick laying on the open-faced roasted bread. But I don't care. I grab the ketchup and smother the dark patty, then slap the sandwich together before taking a big bite. I can barely taste it, but my senses are fired up at the first bite of bread I've had in years.

"It's really good," I say around my burger, my mouth completely full. I take another bite, a little more aware of the burnt parts, but not completely caring. "It's a bit overdone, but good."

"Listen, I'm going to head out," Ashton says, then takes out his wallet. "Let me take care of your meal. Are you staying at the hotel? Can you walk there okay?"

I smack his wallet out of his hands, then laugh when it lands on the floor. "Don't pay for my meal. I got it. I got everyone's tab." I smooth my hair back from my face, wobbling a little as I turn to the bartender. "Griffin, take my card and charge everyone's bill to it. It's on my boss, for making me stay in this shithole that smells like shit and treats me like shit and is a shit place to stay. I might as well pay for everyone's meals since all you clueless country hicks are forced to stay here, and I'm just here until I finish my job. And god help me, I plan to finish it fast so I can get the hell out of here."

I toss the card across the bar, and Griff catches it with a grin. "Well, darling, that's awfully nice of you. Everyone, Jordy here thinks we live in a shithole, but she's paying for all your meals."

The whole restaurant pauses, and then one guy whoops before everyone else joins him in applause and cheers. I grin, feeling like a million bucks.

Until I don't.

"Oh god." It's all I can get out before I lose the little bit of burger I ate all over my beautiful shoes and the concrete floor.

3

Felix Family Farm

Ashton

"Whoops, I got you." I leap up, pulling Jordy's hair back as she vomits again.

"Shit. Get her out of here, Ashton."

"Chill, dude. You gave her three strong drinks in an hour, what did you think would happen?" It serves Griffin right. I watched him make her Manhattans doubles, but I'd said nothing, so I'm just as much the asshole as he is. I even found it funny at first, but when she started slurring her words and nearly fell, I knew we'd taken it too far. And then she started to talk shit ... well, I was just going to cut and run.

Now I feel like the biggest asshole. The girl has no one on her side in this town, and now she's in a vulnerable situation. I'd received a text message earlier today that, I suspect, was sent to just about everyone in town—a photo of her glaring face with a clear message: *"This woman is with the assholes who took over The Till. You know what to do."*

I've lived in this town for just a few years, and have learned quickly that if you aren't from here, you're an outsider. I've earned a quiet respect from my neighbors, but I'm not exactly on the inside. And this girl? She's obviously the enemy.

Jordy moans, and I scoot her away from the pile she's left on the floor. "Here's her card back," Griffin growls, tossing at me as one of the waiters laid paper towels over the area. The tables closest to us file out of the restaurant. "Tell her I gave us a 20% tip." He glares in her direction. "Now, get her out of here."

I don't feel like arguing. The girl isn't my responsibility, but if not me, then who? I retrieve her purse and slip her card inside, but not before I see the name on it. *Alexander Winslow.* I'd be happy if I never see that name again. Somehow, I know that isn't going to be the case.

"Can you walk?" I ask, and she looks up nods.

"I'm sorry. I'm so embarrassed," she whispers.

"It's not your fault. Come on, I'll get you to the hotel."

Jordy shakes her head. "Won't let me. Said they lost my reservation. No room left."

Goddamn Bernie. I know damn well she has room. That place is barely a quarter filled most nights. "Come on, let's go. You have a room. I'll make sure of it."

It takes us twenty minutes to walk across the street to the Lahoma Hotel. While the fresh air seems to help Jordy's stomach, she still moans and limps with every step, her soiled shoes dangling in her hand while I hold her up on the other side.

When we reach the hotel, I set her carefully on the chaise lounge in the lobby, then stalk toward Bernie.

"Ash, doll. What brings you here?" Bernie flashes me a bright smile, her weathered face lighting up as she takes me in. Then it dissolves into an expression of pity. "How you making out these days? I know it can't be easy."

"It's fine," I say curtly. I hate to be sharp with her. Bernie reminds me of my late grandmother, a woman who cured ailments with baked goods and warm hugs. In fact, the hotel lobby always has a plate of Bernie's famous chocolate chip cookies, which she bakes every morning before she arrives to work.

But as sweet as Bernie is, there's also a sharp edge to her, especially when she goes into protective mode. I know that's exactly what she's doing now—protecting our town.

And I suppose, protecting me.

"Listen, earlier today you—"

"What is she doing in here?" Bernie's eyes narrow as she looks past me, then back at me. "That woman is not welcome in this hotel, or anywhere else in Lahoma Springs. If I were you, I'd distance myself from her."

"That woman did nothing to deserve what you and the rest of our town are doing to her. She's only doing her job."

Bernie leans in. "Her job is to dismantle our town, brick by brick. First it's The Till. Then it's replacing our other small businesses with major retail shops, our restaurants with fast food, and our cobblestone streets with a subway system. And you think I'll let her into one of my hotel rooms? Next thing you know, she'll be mocking up plans on how to tear this historic building down and build a high rise for a bunch of out-of-town tourists." Bernie leans back, her jaw tight as she folds her arms across her chest. "I will not house the enemy in this establishment, even if it means she has to sleep on the streets."

I'm not getting anywhere with Bernie. I glance at my watch and wince. It's later than expected. I told Bob and Bec I'd be home an hour ago, though Bec had insisted I stay out later. "You never take time off," she'd said, practically pushing me out the door. "Go see your friends. Do what young people do. Take a load off."

Well, this night isn't exactly what I'd imagined.

"We'll talk about this tomorrow, Bernie," I say.

"There's nothing to talk about." Bernie reaches under the desk and hands me a bag of cookies. "You make sure to give these to that sweet girl of yours." She glares past me. "But don't give any to that piece of trash."

I roll my eyes, but take the cookies anyway. There's no way I'd turn down Bernie's homemade desserts.

"Told you," Jordy mumbles as I make my way over to her. I'm not sure how much she heard, but her assumptions are spot on. I help her stand, guiding her as we walk to my truck parked a block down the road.

"Where are we going?" she asks as she rests her head against the glass window. I drive slowly, not wanting to clean up my truck if she gets sick again. I doubt she has anything left in her since she only got in a few bites of dinner, but I can't be too careful.

"I'm taking you home."

It's not exactly home. Not my home, at least. Jordy is asleep by the time I pull into the gravel drive of the Felix Family Farm, her heavy exhales taking over the noise in the cab when I cut the engine. I brush my hand across her shoulder, but she doesn't stir. I pause, watching her sleep in the glow of the low cabin light. She's an attractive woman, even in her disheveled state. I'd noticed it when our paths first crossed earlier today. Her long, dark hair. Her smooth olive complexion interrupted by a light spray of freckles.

Her smile.

It was so slight and fleeting, as if she didn't give them away often. But when she'd met my eyes in that first encounter, offering that small upturn of her lips, I'd felt the strike of it straight to the center of my soul. It was like seeing the face of someone I'd missed, and feeling that small part of home I'd almost forgotten, but now feels like I can't live without. Just in her smile. Just in the casual way she flashed her brilliance at me, rendering me speechless.

Of course she isn't from around here. Jordy's fancy pencil skirt and six-inch stilettos are a dead giveaway. The way she carries herself, all straight and poised—completely stunning, so damn tall, and way out of my league. Then she dropped the bomb that she worked for Alexander Winslow. If I cave to that smile, even dare to breathe in her direction, it will be the second hugest mistake I've made this month.

Yet here she is passed out in my truck, and I'm moments away from letting her breach the sanctity of everything that matters to me.

I leave her shoes in the cab as I unbuckle her seatbelt and gather her in my arms. She's feather light, and I feel my heart lurch as the smooth warmth of her long legs rests against my arm, her head against my chest. Her hair even smells fancy, all lilac and sunshine in the dead of night.

I rap lightly on the door, then hear Bec's quiet footsteps as she approaches the door. She peeks through the curtain, and her eyes widen when she takes us in. I can only imagine what is going through her mind, bringing some strange woman here, and know I'll have some explaining to do.

"Is she okay?" Bec asks as she opens the door. Leave it to Bec to worry about some passed out girl's well-being before asking where I've been, who this is, and why I thought it would be a good idea to bring her here.

"She will be, once she sleeps this off. I hate to ask, but…"

"Put her in Sasha's room. I just changed the linens this morning."

I do as she says, though my stomach twists at her admission. Bec's hope is enough to fuel the world, even for a daughter who will never return. I was aware that the room remained unchanged for the past year and a half, but I didn't know she was cleaning it, keeping it ready.

Just in case.

Once Jordy is on the bed, I find myself in the strange predicament of what to do next. The outfit she's wearing had to have cost a small fortune, even with the small stain of vomit that soils her blouse. But I don't know the woman, and I definitely don't have consent to undress her.

"I can help," Bec says behind me. "Besides, you have someone who's been waiting up to see you. Now, shoo."

She moves around me, then gives me a light push toward the door.

"Are you sure? Should I—" I point at the clothes in the closet, but her index finger is aimed at the door.

"Ashton, that girl has been asking for you all night. I got this."

I hesitate for only a second longer, but leave and close the door behind me when I realize Bec is not changing her mind.

Bob is reading in his chair in the living room when I enter, and my daughter, Lottie, stands in the playpen. It will be her bed tonight, which really doesn't faze my easygoing girl. She reaches for me, her springy coiled auburn hair all over the place despite the tight space buns I'd pulled it into early this morning.

"What are you doing, sweet girl?" I ask, lifting her into my arms as her face breaks into a huge grin. There's nothing like a toddler in feet pajamas, so cuddly and sweet as she curls into my arms and tucks her head under my chin.

"Daddy," she murmurs. "Daddy home?"

"Tomorrow, pumpkin. We'll sleep here tonight. Did you have fun with Mimi and Papa?"

I feel her nod against my chest, hear her little fingers in her mouth.

"She was an angel, that one," Bob says, "and probably overtired. We had a busy day checking on the cows, covering the beds with mulch, and soaking up the sunshine. I don't remember it ever being this warm this time of year."

"It's always like this in the fall, Bob. You know that." I lay Lottie back in her playpen, and this time she stays down, clutching the small stuffed rabbit I placed in her arms.

"I know," Bob laughs. "It still catches me by surprise every year. I bet Oregon wasn't like this."

"We had our moments."

Oregon feels like a lifetime ago, and sometimes like yesterday. Of course, my crops looked a little different back then. Here it's rows of Swiss chard, lettuce, tomatoes, squash … but over there it was rows and rows of bushy cannabis plants. I thought I was set just keeping my head down and raking in the small piece of the pot, so to speak. Then I met Sasha and everything changed for the better—until it was for the worse.

But was it? Because now I have my sweet little girl, and Bob and Bec feel more like parents to me than in-laws. They've only known me for a few years, but you'd never know it with the way they treat me. And in return, I'd do anything for them.

I glance down at Lottie, and see that her eyes are already closed. Turning to Bob, I gesture toward the hall.

"Want to make a break for it while we still can?" I whisper. He nods, a smirk in his eyes as he lays the newspaper down next to his chair and follows me from the room.

"All right, mister. Tell me why there's a drunk girl in our house." Bec is three steps ahead of us when we join her in the kitchen. Three cups of tea sit on the center island, and I pull up a stool and Bob does the same.

"A drunk girl, eh?" Bob raises an eyebrow at me.

"It's not what you think," I say. "She's working for Mr. Winslow. The town telephone chain has already gone into effect, and every single business in Lahoma has blackballed her, even the hotel. She had a bit too much to drink at Charred, then Bernie refused to honor her reservation. I couldn't just leave her out there to the wolves."

I leave out the part where Griff poured her doubles to purposely get her drunk, and the part where I stood by and watched it happen.

Bec clicks her tongue. "Poor thing. She has no idea what she's up against."

"I think she got a fair preview today." I glance at the closed door to Sasha's room. "But no, this won't be a picnic. I'm afraid she thinks she can just do her business and leave, not understanding that this whole town has been seething since the place was sold to an out-of-town company."

Bob lowers his head, his shoulders hunched inward. "I'm really sorry."

Bec lays a hand on his arm. "We had no choice, love." She takes a deep inhale, glancing at Sasha's room. "We never should have bought The Till in the first place."

"You couldn't have known," I say, even as the burden of guilt remains heavy on my shoulders. I *did* know. At least, the signs were all there. I suppose hope blinds us all. "It wasn't your fault. But it doesn't matter now, what's done is done. We're just going to have to wait until this blows over."

It isn't going to just blow over, though. I know it, and Bob and Bec know it too. If we'd had more time, we could have sold the business to someone in town, or vetted the new owners. Maybe made an exit plan so that The Till could continue to exist, but under new ownership, or even a partnership. But time was not on our side, and Mr. Winslow's offer was enough to undo all the damage that was already done.

And who's to say Lahoma Springs doesn't need a luxury watch shop? It's an odd choice for our simple town, but maybe it can be a step in the right direction.

Or maybe it will bomb, and the space can go up for sale again, undoing the rushed choice we'd made.

"So, tell us about that woman then," Bec says, nodding at Sasha's room. "What's her name? Why is she here? Did she give you any signs on what to expect from Winslow & Associates?"

I shake my head no. "Her name is Jordy, and I actually don't know much about her at all, or how involved she is with Winslow. From what I can tell, she's here to design the new store, and she's close enough to Mr. Winslow that she's carrying a credit card with his name on it. She paid for everyone's meal tonight at Charred," I wince. "Man, I don't know if she realizes what she did. The place was packed, and you know how this town can put away its alcohol. There had to be at least eighty people in there, which means that tab could have been more than $15,000." I look at them, grimacing. "I guess we'll find out what kind of boss Mr. Winslow is if she still has a job in the morning."

And if she loses her job, I had a hand in it.

"I'll call Bernie in the morning," Bec says. "I'll straighten this whole thing out. If I just tell her what happened—"

"No, you can't," Bob growls.

"I don't mean about Sasha," Bec rushes out, but her furrowed brow says differently. "Maybe if I just explain the situation. I mean, that this poor woman is trying to do her job..." She trails off.

"I tried that already," I say. "Trust me, Bernie isn't going to budge, which means Jordy has no place to stay."

"Well, that's easy to fix. She can stay here." Bec looks at her husband, who doesn't return the same hospitality in his grimace.

"Bec…" He starts, but I cut in.

"No, you two have done enough. You don't need to be bringing in every stray that lands on your doorstep." I wink, referring to myself and the day I showed up with Sasha, her belly already protruding over her sweatpants, and no place to go. Bob and Bec hadn't known I even existed, and they still took me in with their daughter. Bob helped me build the house up the hill for our family, enlisting a few neighbors to ensure we had a good roof over our heads, running water, electricity, and a two-minute walk to Mimi and Papa's. And when Sasha left, there was no talk about us leaving. It may have had more to do with Lottie than me, but Bob and Bec are the closest thing I have to family, besides my daughter.

"We can figure it all out in the morning," Bec says. "If you want to take Lottie home, we can manage it from here."

"I'm not leaving you alone with a stranger."

Bec rolls her eyes. "It's not like she's dangerous."

"We don't know that." I highly doubt she's a threat. She's stubborn and difficult, and her attitude sucks. But dangerous? I can't see it. "Besides, Lottie is already asleep and if I have to move her, it will be another hour to get her back down. It's easier if I just take the couch."

"Fine," Bec relents. "But if you're staying, then you're enjoying a Felix family-style breakfast in the morning before you go out in the fields."

She says this as if I'm not here every morning, starting my day with her buttermilk pancakes, bacon, and eggs. Still, my mouth waters at the mere mention.

Bob and Bec retire shortly after, but not before Bec pulls every blanket and pillow from the hall closet for my couch bed. As I lie there in the still of night, my daughter's soft breathing competing with the hooting owls in the nearby trees, I think of Jordy. Is she okay? Will she know where she is in the morning? Will she be pissed to find herself in a strange house wearing strange clothes, stranded in this strange town?

I can't leave it. I get up and pad back to the kitchen, pulling out Bec's notebook she keeps in the junk drawer, along with a pen. Then I scribble out a note. Retrieving a glass of water and some aspirin, I creep to the bedroom where she's sleeping—the room that used to belong to the mother of my child.

I creak the door open, holding my breath as I listen for signs of life. The room is silent, and for a moment, I'm afraid that maybe we've made a mistake letting Jordy go to bed. What if she's too drunk? What if she isn't breathing? But then I hear her sigh, followed by a heavy flop onto her belly. I cover my smile, then feel like a complete perv as I take in those tiny shorts she's wearing that barely cover her ass.

Goddamn, her legs are long.

She doesn't move again as I slide to her side of the bed and place the note on the bedside table, leaning it against the glass of water alongside the painkillers. I want to stay where I am, watch her sleep, watch the way her long lashes brush against her high cheekbones and how her face softens when she isn't scowling. But I feel like Edward in *Twilight*, whose creepy stalking while Bella slept never sat well with me. If it's not right for a hundred-year-old vampire, it certainly isn't right for a thirty-year-old sad sack of a man.

So I leave the room, closing the door behind me, and try not to dwell too much on this gorgeous, impossible nightmare of a woman sleeping a few dozen feet away from me.

4

I Wet My Plants

Jordy

My mouth is like sawdust. I swallow, and it's like jagged glass in my throat. I pry one eye open, the bright sunlight of the room slicing through me like a scalpel, forcing my eyes shut again. I can barely move my head due to the intense pounding, and it's tempting to burrow deeper under the covers to hide from the day.

The covers. They aren't mine. Where the hell am I?

When I open my eyes again, it's to a nightstand with a folded piece of paper staring back at me, my name in bold letters. Rather, blurry bold letters. My head hurts so bad, everything feels like a wavy line.

I pick the letter up, noting the glass of water and three aspirin next to it. Despite my aching head, I ease myself to sitting, dropping the letter as I take a cautious sip of water.

When it stays down, I take another sip, followed by the aspirin, then chase it with more water. So far, so good. My head still hurts, but the water seems to help my vision issue.

I glance at the nightstand again, searching for anything that will clue me in to where I am. There are some crystals strewn across the wood top, a sandalwood and patchouli candle, and a framed photo of a baby wrapped in pink blankets. I pick up the photo, noting the baby's light spray of red hair. She has to be only a few months old, maybe as old as my niece, June. A pale manicured hand rests on the baby's swaddled arms, which is the only clue to who held her.

Every baby reminds me of the one I couldn't have. It was years ago, and I'd never wanted kids in the first place. But somehow, losing her without a choice feels like I've been ripped open then put back together wrong. To think about it too hard means I might fall apart, so I distance myself from any kind of baby, almost as if I'm allergic. To the point that I can't even join my cousin in feeling excited about anything Juniper does.

Yet, I make myself linger on this photo in the privacy of this strange home. Who's the baby, and who's the woman holding her? How does it feel to have such a tiny, helpless being look at you with those big grey eyes? How does she smell? What noises does she make? How does her little body fit so perfectly in this woman's arms?

I take a shuddering breath, placing the photo back on the table face down. That's when I see the framed photo behind it—a family of three, one of them the sweet baby from the first photo, I assume from the same pink blanket. Holding her is a beautiful red-haired woman, her face covered in freckles like she'd spent every day of her life in the sun. Her smile is wide, but I can't help noticing how it doesn't quite reach her eyes. Next to her is Ashton, his hair a lot longer than the close-cut crop he wears now, and the same vacancy in his eyes as the woman beside him. Maybe it's the fatigue of caring for a newborn that contributes to their forced smiles in this photo— or maybe it's something else.

So I'm in Ashton's house, and apparently, he's a father.

Is this his bed? I look around and don't see anything masculine in this room. In fact, it's like an emo teenage girl's room, with pink walls and black curtains, cartoon skulls and panda art, and a giant poster of Blink 182. It's pretty wild, like a room the goth girls at school would have had ten years ago. Not my taste, but not bad either. I can't help thinking of my own room as a teenager, with white walls and white carpet, not a thing out of place, and everything handpicked by our designer. My mom would have had a coronary before allowing me to put thumbtacks in the wall. So while I'm not a Blink 182 fan, I can't help admiring the liberal taste of whoever's room this was.

Whose room is this, though? And how did I not know Ashton was a dad? Or that he's already taken?

Not that it matters. The fact that he has a kid means that any interest I might have had in him is now non-existent. Kids are a deal breaker. I mean, wives or girlfriends are too, but kids? Nope, not happening.

I pull back the covers, noticing for the first time that I'm not wearing my own clothes. Instead, I have on a pair of gym shorts and a green t-shirt with a monstera on it. I hold the shirt out and read it upside down: "I wet my plants."

Weird. Something Nina would probably wear.

And then it hits me. Oh god, Ashton undressed me. He fucking saw me naked. Wait … did anything happen? Whether he's taken or not, I can't guarantee he didn't pull something while I was unconscious.

Hm … What if? For a moment, I drift to that thought. My thoughts becoming glassy as I consider his hands on my body, pulling my clothes off slowly, smoothing his palms over my skin.

NOPE. Not going there. I refuse to entertain ideas of groping, even welcome ones. I chase the thoughts away as I do a mental assessment of my body, then check everywhere for signs of trauma. I find nothing. Besides the normal ache from a night of too much alcohol, I feel fine. Stupid, but fine. Was I really dumb enough to get drunk in a town where I know no one? What the fuck was I thinking? I have so many questions, and I've gotten as far as knowing this is Ashton's house, he has a kid and a wife or girlfriend, and I am crashing in some teenager's room.

Wait. The letter.

I search the blankets around me until I find it, slightly crinkled from getting caught in the sheets. Then I read it.

You're safe.

You had too much to drink last night, and nowhere to go. I took you home so you could sleep it off. We can figure out your next move in the morning, if you stick around.

Here are the things you probably want to know most:

You are in the home of Bob and Bec Felix, owners of Felix Family Farms.

Your phone is charging in the bathroom, which is the closed door directly in front of you to your left.

Your jewelry is also in the bathroom and your clothes are in the washroom. Don't worry, Bec read the labels.

Bec was the one who dressed you.

You are welcome to wear any of the clothes in the closet.

If you want to leave, no one will be offended or try to stop you. But if you stay, Bec is an amazing cook and can make you any food you want.

— Ashton (the asshole)

Damn. It's kind of hard to hate the guy after all that. I remember the night before in fits and spurts, enough that I know I made a complete ass of myself—starting with calling Ashton's town a shithole. Oh, god. And throwing up everywhere. I want to burrow under the covers as memories of the night keep coming back to me, but my bladder is near bursting, and my nausea is returning with every forming recollection.

I wobble out of bed and open the door Ashton referred to, revealing my jewelry and phone right where he said they'd be in a bathroom with black and white checkered floors and hot pink bathmats. The theme might have been overdone, but it's consistent, and it's growing on me. Plus, everything smells nice in here and in the bedroom—like a hotel room or something.

It's like this room hasn't been lived in for years, but has been kept clean and fresh, nonetheless.

Once my bladder is gratefully emptied, I glance in the mirror—and holy shit—I look like hell. My hair is a wild rat's nest, and my mascara creates deep, dark circles under my eyes. The shorts are too small for my long legs, almost like underwear. I consider looking through the closet like Ashton suggested, searching for something less revealing. But it feels weird to rifle through someone else's clothes, especially if they belong to some teenager.

Taking a deep breath, I cross the bedroom and ease the door open. Instantly I'm met with the smells of breakfast—bacon, syrup, coffee—each hitting me with another wave of nausea. I cover my nose and breathe slow until my senses grow accustomed, allowing me to remove my hand. All the while, I take in my surroundings; a large room with exposed beam ceilings, large windows and a door that reveal a porch area that face a large expanse of farmed land, and an open kitchen where an older woman stands, wearing an apron and a warm smile on her face.

"Well, hello there."

"Uh, hi." I feel naked all of a sudden, wearing this tight t-shirt and tiny shorts, especially as I see the young toddler in the highchair near the counter, her chubby hands grabbing at cereal on the tray. "I'm Jordy," I say, then feel stupid. "You probably already knew that. And you're, uh, Bec?" I hesitate, recalling the name from Ashton's note.

Bec beams and nods. "That's right. And this little cherub is my granddaughter, Lottie. Aren't you, sweet thing?" Lottie grins around the finger in her mouth, then grasps more

Cheerios with her slimy hand. "You know Ashton, and you'll meet my husband Bob in a few. They head out early to tend to the animals, taking a half pot of coffee with them, I swear. Did you want coffee? Did you get enough sleep?"

I'm sure the bags under my eyes say otherwise, and I shrug as I pull at the hem of my shorts, trying to appear less naked.

"Oh, sorry about the clothes, I just grabbed what I could find. Let me get you a robe, if you're uncomfortable. You're probably cold anyway."

I'm trying to put the puzzle pieces together. Bec is grandma to the toddler in the highchair, which makes her...

"Are you Ashton's mom?"

Bec throws her head back, her laugh coming straight from her belly. I feel dumb immediately as I take in Bec's pale ivory features that contrast with Ashton's smooth brown skin.

"Lord, I wish I was mom of that boy. He's the kindest, gentlest soul I know who would give anyone the shirt off his back. But no, I'm not his mom."

She wipes at the tears in her eyes, her smile wavering a little as something dark crosses her expression. Then she waves her hand as if to brush away whatever bothered her in that moment.

"Oh dear, that robe. I've done talked your ear off. Let me get it for you. Watch Lottie for me, okay?" she asks, then scoots out the door and down the hall.

Watch Lottie. Watch her do what, exactly? I sit on the barstool and stare at the toddler, and she stares back. I realize quickly that this is the same child as the one in that photo, just a few years older. The soft auburn spray of hair from the photo is now a full blown fluff ball, which I have to admit is kind of cute. I mean, cute for an obnoxious, gross toddler. But cute, nonetheless.

Lottie picks up a Cheerio and holds it out to me.

"More?" she asks. I balk at the outstretched hand, then mentally chastise myself. This is a child, not a monster. I take a deep breath, then grimace into a smile—as if that will make me appear friendly instead of allergic to children.

"You want more?" I look around the kitchen, feeling out of my element until I spot the cereal box on the countertop. I start to reach for it, but then second guess the move. What if the amount on her tray was pre-measured? My mom did that when I was a kid so I wouldn't eat too much, and she went ballistic if I ate even a bite more than what was given to me. What if Bec felt the same way?

I look back at the little girl and shake my head. "You have more on your tray."

"More?" She continues to hold out her hand, and I see the slimy Cheerio in her hand and suddenly understand. I hesitate for a moment, then with cautious fingers, I take the Cheerio she holds out to me. She grins, her little teeth like pearls in her mouth. Then she gets another Cheerio off the tray and shoves it in her mouth, watching me the whole time. I pretend to do the same, and she laughs as I make chewing noises. The sound is like a bell, and it goes straight to my heart, sending chills through my veins on the way.

Oh, that sound. It both breaks and warms my heart. I focus on the latter, burying my pain as I grin back at her. A real smile, this time. She laughed at something I did, and it's as if a bird flew from the sky and landed on my open palm.

Bec returns just as I take another Cheerio from Lottie's outstretched hand.

"Ah, I see she's included you in her little game. Sweet Lottie, you're such a giver!" The little girl squeals as Bec bends down and peppers her with kisses. "Here's my robe. It's probably too big for you, but at least you'll be warm."

She hands over the robe and I slip it on. It's a little worn, but the weathered fabric feels smooth against my skin. There's a comforting odor to it—like laundry detergent and the faint scent of cookies. The scent reminds me of my Grandma Dot, who used to putter around her house in the morning in her own worn robe while Nina and I took over the couch and watched cartoons.

"So, Jordy." Bec hands me a cup of coffee, along with the creamer and sugar, both of which I wave off. "Is that short for something?"

"My full name is Jordan, but no one really calls me that."

"I like that name," she says, then smiles at me. Her smile is so inviting, I feel something soften inside me. This is the first time anyone has been welcoming to me in this town, and I haven't realized how much I need that. I wrap her robe around me, then with a wary glance at Lottie, I choose the furthest barstool at the kitchen island with my coffee cup in tow. When I take a sip, I grimace at the bitterness of the black.

"Do you have almond milk?" I ask, and she shakes her head.

"No, but the cream is fresh. Straight from the cow this morning." She nods at the carafe she'd offered earlier, and I lift it reluctantly. I haven't had milk in ages, mostly because I can't stand the taste. I sniff at it, pour a little in my cup, then

I take another sip—and damn, if it's not the smoothest, creamiest coffee I've had in ages.

"Pretty good, huh?"

"This is milk?"

Bec laughs, nodding. "Tastes way different than at the store, huh?" She pulls a plate from the cabinet, then the pan off the dish rack. "Can I make you some breakfast? We all ate a few hours ago, but you're probably starving. I could make you some eggs and bacon, some hash browns, some…"

She trails off, probably noticing the green tinge to my expression. Yes, I'm starving. The little bit I ate last night was lost on the restaurant floor, and it's now nearing noon. That means it's been about twenty-four hours since my last decent meal.

But eating something? I can't stomach anything right now.

"That probably sounds terrible," Bec tuts, and I nod.

"I'm sorry. Any other day and that would be amazing, but right now, I think I just need water and nothing else."

"Darling, you need more than water. If you don't get something in you, you're just going to feel sick the rest of the day. Do you trust me?"

I do not know this woman. But I nod anyway, because yes, I trust her. I've known her all of ten minutes, and she's already the motherliest woman I know. Of course, my own mom doesn't have a motherly bone in her body, so this isn't exactly a fair assessment. But Bec is made of mom material. She's housing me in her home, a total stranger. She's feeding me. She trusts me around her granddaughter, even if I don't trust myself.

Still, it doesn't stop my curiosity about the girl—partly because she's Ashton's daughter, but also because my horror around kids is a like train wreck. They terrify me, and I also can't focus on anything else when they're around.

"Is Lottie her full name? Or is short for something?" I ask.

"Charlotte Rebecca Felix. Named after my mother, who was also named Charlotte, and me. Though I'm pretty sure Sasha was actually naming her after that sweet spider in *Charlotte's Web*. She used to love that book when she was little, and made me read it to her every night."

Sasha. This must be Lottie' mother. Bec's daughter, maybe?

"Does Sasha read it to Lottie now?"

Bec's smile freezes. She turns quickly back to the counter where she's preparing food, but not before I see her smile drop.

"No, but I do. This girl loves to be read to. She just turned two over the summer, and she got piles of books from her Papa and me. She makes me read her exactly three books before every nap. Any less, and she throws a fit. Maybe it's the reading, or maybe because she's this big two-year-old now, but it's like this little light bulb went off. She's growing like a weed and trying out new words. But mostly she just babbles at us and expects us to understand. Which we do sometimes, right sweet girl?"

Lottie looks up, and it's apparent that "Sweet Girl" is as familiar a name to her as her own given name.

"You are obviously so proud of her."

Bec blushes, waving her hand. "I'm sorry. I'm gushing too much, aren't I? She's our first grandbaby, and we just love her to pieces. We're so lucky that Ashton has remained close with our family and lets us be such a huge part of her life."

She doesn't have to say it, but it confirms what I've started to suspect.

Sasha is not part of the picture anymore.

Ashton tromps through the front door at that moment, followed by an older man with a large grey mustache and a wide-brimmed hat, both of them covered head to toe in dirt as if they've rolled in mud. The dirt doesn't distract me from Ashton, however. I hold my breath as my eyes take him in, dazzled by his grin as he goes straight for Lottie. Goddamn, that man is gorgeous. He's wearing a flannel shirt, rolled up to reveal dark forearms, one of which sports a black and white lion tattoo. Even with the shirt on, I can't get over the size of his arms, the way his muscles strain against the fabric, the broadness of his shoulders as if he were a football player instead of a farmer working the field. He is so beautiful, I have to tear my eyes away. Even then, I'm overwhelmed by his scent—a mixture of intoxicating, woody sweat mingling with the smell of grass and gasoline—all testosterone and male— leaving me breathless.

What the hell is wrong with me?

"Bob, this is Jordy," Bec says, interrupting my inner turmoil as she introduces her husband. I look up, hoping my smile hides the fact that I cannot breathe while Ashton is in the room.

"Ma'am," the older man says, nodding his head before kissing Bec on the cheek. She leans away from him in an effort to not get dirty, even as her eyes crinkle with affection. He gives me another nod, then disappears around the corner towards the bedrooms.

"And you know Ashton," she continues.

"That might be too familiar a term, but she did throw up on my shoes, so I guess we're friends now."

I feel my face burn, but I stay silent as I narrow my eyes at him, even as my heart is still recovering from the way his presence takes up the whole room. The corner of his mouth twitches, and then he winks at me—a move so unexpected that I don't anticipate the way my heart flutters, or the way I have to avert my eyes to keep from staring at the easy way he smiles at me. *Get a grip, Jordy. He's a stranger in enemy territory. And he has a kid.* When I look back, the expression on his face is only more amused.

"I see you survived the night," he teases. "I thought you could handle your Manhattans, New York."

"Ha ha." But I'm mortified, especially as I remember heaving my dinner all over my shoes.

"Enough," Bec orders. "You, in the shower," she says to Ashton. Then she turns to me, "and you, get some food in that belly of yours."

She sets a bowl of applesauce in front of me, some rice, a half bananas, a piece of toast, and a large glass of cloudy water. "That's electrolyte water, with lemon juice and salt. I expect you to drink all of that."

"You better listen," Ashton mocks, then leaps out of the way when Bec snaps a towel at him.

5

Just a Small Town Boy

Ashton

Let me tell you something. Jordy can make even the rattiest bathrobe look like lingerie. When I walk into the house, the first thing I see are her long legs peeking out from beneath Bec's ancient robe, those tiny shorts riding high on her golden thighs. It's hard to tear my eyes away—even after everything.

She's wearing my ex's clothes and my mother-in-law's robe. I'd spent the evening dodging her puke, and still, she's the sexiest woman I've ever laid eyes on.

Too bad she's completely off-limits.

I'm already in enough hot water with this town for selling The Till. If they find out I'm even thinking about Jordy this way, I might as well set myself on fire. But seeing her chatting with Bec, sitting next to my daughter at the breakfast table—

it's like catching a glimpse of a life I didn't even realize I wanted.

Ridiculous.

Jordy's a stranger, a corporate shark's errand girl, and she lives on the other side of the country. And me? I'm a single dad, the town's favorite topic of conversation, tied to a relationship that ended long ago. Dating anyone in Lahoma is impossible. As far as this place is concerned, I'll always belong to Sasha, even if she's gone. The town's loyalties run deep, and as long as I stay here, I can kiss my dating life goodbye.

But Jordy? She isn't from here. She has nothing to do with my past. She's like fresh water in the desert, but I'd be an idiot to take a sip.

By the time I'm out of the shower, Jordy's dressed in another of Sasha's outfits, her damp hair smelling like chamomile shampoo. She'd swapped the bathrobe for a pair of old jeans with sunflower patches and an orange t-shirt that reads, "Cluck around and find out" with a cartoon chicken. The jeans hit just above her ankles, where Sasha used to have to roll them at the hem.

"Nice fashion choice," I tease, immediately regretting it when she shoots me a stony glare.

"It's not like I had a choice. My suitcase is in my car, and my clothes from last night are a mess. Bec offered to wash them, but they're dry clean only." She huffs. "But maybe it doesn't matter. I don't think puke and silk go well together. I'll probably just throw them away."

She glances down at the t-shirt, sighs again, and crosses her arms over her chest. I wonder if this is normal for her—

jeans and a t-shirt—or if it feels as foreign as she looks wearing them.

"I can take you to the dry cleaners on the way to pick up your car," I offer, scooping a happy Lottie out of her highchair.

"It's fine. I'll figure it out."

Her gaze flickers to the bag on the counter—her ruined clothes, wrapped up and useless. A twinge of guilt hits me. I brush it aside and nod toward her empty plate.

"Do you feel any better?"

"Tons." Jordy's shoulders relax for the first time all morning. "I wasn't sure I could stomach it, but Bec didn't give me much choice. I guess she was right because I don't feel nauseous anymore, and my head doesn't hurt."

She stands and carries her dishes to the sink, washing them and setting them on a towel to dry. Efficient. Like she doesn't want to owe anyone anything.

"I really need to get going, though. Could you drive me into town?"

"Sure. Let me just get Lottie's car seat out of Bec's car. Do you mind watching her?"

I don't wait for her answer, just hand Lottie over without thinking. But the second Jordy takes her, I see it—a flicker of something sharp in her expression, her whole body going stiff.

I frown. "Sorry. I just assumed—"

"No, I'm fine," she cuts in, but her voice is tight.

She holds Lottie like she's holding a live grenade, barely moving as my daughter grabs for her necklace. The expression on Jordy's face is stuck in a grimace as she eyes Lottie.

"You can put her down," I say. "She walks."

"Oh. Right."

She lowers Lottie to the floor immediately, stepping back fast like she needs distance. She watches her, but not like she's making sure Lottie's safe. More like she isn't sure how to exist in the same space as a child.

"You haven't been around a lot of kids," I muse, half-laughing. But when I see the offense darken her expression, my smile fades.

"I've been around plenty of kids," she huffs, then she hesitates. "I just don't particularly like…"

She trails off, pressing her lips together in a tight line.

"So you haven't been around kids," I repeat.

Her jaw tightens. "My cousin just had a baby girl."

"Oh, that's great. So you babysit her a lot?"

Her eyes narrow, something unreadable flashing across her face before she looks away.

"We're wasting time, and this conversation is boring me," she says, voice flat. "Just get the car seat so I can get to work."

We leave the farm with Jordy sitting in the passenger seat, scrolling through her phone, and Lottie babbling in her car seat in the back. My daughter's hair is extra wild this morning, though I'd managed to pull it tight into floofy poms on the side of her head. She got the auburn shade and pale freckled skin from her mother, but those coiled spirals are all me. Thankfully she's learned from an early age to just sit still while her daddy pulls at her hair—just like my own mother used to do for me back when I was young and wore my hair long.

Jordy's stilettos lay on the floorboards at her feet, hosed off and dried before I returned them to the truck. Hopefully water won't ruin them, but I choose to not tell Jordy, just to be on the safe side. I'm starting to understand that Jordy is very particular, and all of this is outside her comfort zone— from the sunflower jeans to the kid in the back seat.

Jordy is a puzzle I'm not sure I want to solve, but damn if I'm not fascinated by her—and attracted. Way too attracted. Even though I barely know her, I can tell we are two entirely different people, and yet, I'm drawn to her like a bird to open sky. There's something about her that calls to me, and I can't quite name it. Maybe it's because we're both outsiders in this town, though I doubt she sees anything in common between the two of us. Maybe it's the way she carries herself—tough on the outside, but with something fragile just beneath. Or maybe it's the fact that she isn't throwing in the towel, even though this town has given her hell from the moment they learned who she is.

All I know is that every moment I'm next to her, I feel both the excitement of our nearness, and the pain of not quite reaching her.

Of course, my complicated feelings toward her hardly matter. She's here for only a few weeks—just one more reason why I need to keep my attraction in check.

That, and she's working for that asshole.

Besides, we didn't exactly get off on the right foot, and the way things are going, that's not going to change.

I turn the radio on to help break the silence in the front seat, trying not to feel affected by the wall between Jordy and me. Leon Bridges fills the cab, doing little to change my mood. I can't place why I even care. After today, I plan to never see her again. She'll get to work, I'll go back to the farm, and that will be it. How this town treated her isn't my business, or my problem. Her obvious disdain for children has nothing to do with me or Lottie, and isn't something I need to feel offended by or try to fix. I'm just the idiot who brought her home last night in her hour of need. I did my part, now my part is done.

"Where is Lottie's mom?"

Jordy's question surprises me. Her curiosity is normal, but given the way she shut down, I didn't expect to be quizzed about my life … especially about that part.

"I don't know."

She turns to me, and I glance at her long enough to see the confusion on her face.

"What do you mean, you don't know? Lottie is two, right? You mean to tell me that her mom had her, and then up and left?"

Pretty much.

But to Jordy, I just shrug. "It's a bit more complicated than that."

I can feel her questions mounting. *What kinds of complications? Why did she leave? What kind of person abandons their child?*

But all she says is, "It's nice how involved Bec and Bob are with Lottie."

I breath out a sigh, my shoulders lowering with my defenses. "They've been like parents to me, and they love their granddaughter." I look at Lottie in the rearview mirror. She's busy studying her hands, talking softly in her own little language. I smile, my heart expanding like it always does when I feel overwhelmed by the love I have for this little girl. "Honestly, I wouldn't be able to do it without them. They let us move in before Lottie was born, and then after…" I pause, my eyes shifting to Jordy, then back to the road. "Let's just say I owe a lot to the Felixes. Bob and I built a small house on the property around the time Lottie was born, and it's where we live now."

"Just you and Lottie."

I keep my eyes on the road as I nod. It's been years, and I still feel that weight of anger building in my gut whenever it comes to Sasha and all the allowances everyone makes for that woman—especially the excuses I've internalized about her. But enough time has passed that those excuses were weak. Every morning that I wake up to my daughter is a reminder of everything Sasha willingly gave up. Most days, I don't think about forgiving her anymore. On the best days, I don't think about her at all.

Jordy says nothing for a moment, long enough that I think the conversation is over. But then I feel her eyes on me.

"Did you grow up here?"

I shake my head. "No. I lived on a farm in Oregon for a few years before Lottie was born. Before that, I grew up in Louisiana. I've been in California for just about three years."

Jordy makes a noise in her throat, saying huh without uttering a word. Again, silence fills the cab except for Lottie's soft singing in the back seat and the music on the radio.

"So, you're kind of an outsider here, huh?"

Bingo.

But I can't help the laugh that stays in my chest. "You're awfully curious. What about you?"

"What about me? I'm definitely an outsider."

"No, silly. I mean, what's your story?"

She shakes her head. "Not much to tell. I live in a cramped apartment in New York, and before that, I lived in Southern California."

"Ah, a native. So this isn't some strange place to you."

She laughs, and I feel her relaxing next to me. "I mean, kind of. SoCal and NorCal are so different, they might as well be different states. But yeah, I grew up on the West Coast, so there's that. But it was Santa Barbara, not a small town like Lahoma Springs. So this whole town loyalty thing is pretty foreign to me. Especially now that I live in New York. God, everyone there is out for themselves." She huffs a laugh. "The irony is that I was almost a small-town girl."

"How so?"

I feel the layer of hesitation immediately. The way she shifts in her seat. The pause in her breath. Then she waves her hand.

"It's not important."

I want to leave it alone. I really do. But the sudden shift in the cab eats at me. "If it wasn't important, you wouldn't have said it."

She looks at me, and I hold my breath under the weight of her gaze.

"I suppose you're right."

Then she turns back to the window.

Obviously, my job is just to be a good chauffeur and drive her into town. But it seems unfair that she gets to ask me all these questions and I can't even make small talk with her. She's so guarded, and while it should repel me, it only makes me lean in more. What's eating her? The longer she stays silent, the more I need to know.

But I've done that before—pushed when I should have let go—and it cost me, more than I care to admit.

So I keep quiet, biting my tongue as we near the corner of Main Street, and drive the rest of the way into town without another spoken word.

6

The Till

Jordy

Ashton stops behind my car so I can do a quick inspection, just to make sure nothing happened to the loaner. He looks slightly amused when I tell him I want to check for damages, but I wouldn't hold it past these people. He didn't see the way they looked at me when I entered The Till, how they held their cameras up like paparazzi, or how they later kicked me out of every establishment. I'm surprised I didn't see Wanted posters with my photo on every street pole, though I suppose they don't need that in this digital age. Word sure got out fast about my arrival, because everyone knows who I am.

Luckily, my car is fine. I throw my stilettos in the backseat then head back to the truck.

"I can take it from here," I say. "Thanks for your help." I start to close the door, but he stops me.

"You don't even have a place to stay yet," he points out. "Just wait there."

I want to argue—I really do—but I watch as he does a U-Turn and then parks in front of The Till instead. The protesters are still there, but they stop when he gets out of the truck.

"Hey, Ash, how's it going? Hanging in there?" One of the guys claps Ashton on the back as a woman puts her sign down to help get Lottie out of the car. For someone who said he was an outsider, he sure has a lot of friends. Does he not see how much this town likes him?

I pretend to scroll my phone when Ashton starts across the street, stroller in front of him. I look up as he approaches, noticing that the small crowd is watching him join me at my car.

"All right, where to first? The hotel to try again?"

By now the people are whispering amongst themselves, and I feel this tight ball form in the pit of my stomach.

"Forget them," he murmurs, "they're just thrilled to see something new to talk about."

"Well, I'm pleased to be their entertainment, I suppose."

But I do as he says, keeping my head held high, walking beside Ashton as he pushes Lottie in the stroller.

Third try is *not* the charm. Bernie takes one look at me and points at the hotel door. I recall bits and pieces of the night before, including Ashton at the counter, trying to talk some sense into her. But she didn't budge then, and she won't budge now.

"It's fine," I say as we leave. Normally I'd put up a fight. I'd tell Bernie what she could do with her Farah Fawcett hairstyle and paisley polyester blouse, and how her old hotel smells like cheese. But I'm tired. Defeated.

Alone.

I haven't even started work yet, and I'm ready to leave this place. The best thing I can do is get my work done and leave this hell hole, even if it means I have to sleep on the concrete floor of the vacant shop. "I'll find a place to stay in the next town over. It's not like this is the only place to stay." Even though I know it is.

So does he. Ashton pulls up his phone and searches out hotels, then shows me his screen. The nearest one is sixty-seven miles away.

"It's fine," I insist again. But it isn't fine. None of this is fine. And before I can stop it, I feel the tears prickling my eyes. I quickly turn my head so he won't see. "Thanks for everything, Ashton. You don't have to babysit me anymore, though."

I leave him standing in front of the hotel as I stalk toward The Till, soon to be Timeless. I don't break my stride as I plow through the small group of protesters out front. "You all are on private property," I hiss as I unlock the door. "If you don't vacate the premises immediately, I'll call the authorities to haul you away."

"You mean Officer Ted?"

I glance at the lady who spoke, the same one who'd lifted Lottie out of her car seat. Bernie's threats come back to me, including when she called this Ted guy to teach me a lesson.

"What, this whole town is on a first name basis with this officer?" I roll my eyes. "You all need to get a life."

"Well, I have a life," the woman says, then pulls her phone out. "With Officer Ted Shanigan, my husband. Should I get him on the phone for you so you can tell him to haul us away?"

The words sink in my stomach, my face growing hot as a few people snicker around me. Fucking incestual town. I turn away from her, feeling the weight of their laughter as I unlock the door and then close it behind me.

I'm afraid they'll stay outside the shop, caging me into this fishbowl. But they disperse soon after, leaving me alone to start my work.

The thing is, my heart isn't in it. Usually when I come into a blank slate like this, the ideas start pouring in faster than I can jot them down. But this time, there's nothing. I have a few preliminary ideas I'd sketched out with Alexander in his office before I'd left New York, but looking at the space now, I know there's so much more potential. My earlier ideas won't do the light and architecture justice.

Maybe I'm in over my head. I thought I was made for designing spaces, but I'm still new to the business. The biggest job I've had was designing Nina's boutique in Sunset Bay, a project I'm still proud to have created. Beyond that, I've had a few storefronts and several office spaces, including Alexander's. Apparently I'd impressed him enough that he was willing to fly me across the country to design this shop in a nowhere town.

But why choose Lahoma Springs? What's his reasoning for introducing a luxury watch shop to a small town that thrives on family-owned businesses?

I pull out my phone and touch Alexander's name on the screen, then put it on speakerphone.

"Hey sweetie, how's it going? You've obviously been busy."

The tightness in my chest increases at the unsolicited pet name. But I let the *sweetie* slide in favor of my confusion. "Busy? How so?"

"Well, there was that huge order you placed yesterday. Let me find it."

I can hear him clicking on keys, along with talking to whoever is in his office. "Here it is. A charge for $13,517 at Charred. Is that one of those natural wood places that burn their etches into the art pieces? I love the direction you're going."

A cold chill washes over me as memories of my evening hit me with an icy blast. Mother. Fucker. I groan as I recall the moment I whipped my card out, paying for everyone's meal. There must have been a hundred people in that place. Maybe more.

There's no getting around this one. I could play it off, feeding into his assumption that I'd bought some fancy piece of furniture. At the end of the day, Alexander is so rich that he wouldn't even notice what's in this store or not.

I can't bank on that, though. More than that, I *hate* lying. I've been lied to enough in my life, and I fucking hate liars.

"That was at a steak house, actually," I say, then hold my breath.

He doesn't speak for an eternity. Then he lets out a heavy breath.

"Was it a twenty-pound wagyu wrapped in gold foil?"

I'm going to be fired. I just know it.

But maybe that isn't so bad. I can just go home, pack up my things, and move back in with my parents while I try to figure out what I'm doing with my life.

Just the thought of living with my mother again makes me shudder.

"No, not that. I got carried away." My stomach sours at the thought of all those Manhattans, not to mention my coming admission. "Let's just say that one thing led to another, and I told everyone that dinner was on me."

"Everyone. As in…"

"As in everyone that was dining out last night at Charred."

More silence. Then a low chuckle.

I don't know what's scarier. Alexander not saying a word, or Alexander feigning amusement before he rakes me over the coals. To be fair, he's never said one stern word to me. He's never had the reason—before today, that is. But I walked in on him once when he was in the middle of a meeting, his finger jabbing the chest of some guy in a business suit while he read him the riot act. I saw the way his employees sucked up to him, and rushed to meet his needs.

He may be nice to me, but it's only because I haven't fucked up.

Until now. Until I've pissed him off so bad, all he can do is laugh before he rips me a new one.

"Brilliant," he says.

My chest tightens. "Brilliant, as in, you can't believe you hired an idiot like me?"

"Come on sweetheart, give yourself a little more credit. Or at least, give me some credit. I hired you because you think outside the box, and obviously that's what you're doing now." He laughs again. "It's not easy connecting with people in a small town."

"You have no idea," I mutter.

"But treating them right off the bat is a clever move. It gets them to trust you, maybe even welcome you, and by extension, it will get them to welcome Timeless when it's up and running. I like your style."

I'm about to tell him otherwise, but the sound of the door closing behind me almost makes me drop the phone. I whip around to see Ashton re-locking the door while Lottie sits in her stroller next to him. When he turns around, he has a sheepish look on his face while holding up the keys that let him in.

Keys he shouldn't have.

"Listen, I need to go," I say, my eyes never leaving Ashton's.

"I get it. Busy at work, that's my Jordy. I look forward to seeing what you come up with. I should have the management team in place soon. I want you and me to be the leads on this project, but we can start including them in these conversations once they're up and running."

"I look forward to it."

Once I hang up, I glare at Ashton.

"What? This town is not only in each other's business, but you all have keys to each other's businesses as well?"

"Nope. Just me and you." He twists the key off the ring, then holds it out to me. I stride over and snatch it out of his hand.

"And why would you have a key?"

It dawns on me as soon as the words leave my mouth.

"It was your store."

"It was my store," he agrees. "Well, it's actually Bob and Bec's store. But I managed it until the end."

It's then that I remember my conversation with Alexander yesterday. The names he said.

Mr. Felix. Like Bob and Bec of Felix Family Farms. Which means...

"You're Mr. Elliot."

Ashton nods. "That's the last key I have, as far as I know. But your employer will probably change the locks anyway."

"Likely." I have so many questions, none of them important and all of them completely nosy. "Why did you sell?"

"Good question."

Lottie begins fussing, twisting in her stroller. He starts to unbuckle her, but then stops. "We usually let her go free in the shop. Do you mind?"

I shake my head, and he unbuckles her the rest of the way and lifts her out. Once free, she starts toddling around the cavernous space.

"I just don't understand," I say. "This whole town is picketing as if the place was stolen from them. But you and Bob were willing parties in this transaction." I gesture my hand toward the windows, toward the whole town. "They all think *I'm* the enemy. If they're so pissed about the sale, why aren't they mad at *you*?"

"I don't know," he says, rubbing the back of his neck.

"You don't know, or you're not telling me everything?"

He looks away, and goddamn it, I want to shake him. To force some real answers here. But when I look at him, he's watching his daughter, and something in his face gives me pause. The sadness. Almost like he's lost.

It's hard to break someone who's already shattered.

My eyes drift to Lottie, watching as she bends to pick at a spot in the concrete. She wobbles, then plants her butt on the ground and starts smacking it. I have to admit the kid is cute, in an almost non-scary way.

"Look, I know it's none of my business why you sold, and under normal circumstance, I'd just do my job with no concern for you or the details of the sale. But the thing is, nothing has been normal about this job since I got here. I've been blackballed by everyone here, as if I've done something wrong. This leads me to believe that no one knows the details of the sale, and they are unfairly targeting me and my employer when they really need to be pointing their fingers at you. So tell me, Ashton Elliot, why did you sell The Till, and why does everyone in town believe we're the villains and not you?"

He looks down, and I feel a pang of sympathy at the flash of discomfort that crosses his face. But then I harden my heart, followed by my expression once he looks up again.

"It's complicated," he says, repeating what's proving to be a popular answer. Then he lets out a sigh before meeting my eyes.

I shake my head. "Nuh uh, I need more than that."

Ashton looks at Lottie, who's happily babbling in her own little world. "We were about to lose the farm," he finally says. "The investment was a rocky one from the start, and it was never a money maker. But Bob and Bec loved the place. They bought the building not long after Sasha and I moved in, and Sasha was placed in charge of the store."

He looks out the window, and I follow his gaze. Bernie was out there in front of the hotel, leaning down to hand a cookie to a little girl with her mother. The smile on her face almost makes her look young. So different from the woman who threw me out of her hotel.

"The Till held its own for a little bit. We sold seeds we got from a catalogue, and opened up the front of the store as a co-op for small businesses. It was charming and sweet, and Sasha loved the place. But soon, the money started bleeding out. We kept pulling from the farm to keep it alive. At one point, the electricity was turned off when the checking account went negative and a check bounced. And then Sasha…" He pauses again. I don't say anything, just wait for him to finish. "Well, she left and we were left holding the bag. There was no choice but to sell, and Alexander popped up out of nowhere with an offer we couldn't refuse. The money was enough to pay off our debts. It let us walk away clean—and fast. We had to take the offer."

"And you didn't tell anyone about the reasons why," I muse. He shakes his head. "Ashton, this town failed you. You all wouldn't have gone under if they'd bought enough to keep you afloat. They are acting like victims when really they're the ones to blame."

"It wasn't them." He glances at me, then at Lottie. "It's a long story."

"I have nothing but time."

He closes his eyes, and I'm suddenly aware that I'm prying into things that are none of my business.

"I'm sorry, I shouldn't—"

"Sasha cleaned us out," he says, his voice low, even though we're the only ones in the shop.

"You mean she *stole* from you? From her parents?"

"From all of us," he says, meeting my eyes. "She took off in Bec's car, but not before emptying the business account. Most of it was Bec and Bob's retirement fund, which they'd invested in The Till, and all of it was gone. We haven't seen her since. Without that money, we had no choice but to sell The Till. The offer from Winslow & Associates came in at the perfect time, and it was enough to pay back everything Sasha took and more. Basically, we had no other choice."

I look down at Lottie, feeling my breath grow sharp and hot as I watch Ashton's daughter—Sasha's daughter—play happily at our feet. Why do I feel enraged by this information? It's not like I have any vested interest in The Till. But I can't help feeling protective over Ashton. Over the Felixes. Over this tiny innocent child with a mom who just up and left her without a second glance.

"And no one in this town knows a thing." I shake my head. "Man, you all must be saints or something, because I'd be blasting my ex's name all over town if he'd pulled a stunt like that."

"It's not that simple," he says.

"Really? Because from where I stand, it's very simple. She embezzled from the family business and then abandoned you all to pick up the pieces. She sounds lovely."

Ashton crouches down, then sits next to Lottie who immediately climbs into his lap. I join them on the floor, then sigh.

"I'm sorry. I mean, I'm not sorry about judging your ex, but I'm sorry for prying. None of this concerns me. How you all handled it is not for me to say."

"You're right, it's not," he says. As much as that pisses me off, I have no argument against it. "And you're also right that we've let her get away with all this by keeping it under wraps. But we're talking about Bec and Bob's daughter here. We're talking about Lottie's mom."

"We're talking about a woman who didn't think twice about stealing your livelihood." Then I shake my head. "There I go again. Sorry."

"It's more than that," he says, waving a hand as if to excuse my intrusion. "We'd been fighting nonstop, and she wanted nothing to do with Lottie. She couldn't even pick up at the house. I was working my ass off, and I'd come home to Lottie in the same clothes she'd slept in, her diaper leaking, and the house a complete wreck while Sasha rotted on the couch. The worst part? Lottie didn't even cry anymore. Six months old, and she didn't cry. It was like she gave up." He looks down at his daughter, twisting a piece of her hair while she leans against his chest. "To top it off, Sasha started smoking pot again. It wasn't anything new. We both met at a cannabis farm we worked at in Oregon, and both of us had been heavy smokers. But when she got pregnant, I'd stopped smoking alongside her in solidarity. I thought we'd quit altogether, but then she started up again after Lottie was born. While I was working, and while she was in charge of our daughter. And it pissed me off. I was giving up everything for our family, and she was just getting high and letting Lottie sit in her shit."

"Ashton, you don't need to tell me anything else," I say.

"No, I do. I've held this inside for way too long, and I'm fucking tired of keeping all of this in." He looks at me. "I blamed it on the drugs. I wasn't sure what else she was on. Honestly, I still don't. All I knew was that I couldn't take it anymore. I was fucking tired, and I worried about our daughter. I mean, Sasha wouldn't even let me involve her parents, so I was completely on my own." He lets out a breath. "I finally came to my senses and went to Bec and Bob with all of this. I was in way over my head. This wasn't the Sasha I knew, and I couldn't do this anymore."

"What did they do?"

"They took her in," he says. "Packed a bag of clothes and had her come to their house. It was just across the way, but she wouldn't see us anymore. Not even Lottie. Bec put a name to it, and I felt like the biggest asshole because all the signs were there."

"Postpartum depression," I whisper, feeling the words ice over my like a ghost. He looks at me quickly, and I avert my eyes.

"See, even you know what it was. I had no fucking clue."

Of course I know what it was—I know *intimately* what it was. But I can't tell him that.

"Maybe you're right," he continues. "I shouldn't be dumping on you. You hardly know me."

"Maybe that's what makes it easier to let it all out," I offer, shaking myself from my thoughts.

He ponders this for a moment. "Maybe," he says. "It's just that everyone in this town knows everything about everyone else, and as you've noticed, loyalty runs deep. They don't know why Sasha left, but they'd take her side over mine in a heartbeat, even with everything that happened."

"I don't know about that."

He laughs, but it doesn't reach his eyes. "Sasha went to the same school everyone else did. She was on the same soccer team. She hung out with the same friends and knew everyone's parents. This town watched her grow up, and they grew up alongside her. But me? I've been here a whole two and a half years. They know me as Sasha's boyfriend, or as Lottie's dad. But as Ashton?" He laughs again, this time looking up at the ceiling, at the ornate architecture that serves as our sky. "I don't have a real friend in this town. Not one person. If it came down to a choice between me and Sasha, no matter what she did, she'd win."

"But her parents—"

"You didn't see it." He takes a deep breath, looking down as if remembering his daughter in his lap. "When we showed up in Lahoma, everyone was so delighted to see her again. They looked past her half-starved body and dull skin from months of living in my car. All they saw was her pregnant belly and the fact that their prodigal daughter had returned."

Lottie squirms, and he releases his hold on her, letting her wobble to standing before taking off to run circles in the center of the room. "I saw the side glances that came my way next," he continues, his eyes never leaving his daughter. "No one said it, but I know what they were thinking. It was my fault she'd left. My fault she looked the way she did. And now she was back, unmarried and pregnant, and I was to blame. If this town found out what she did, it's not her they would hold liable. It would be me."

"I don't know," I say. "She stole from her family, enough to make it hurt. It's her fault you all had to scramble and sell the store. Of anyone, they should picket against her instead of blocking me out of this store or blaming my employer for snatching it up. I mean, did any of you even search for her? Send the police after her? Do anything to make her pay for how she royally fucked all of you?"

Ashton closes his eyes, and I know the answer.

"God, Ashton. Even if Sasha was suffering, it doesn't excuse the fact that she stole that much money."

"People do crazy things when they're depressed."

I say nothing. Because, more than he knows, I understand. Yet, even knowing that kind of pain, I want to disagree. When it happened to me, I didn't steal from my family or abandon everyone I knew.

But the past has its own way of rotting through a person, and who am I to pretend otherwise?

"I suppose," I finally say, my tone unconvinced as I leave the rest to fester like an old wound.

Bernie's Town

Jordy

Ashton sticks around while I sketch ideas on my tablet, experimenting with colors for the shop. He'd asked if it was okay, and I'd shrugged like it was no big deal. But inside, I'm relieved to have him here. The picketers outside are getting louder, their voices an unsettling backdrop. Having Ashton close—chasing a squealing Lottie around the empty space—is both comforting, and admittedly, a little entertaining.

But more than that, I feel an unexpected closeness to him—protective, even. Maybe because he let his guard down, sharing so much with me when we're still practically strangers, or maybe because he's the only one who took me in last night when no one else would.

Honestly, though? Just these few hours with him, and I'm realizing just how kind Ashton is; a wonderful dad to Lottie, still close to his ex's parents, and even after everything Sasha has done to him, after all the ways she's wronged him, he still reserves some grace for her.

I don't understand it, but some part of me clings to that forgiving nature—because, whether I like it or not, I'm going to need it. This town hates me. Sasha may have been the one who started this mess, and Ashton and the Felixes finalized it. But I'm the easy target.

Not that I enjoy being the scapegoat for their family drama, but I'm a temporary resident of Lahoma Springs. I'll be gone in a few weeks. Ashton and the Felixes are here forever … and the only ones who have been nice to me in this whole town.

If taking the brunt of the town's anger means they get to dodge some of it, well … I suppose I can take the bullet with a tight smile.

I shut my laptop and push to my feet, brushing the dust off my ridiculous sunflower jeans. The fact that I'm still wearing that bitch's clothes just about kills me.

"All right," I announce, "I'm tapped out for today. Time for plan B—finding somewhere to stay. Any ideas? Airbnb? Couch Crashers dot com?"

Ashton scoops up Lottie before she can bolt, expertly tucking her into the stroller and handing her a sippy cup before she even has the chance to protest. It's so smooth, so second nature, that I catch myself staring. I've never thought of myself as someone who was impressed by parenting, but I have to admit it's a skill—and Ashton has it down.

"We could ask Bob and Bec if you could stay in Sasha's old room," he says, buckling Lottie in. "Bec already offered."

I snort. "Yeah, I'll pass on that." Staying in Sasha's bed, in Sasha's house, while wearing Sasha's clothes? Hard no. "What else you got?"

He hesitates, then says, "You can stay with me."

I freeze for half a second. I mean, it's an option. It's convenient. Close to the store. Hassle-free.

So tempting…

But I've already taken more than enough hospitality from this family. They owe me nothing, and the last thing I want is to feel like I owe them anything back.

"I'll just stay here," I say, sweeping my hands to indicate this huge, empty building. "There's electricity, a bathroom, and a heater, plus a whole street of restaurants." Restaurants that won't serve me, but he doesn't need to know that.

"And a cushiony spot on the concrete floor while the whole town watches you sleep from the windows." He rolls his eyes. "Come on, Jordy. My house is big enough for the three of us. Plus, you'd get to enjoy Bec's home-cooked meals. Which yes, I eat almost every single night, and you should too. Do you really want to say no to that?"

There are plenty of reasons to say no—starting with the fact that he's already done so much for me. I can't take more of his generosity.

Plus, he smells so fucking good…

No. Nope. Absolutely not. I did not just think that about him.

No way am I getting snowed in by his charm and hospitality. No way am I letting myself admire his solid jawline, his broad shoulders. No way am I inhaling his scent after he works the fields all day. And absolutely *no way* am I entertaining the thought of tasting the salt on his skin…

No. Fucking. Way.

I can't stay with him because I know myself. I'll get too wrapped up in how much I want him, and it will make me forget my number one rule: no dating guys with kids.

I'm already struggling to ignore the way he looks at his daughter. How he treats her—not as an interruption, but as an addition to everything he does. How happy Lottie is, even without a mom, because Ashton and her grandparents have created a life where she's safe and wanted.

I've never known what that feels like. And I want to.

"I don't want to burden you," I say.

Ashton shakes his head. "You wouldn't be a burden. If anything, this is my way of making it up to you. The way this town treats you is my fault, and I'll tell everyone as much if it gets them off your back."

"Don't do that." The words are out before I can stop them. But I mean it. "Bec and Bob have been through enough. You too. And Lottie. I'm just a temporary citizen here to do a job before I leave again. It doesn't matter if they hate me."

It really doesn't—I'm not here forever. But I also do need a place to stay, and arguing with him was getting us nowhere.

"Fine, I'll stay with you." I try to ignore the flutter in my chest when his face lights up in a grin. "And I won't tell these people anything that's not their business, even if your ex is a piece of shit." I glance outside, noting that the picketers are still going strong. It makes me furious just seeing them. I want nothing more than to go out there and give them a piece of my mind. But they already have a vendetta against me, and acting out my rage isn't going to help.

I turn back to Ashton. "If I'm going to get anything done here, I need to clear out these protesters. Will you back me up?"

He points the stroller towards the door, then nods in its direction.

"Let's get to it," he says.

I march to the front door, unlock it, and stride straight to the center of the picketers' slow-moving circle.

"Listen up," I call out, planting my feet. "I get that you're angry, and that you want someone to blame. But blocking the entrance is not going to change what happened."

"You're the one changing our town," a man shoots back. "You and whoever you work for."

I narrow my eyes at him, feeling the agitation rise in me as the others murmur around him. "I was hired to do a job," I point out. "I didn't buy this place, and I didn't sell it either. But you're sure as hell making me the villain because it's easier than facing facts."

"There's freedom of speech laws, lady," another one calls. "We can protest wherever we want."

"Sure," I say, "but the law also says you can't obstruct a place of business, and my boss has lawyers. So unless you're ready to get sued for trespassing, I'd rethink this little stand-off."

A few of them shift uneasily, but a woman in the front steps onto the street and spread her arms wide. "Then we'll just move to the road."

Before I can fire back, Ashton's voice cuts through the tension. "Jordy is not the bad guy here."

All eyes shifts to him, including mine. Lottie sits in her stroller, her juice forgotten as she stares wide-eyed at the crowd. I have this momentary urge to stand in front of her, shielding her from all the negative energy this crowd is directing our way.

"She's an independent contractor," Ashton continues, his voice steady. "She didn't make the decision to sell. I did, and the Felixes did."

"Ashton," I murmur, but he doesn't stop.

"I understand your frustration. You loved The Till. I did too. But there wasn't another choice."

"You could have talked to us," the woman in the street snaps, though her tone is lighter than it was with me.

"We could have done a lot of things," Ashton admits. "But what's done is done. Taking it out on Jordy won't bring The Till back. And whether you shop here or not, this new store is coming. Protesting won't change that."

A beat of silence passes, and I feel it in my static breath. I hate that I'm nervous, that I even care enough about their response to be nervous.

"We won't spend a dime here," the woman finally says. I breath out as a murmur of agreement ripples through the crowd.

"That's fine," Ashton says. "But let Jordy do her job. She's not the one you're mad at."

The crowd continues their grumbling, casting a few sideways glances at us as they disperse. I turn to Ashton, feeling my shoulders lower as I let down my guard. My whole body loosens, making me realize how tightly wound I've been.

"I can't believe that worked," I mutter.

Ashton nods, blowing out a rush of air before shooting me a crooked grin. "Me neither."

"Want to try that on Bernie at the hotel?"

He shakes his head. "Bernie is a tough nut to crack. I think she tolerates me only because of Lottie. But she's obviously dug her heels in about this, and when she digs her heels in about something, there's really no way of turning her around." He bumps my shoulder then, giving me a side grin. "Besides, you're about to stay at Chateau Elliot, run by yours truly. You really want to turn that down?"

No, I really don't, though I should. The way his smile is making my butterflies do somersaults, I should run the other way. But the thought of sharing space with him for weeks on end makes this whole chaotic shitstorm worth it.

"Guess you have a new roommate," I say, bumping him back.

I spend the rest of the afternoon in a nearby coffee shop, amending sketches to fit the space while Ashton takes off so that Lottie can take her nap. The shush of the coffee machine and the burst of caffeine in my veins helps me transition from the chaos of this morning back into work mode.

I compare my earlier designs with some of the new ones I'd worked on this morning. My original ideas include chandeliers and tapestries, bronze sculptures and elaborate murals. It was to be extreme luxury meets 17th century, and honestly, it would have looked exquisite in the space. But having met with the town's fierce loyalty, I feel like it's more important to match the spirit of Lahoma Springs. Sure these people have been assholes, but it's not going to help business if I create something that clashes with the rest of the town.

It's clear that my focus has to do a 180. The new shop needs to infuse the local flavor, and the only way to do that is to explore the neighboring businesses. I just hope they'll let me, but with the way I've been treated so far, it will be a tall order.

I leave the coffee shop and pause outside for a moment, planning my course of action. Taking a deep breath, I close my eyes, willing my heart to calm down. Somehow, I'm going to have to charm this town just so I can get my job done.

Starting with the store next door.

The shop is called Leaf, and it's brimming with leafy green plants from floor to ceiling. When I walk through the open doors, it's like a breath of fresh air. Everything smells mossy and fresh, the air moist as if the plants have just been watered. I'm ready to buy everything in the store. But when I turn to the man at the counter, the air turns frosty with a biting chill.

"Hi there," I say. He remains silent as he peers at me over the top rim of his glasses. "I'm—"

"Jordy Gallo. I know. The designer for that soulless company, Winslow & Associates."

I pause, momentarily stunned, though I shouldn't be. Of course he knows who I am.

Then I recognize him. He was one of the protesters, the well-dressed one who'd left early. And apparently, this is his shop.

"Yes," I stammer. "You probably know that I'm designing the store next door to you, a luxury watch company. I'm planning to give it a Lahoma Springs look to help it fit in with the rest of the town, and—"

"Honey, that store will never fit in with the rest of the town." He says it with a flourish of his hand, as if to dismiss me right out of his store. It's not like I expected any of these shopkeepers to be an easy sell, but his biting tone and stony stare reveal this might be a near impossible task.

I'm not ready to give up, though.

"I get why you think that," I say slowly, "and I admire your loyalty to Lahoma. Honestly, I don't blame you."

He tilts his head ever so slightly, but says nothing.

"If I'm being completely truthful, I wouldn't trust an out-of-town business owner either, if I lived in a small town like this. I mean, you all have a lot going for you, the quaint charm and absolute preciousness of this town."

"Are you mocking us?" His eyes narrow, and I widen mine in response.

"Absolutely not!" I lean forward, reading his nametag. "Michael, I'm agreeing with you. No one should come here and threaten your way of living by introducing a store that clashes with the aesthetic. It would make it stand out, possibly even get people to come in out of curiosity, which is incredibly unfair to all of you who have poured your blood, sweat, and tears into these shops. I mean, your family lines live in these stores, and some outsider is going to come here and act like they're better than all of you by appearing way different?"

God, even I'm eating up my own bullshit. Yet, as Michael continues to look at me unblinking, I start to doubt there's a chance in hell I'll break through. Then he scoffs and shakes his head.

"Goddamn, you're good." His face relaxed into something warmer and a little bit smiley.

I smother a grin under my hand, and he pauses long enough to shake his head. "Don't get smug. I still don't trust you, but I also agree with your little ploy there. I'll be damned if some luxury watch shop overshadows any of the businesses on this strip, especially mine. If there's no stopping this shop from opening here, I might as well make some money. So tell me honey, which plants should we charge to your boss's credit card?"

An hour later, Michael not only helps me spend over a thousand dollars on plants, but also turns the closed sign on his shop so that he can help me on my mission. The man may not trust me, but he sure knows how to use that credit card. By the time we've reached the last store, I have just about everything I need.

The final store is Lock & Key, this French Country antique store full of artisan treasures. I do a slow circle as I take in the historic pieces, feeling breathless at the stories each item whispers to me. The ceramic white milk jugs and the painted wood framed windows. The chicken nesting boxes holding plates and interesting bottles in the hay-filled sections. The old ladder with colorful material draped over each rung. The hundred-year-old stove and the handmade Christmas ornaments.

Timeless.

I want to scoop up every item and carry them over to the new shop. The mix of modern time pieces with farmhouse vintage goods make the most sense in the world.

"You need this," Michael breathes, running his hand over a Civil War-era armoire. One look, and I know he's right. It has cabinets that open to drawers and shelves. On the side are hidden chambers, practically invisible if you're not looking for them.

This is a centerpiece of a furniture item, and I know it belongs in Timeless. But I wince when I see the price tag. $24,000. Alexander might have overlooked a $13,000 dinner bill, but charging this much not even twenty-four hours later feels like a one-way ticket out of a job.

"It's one of a kind," someone says behind me. I turn to see a girl of about twenty standing there shyly, her lips painted red and her blonde hair swept up in a ponytail. Her nametag says Grace Dalton, and she has a kind of Taylor Swift vibe to her in her cardigan and short skirt. "The owner keeps it mostly for bragging rights," Grace admits. "It's been in her family for years. She keeps saying she'll let it go to the right buyer, but so far, no one has even made an offer."

"Well, it's her lucky day," Michael says, and I glance at his beaming face and shake my head. "Stop," he hisses to me, then charms his smile back to Grace. "She'll take it. It's for that shop on the corner, you know, the one that used to be The Till."

Grace raises an eyebrow, then looks at me. But instead of the usual scowl these shopkeepers throw my way, she looks amused.

"So, you're the famous Ms. Gallo," she says.

"In the flesh." I give a mock curtsy. "But I think I need to put some thought into whether or not I get this piece." My logical side knows there is no way I can buy this, but the more my eyes linger on the armoire, the more I feel like I don't have a choice. It's just the kind of showstopper I was looking for. "For something of this size and cost, I really should get approval from my boss."

"Don't bother, it's not for sale," a woman shouts from across the store. I turn, then groan when I see who the voice belongs to. Good old Bernice Lahoma. Judging by her position behind the counter, this is also her store.

"Of course this is Bernie's shop," I mutter. "I forgot she owns the whole town." Seeing her in Lock & Key is a punch to the gut. I'm already in love with this store, but I don't want to give Bernie any business with the way she treated me.

"Not the *whole* town," Grace says. "I mean, she inherited a lot of the shops here. But she's let go of a few businesses in recent years. All she has left now is the Lahoma Hotel, Lock & Key, and Charred Steakhouse."

"Oh, that's all?" I scoff, side-eyeing Bernie who seems intent on staring me down until I leave. I turn my back to her.

"Well, she's not getting any younger," Grace says, oblivious to my sarcasm. She turns to Michael. "Say, didn't she own The Till for a time?"

Michael nods. "She did for years, and then she sold it to the Felix family when they expressed interest."

Things suddenly make sense. I realize now why Bernie has such a vendetta against me.

"I wonder why the Felixes didn't just sell the shop back to Bernie," I muse.

Michael raises an eyebrow. "That's the question of the century."

Everyone Has a Back Story

Ashton

Jordy's a lot more talkative as we gather around the table for dinner at the Felix house. Gone is the woman who'd woken up hungover and a bit defeated this morning. Now, she's animated and full of smiles, sharing details about the friends she made, the stores she visited, and how Timeless is really coming together.

It's hard to hear. Her excitement is understandable, but it's also a nail into the coffin of our decision to sell.

I hide my leftover guilt, however, leaning in as she continues sharing about her day.

"Once Michael realized he could spend my boss's money, he became the biggest help," she says. "Of course, Alexander is going to regret the free rein he gave me for expenses—especially after that pricey meal I charged last night."

She shoots me a pointed look. I wince slightly but hold my ground.

"Hey, I didn't even suggest you pay for everyone's meals," I protest. "That was all you."

"And those magic Manhattans you insisted I try," she counters, one eyebrow lifting meaningfully. "The ones that kept appearing in front of me while my dinner was mysteriously delayed."

Fuck.

I flick a glance at Bec, who is now eyeing me with quiet judgment.

"What did you do?" she asks, her voice sharp with suspicion.

"I didn't do anything." I turn back to Jordy, who clearly doesn't believe me. "Okay fine, I may have been aware that Griffin was pulling shenanigans last night. He, uh … kept forgetting to put your dinner order in."

Jordy snorts. "Forgetting. Right."

"And," I add reluctantly, "he may have made your Manhattans doubles."

Her eyes widen. "That ass!"

Then she slaps a hand over her mouth, glancing at Lottie, then Bec and Bob. *Sorry*, she mouths.

I shake my head. "Trust me, these two have heard me say worse. But seriously, I should've put a stop to it sooner. I saw what Griff was doing, and I let it go on way too long. I'm sorry."

Jordy shrugs. "I should be more pissed," she admits, "but I also should have known better than to drink anything in a town full of people who hate me."

"Well, *I* don't hate you," I say firmly.

"And neither do we, dear," Bec adds. "We're just sorry our town is so resistant to change. It's not like we sold the whole town. It was just a store."

She glances at Bob, who stays silent, focused on his food.

When I look at Jordy, I can tell she caught the exchange. This isn't just about a store.

Jordy lets the moment settle before shifting the conversation.

"Bec, this is the best meal I've ever had," she says, her voice lighter now. "My grandmother used to make stew, but it never tasted like this. What's your secret?"

Bec's cheeks flush under the compliment. She made us pot roast stew with buttermilk biscuits—the kind of meal that settles deep in your belly, warming places you didn't even realize were cold.

"Oh, it's just an old family recipe," Bec says with a modest wave of her hand. "Stew always tastes best at the end of a busy day."

"Don't listen to her," Bob grunts. "She sweats the onions in a quarter bottle of wine, then adds a few extra dashes of Worcestershire, and she thickens it with mashed potato instead of flour."

"Bob, you're giving away all my secrets." Bec swats his arm playfully, but her eyes crinkle with affection.

Across the table, Lottie is wearing more stew than what she put in her mouth. Bec sighs. "Well, I see someone's going to need a bath after this."

For Lottie, I always mash the stew up extra fine, then tear up a biscuit so she can grasp the pieces with her tiny fingers.

She likes feeding herself—insists on it—so meals like this always end in a bath. But just like the rest of us, this is one of her favorites, and she hums quietly as she works at the bowl in front of her.

Bec sets her spoon down, her expression darkening. "I'm going to have a talk with Griffin next time I'm in town," she mutters. "Or maybe I'll bring it up when I play Bridge with Bernie—let her know what her son's been up to."

Jordy groans. "Wait, Bernie is Griffin's mom? My god, is everyone related in this town?"

Bec chuckles. "No, but I know it seems that way."

Then, after a pause, her voice softens. "I think you know that our daughter used to manage The Till before she…"

She trails off, glancing at Bob.

He inhales sharply, then clears his throat, all without looking at her.

"Excuse me," he says, pushing back from the table. "Thanks for dinner, honey."

He leans down, pressing a kiss to the side of her head, then takes his bowl to the sink and disappears down the hall toward the family room.

Bec lets out a slow breath, her fingers tightening around her napkin.

"Sorry," she whispers. "He doesn't like talking about Sasha." Her voice wavers. "I guess neither of us do."

Jordy is quiet for a moment, studying Bec with a look of quiet understanding. Then she says gently, "You don't have to tell me anything."

She glances at me, something unreadable flickering in her gaze before turning back to Bec.

"But I know that this town loved your daughter, and that you all miss her very much." Her voice is steady, but there is something raw beneath it. "And I know it must be hard to see me transforming a space that Sasha once designed and managed. Loyalty runs deep here, and while it's been hard to navigate as an outsider … I'm also a little in awe of it."

She hesitates, then adds, "Where I come from, loyalty often comes with collateral. Even my own mom would sell me out for the right price."

Bec sucks in a quiet breath.

"Oh, honey, that's awful." She reaches across the table, squeezing Jordy's hand.

Jordy flinches at the show of comfort, then looks at Bec's hand and softens. She shakes her head as if shaking off the weight of her own words. I get the feeling she isn't used to empathy.

"Sorry," she says quickly. "That's not how I meant it. My mom isn't some evil monster or anything. I just mean that I admire the way people here stick up for each other, how you have each other's backs."

"That's generous of you," I say, holding her gaze. "But just know that we have your back too, and as long as you're here in town, you're safe."

Jordy smirks. "As long as you're not in charge of mixing my drinks."

Back at home, I ease Lottie's door shut once she's settled, then turn to see Jordy at the kitchen counter poring over her sketches. She traces the rim of her wine glass absentmindedly, her brows furrowed in concentration.

I lean against the doorjamb, watching unnoticed. Even in sweats and her dark hair piled into a messy bun, she's stunning. The last twenty-four hours have been chaos, yet it feels right that she's here.

Besides Bec, no woman has been in this house in a long time. Dating has been the last thing on my mind.

Until now.

I shake the thought away before it can take root. Jordy is here because she has nowhere else to go, not because I have some ulterior motive, and as far as I can tell, she's not interested. She seems grateful for a place to stay—nothing more.

I cross the room, pulling out a stool. She looks up as I sit. Between us is the bottle of wine and her now empty glass, which I fill before pouring my own.

"That's not a double, is it?" she jokes.

I groan as she laughs.

"I can't tell you how sorry I am about that."

She shakes her head. "You weren't the one pouring, and I shouldn't have brought it up in front of Bec and Bob. It was petty and I'm sorry."

"You have nothing to apologize for. It was an asshole move—whether I did it or just let it happen."

Silence stretches between us, thick but not uncomfortable. Then Jordy scrunches her nose. "From what I remember, it was the best Manhattan I've ever had. A little strong, but the best. What can I say? I'm a whiskey girl."

"Told you." I smirk. "We'll have to go back sometime so you can—"

"Oh, hell no," she cuts in. "Now that I know Griff is related to the Wicked Witch of the West, that's a hard pass. No way am I risking getting poisoned by Bernie or her son."

"That's a little extreme, don't you think?"

She shoots me a glare. "The town sheriff is married to one of the protesters, and Bernie's tight with him. How hard do you think it'd be for them to hide my body?"

I snort into my glass. "That's ridiculous."

"Is it?" She arches a brow.

"You've made a couple friends here," I point out. "If you can do that, despite the hostility this town has thrown your way, I'm fully confident you'll have the rest of this place eating out of your hand."

"I don't know about *friends*," she says. "Michael was only interested because he could spend my boss's money."

"As much fun as that must have been, Michael would not have spent the day with you for just that."

I take a sip of wine, then lean forward. "Here's what you don't know about him … two years ago, he battled an aggressive form of cancer that cost him all his hair and a shit ton of weight."

Jordy's eyes widen. "Oh my god, seriously? I never would've guessed."

"He's fine now," I assure her, "but he wasn't back then. He had to close Leaf for a few months because he was too weak to manage it, and he had no other staff. His boyfriend, Dominic, moved in with him and took care of everything. But it wasn't long before it became too much. One night, Dominic just took off—right when Michael had finally let himself trust someone to take care of him."

Jordy's expression darkens. "*What the fuck.* That's awful." She shakes her head, gripping her glass tighter. "Did the town step in? Please tell me someone helped him recover."

"Not at first. Michael's good at knowing everyone else's business, but when it comes to himself, he keeps things locked down. We all assumed Dominic was taking care of him, it wasn't until Bernie dropped off a casserole that she found out what happened. She organized a meal train, housecleaning, rides to appointments—the whole nine yards." I sigh. "He's grateful, but he trusts no one now. Doesn't spend time with anyone. Just his plants. So yeah, maybe he tagged along for your boss's money. But the fact that he stuck around? That says something else."

Jordy takes a long sip of wine, her expression troubled. "I don't know what's worse … the fact that Michael's ex abandoned him, or the fact that you just ruined my view of that bitch, Bernie."

I laugh. "She's protective, it's her nature. I'm confident she'll warm up to you before you have to leave. You two might even end up being friends."

Jordy snorts. "Sure. Besties. We'll braid each other's hair—if I knew how to braid."

I don't mean to, but my gaze drops to her hair, imagining the strands sliding through my fingers. How it would feel. How it would look pulled back in a braid.

I force my focus back to my wine.

"What about Grace?" she asks. "Besides you and the Felixes, she's the only other person who didn't bat an eye when she found out who I was. Is she one of those silent backstabbing types? Should I arm myself?"

I chuckle. "Grace is honestly the nicest person in this town. You could slash her tires, and she'd offer to help you with whatever's ruining your day."

Jordy tilts her head. "Is she seeing anyone? You seem to have a high opinion of her. Have you asked her out?"

I nearly choke on my wine. "*She's like twelve*," I manage.

Jordy smirked. "She's in her twenties, right?"

"Doesn't matter. I'm not interested."

Her expression is unreadable, but something about the way she asked doesn't sit right with me.

"Okay," she says slowly. She sips her wine, her eyes staying on mine. "But have you thought about moving on?"

A thrill goes through me at the words, some fluttery foreign feeling I brush aside before it can take root.

"Sure, I've thought about it. But between Lottie and the farm, there's not much left for anything else."

"I don't buy that." She tilts her head slightly. "I mean, you're here with me now. You've been more supportive than you needed to be. Some girl would be *very* lucky to get this kind of attention."

She runs her finger along the stem of her wine glass, absentmindedly tracing the edge. My gaze follows the movement, and for a split second, I imagine that same finger trailing over my bare chest. Heat curls in my stomach before I shove the thought away.

"You clearly have the time to go out," she adds. "I mean, you were out last night while Bec watched Lottie."

"I'm not saying I *can't*," I say. "I'm saying I just haven't *wanted* to. Last night was a rare thing."

"And was it really so bad?" She gives me a pointed look, raising an eyebrow.

I smirk. "You tell me. First night out in months, and I got a girl drunk, got her kicked out of a hotel—again—and ended up taking her home to meet the folks."

Jordy laughs. "You move fast."

She says it so casually, without a hint of flirtation, but the words stick. I *did* move fast … with Sasha, and now with Jordy—this beautiful, sharp, complicated woman who is living under my roof for at least the next month.

I need to keep my head straight.

"Well, roomie," I say, pushing back from the stool, "the only place I'm moving fast is to bed—so we can do this all again tomorrow."

I drain the rest of my wine and move to the sink. When I turn around, she's suddenly there. Before I can react, her arms wrap around me, and my breath stalls.

She presses her head against my chest, her hands resting lightly on my back. For a split second, I freeze, my arms hovering in the air. Then instinct takes over, and I pull her in, my hands settling on her waist.

She fits against me too damn well, every soft curve molding into me like she belongs there. And *fuck*, she smells good—like lilacs and something warm, something unmistakably *her*. I let myself inhale—just once—before forcing myself to focus.

"What's this?" I murmur, my voice lower than I intend.

Jordy doesn't lift her head. "Just … thanks," she says, her words muffled against my shirt.

After a long moment, she pulls back, her hands slipping away from me. Her cheeks are tinged pink, like she's just realized what she did, or maybe she regrets it.

All I know is that I already miss her warmth.

"I had no idea what I was walking into when I came here," she admits. "This could've gone *so* badly. But you didn't just make it possible for me to do my job, you made sure I was comfortable. I don't know anyone who would go this far for a total stranger."

I let out a slow breath. "I think we're past strangers."

She smirks. "I mean, you *did* hold my hair while I puked."

"There's a *lovely* visual," I say dryly.

She laughs, shaking her head. "But really, I'm lucky I ran into you yesterday. It helps to have a friend like you."

Friend.

The word settles between us like a barrier. A safe boundary she's setting.

I nod, forcing a grin. "Yeah. Lucky."

9

Not Friends

Jordy

Friend.

That's what I called Ashton before heading to bed. I saw the way his brow furrowed, like he couldn't stand the thought of being friends with someone like me.

He'd been nice to me, more than nice—I'm literally sleeping in his house. But I can't shake the feeling that he's doing all this because he's a good guy, not because he likes me.

I've never cared this much about what someone thought of me. I've held my head high through worse—when I found out Brayden was cheating on me with my cousin, when I moved to New York and clawed my way into a career that wasn't easy to break into, when I walked into businesses and watched people take one look at me and dismiss me outright.

I do not bow to anyone's misconceptions about me.

But my confidence also means people get the wrong idea. They think I'm bitchy. Too single-minded. Hard to work with. The kind of person who doesn't need friends.

And yet, something about Ashton unnerves me.

The way he listens—really listens—like he actually cares about what I have to say. The way his hand lingers at the small of my back when we walk. The way he acted as a buffer with Bernie, like he was standing between me and whatever threat she posed.

It's making it hard to keep my walls up.

But that look on his face when I mentioned being his friend? That's all the reminder I need. This is still a business transaction. The Till has been under his family's care. That makes him invested in my success. Maybe. Or maybe he doesn't care about Timeless at all. Maybe I'm just the offering to make up for his mistakes—his way of making peace with Sasha's absence.

Whatever it is, we aren't friends.

I'm still repeating this to myself the next morning as I grab my coffee—only to come face to face with Ashton's entirely too perfect bare chest.

Holy hell.

Dark, defined muscles. Chiseled abs. Flannel pajama pants slung so low on his hips I almost forget how to breathe.

"Morning," he says, and when I finally tear my gaze away from his torso, his eyes are amused.

I clear my throat and edge around him carefully, avoiding any sudden movements that might involve grabbing onto his shoulders like some sex-starved lunatic. How long has it been? Faced with Ashton's half naked body, entirely too long.

"Morning," I squeak, reaching for a coffee cup.

"Did you sleep well?"

Did I ever. He'd changed the sheets before insisting I take his bed while he slept on the couch. I'd fought him on it, but he was more stubborn than me, and I'd eventually given in.

Even with fresh sheets, his bed had *still* smelled like him.

That scent distracted me way too much, to the point where I had to slip a hand into my underwear and deal with my frustration before I could even fall asleep. When I woke up, I was rested—but also very aware of the fact that the first thing I did was inhale deeply, just to smell him again.

"I was comfortable," I say, keeping my voice as even as possible. "Thanks for giving up your room. Did you sleep okay?"

"Like a rock." He grins. "That couch is way comfier than it looks."

I'm not sure what to do with myself in this moment. Do I take my coffee and retreat to my room? Or do I stay out here, sipping slowly while sneaking shameless glances?

Before I can overthink it, Lottie's muffled cries sound from her room.

"Right on time," Ashton says with a laugh, setting his coffee down and heading toward her door.

I watch him walk away—and oh my god, he has the nicest ass. Two perfectly sculpted mounds that make me want to squeeze, maybe take a bite out of, if I'm being honest with myself.

I'm still recovering from that revelation when my phone rings.

Alexander.

I sigh, staring at the screen before answering.

"How's everything going?" he asks. "Is the store ready to be staged?"

"Not quite," I say with a small laugh.

Ashton re-emerges, carrying a sleepy Lottie in his arms. She's wrapped in a blanket, clutching a stuffed elephant, curled up against his bare chest like she belongs there. And I melt. There's something so impossibly sexy about seeing a strong, muscular man being completely soft with his kid. Like it's the most natural thing in the world.

I inhale sharply, forcing myself to focus.

"I ordered just about everything we need from the small shops around town," I say.

Alexander sucks in a breath. "I don't know about that," he says. "We want Timeless to stand out, to be the place where tourists gravitate. This is a new brand, Jordy. We're not trying to blend in with the local mom-and-pop vibe."

I stiffen, then glance at Ashton who is scrolling his phone while Lottie snuggles against him. The scene is so peaceful, so easy—the exact opposite of the frustration brewing inside me.

I pick up my coffee and head to my room, shutting the door behind me.

"You told me you trusted my vision," I say tightly. "That I should move fast and make decisions on my own. That's what I remember from our conversation last week."

"We had ideas last week," he counters. "Luxury. Elegance. Not whatever you're currently cooking up."

"You don't even know what I have planned." My voice is rising. "And as far as I can tell, you haven't even been to this town, so you have no idea what it's actually like."

Alexander sighs. "Sweetheart, I grew up in that town."

I freeze. "What?"

"It was a long time ago," he admits. "My family doesn't live there anymore. But yeah, I lived there until eighth grade. And I'm telling you—if it hasn't changed in twenty years, it should. We can be the force that brings Lahoma into the modern era."

My chest tightens. I don't want to be that force. I don't want to rip this town apart just to turn it into another generic tourist trap.

"Maybe I'm not the right person for this," I say finally.

"Honey, no. You *are* the right person."

"Then why are you dismissing everything I'm telling you?"

Silence.

Then, a long sigh. "You're right." A pause. "But can you at least incorporate some twenty-first century design? Something that leans more toward luxury than barnyard?"

A slow smile spreads across my face.

"I can do that," I promise. "But you'll have to keep an open mind. I think you're really going to love this."

10

Parenting 101

Ashton

Jordy emerges from the bedroom just as the bacon finishes crisping in the pan. Her cheeks are flushed, and a huge smile lights up her face. Something inside me tightens just knowing she'd been talking to Alexander. The conversation had sounded tense, but now she's smiling as if everything shifted.

What if this is more than just a working relationship?

And if it is, why the hell do I care? I have no reason to feel jealous.

So why the fuck am I?

"God, that smells good," she says, stepping into the kitchen. "With all you've done for me, I should be cooking for you. Is there something I can do to help?"

I nod toward the toaster. "You can push those down, then butter them when they're done. How do you like your eggs?"

"Any way is fine." She presses the toaster lever, then turns to face me. "Just make them however you're making them for yourself."

I struggle to keep my eyes from lingering on the way her shirt hugs her chest, or the way her tan legs look impossibly long in those tiny shorts beneath her open robe.

"Okay, hard fried it is," I say, giving her a wink. "Come on, everyone likes their eggs a certain way."

"How do *you* like them?" she asks, a playful glint in her eyes.

Touché.

"Why should I tell you when you won't tell me yours?"

She laughs, her voice light. "This is like a 'I'll show you mine if you show me yours' argument."

Fuck. The thoughts that line brings up are dangerous. Is she trying to kill me?

"Fine, brat," I growl, and she grins at the nickname. "I like them different ways, but with bacon, I like them cooked over medium so the yolks are just a little firm but mostly like jelly."

Her eyes widen. "What a coincidence!" She offers a crooked smile. "That's exactly how I like them."

I roll my eyes, cracking the eggs into the pan, now greasy from the bacon. She finishes the toast, and I plate everything, including a small bowl of chopped up egg, toast, and bacon for Lottie. I notice again that Jordy takes the seat furthest from Lottie. It's not a big deal. I mean, I always sit by my daughter, but it's like Jordy is avoiding her. She watches her from a distance though, especially when she thinks I'm not looking. It's like she's fascinated and terrified at the same time.

"So, besides shopping, designing shops, and liking eggs exactly like mine, what else do you do?"

Jordy takes a bite of breakfast, humming with satisfaction. "This is really good," she says, wiping her mouth with a napkin. "I don't know. Lately there hasn't been much time for anything else. When I'm not working, I'm usually researching style trends or posting about designs on social media to gain more clients or interest." She tilts her head slightly. "I like reading, if you count opening a book before bed and falling asleep within two pages."

"I can relate," I laugh. "I've been trying to get through *The Martian* for three months now. I think I like it, but it's hard to say when I only get through a chapter a week."

"So, you basically eat, breathe, and dream design and that's it? Do you have a favorite color? A place to unwind? A favorite vacation spot?"

"Italy," she says, then takes another bite. "I lived there for a month two years ago."

"Wow. I've never ventured beyond the West Coast. What did you love most about it?"

"The escape." She breathes a soft laugh, but there's something sad in her eyes. I can't ignore it.

"What were you escaping from?"

She hesitates, her fork halfway to her mouth. I know she's uncomfortable, but I refuse to back down. "Come on, I've pretty much told you my whole story, and you've been sitting here like a closed book. You've got to give me something here."

Jordy shoots me a withering look, then rolls her eyes. "A broken engagement," she mutters.

"Ouch."

"Not finished." Her eyebrow quirk. "My fiancé left me for another woman, and not just any other woman." She pauses, a wince in her expression. "He left me for my cousin."

I suck in a breath.

"And now, they're married and have a baby."

"Wait." I think back to yesterday. "Is this the same cousin you were talking about? The one who just had a baby?"

"The one and only."

I let out a long, heavy exhale, shaking my head. "Damn, no wonder you don't like kids."

"I never said I didn't like kids," she protests, though she rolls her eyes. "I don't hate them. It's just that…" She trails off, leaving the unspoken words hanging. I don't press. "At any rate, I spent five years shaping my life around that relationship. I stayed near home when all I really wanted was to travel, to see the world and make a name for myself. After it ended, I packed up what I could and traveled through Europe for three months before finding a place to live in New York."

"And Italy was your favorite. What was the best part?"

"The food," she says with a smile, "I've spent my whole life eating clean and healthy. My mom's always been on my case about what I eat, how much I exercise. She wanted me to be an actress. *Her* dream. I'd be the star she could brag about."

She takes a sip of coffee, looking at me over the rim, her eyes distant.

"I'm a huge disappointment to her."

"But how? You've managed to make your life what you want, especially after a bad breakup. I'd think she'd be proud of you."

"You'd think," she mutters, then laughs bitterly. "You don't know my mom. Let's just say nothing is easy with her. I'll always fall short."

She nods toward Lottie, who's busy playing with her food. "But I get it now. You'll see. Your daughter's easy now, but at some point, she'll have her own ideas and goals. They won't align with what you want for her. You'll feel like you've invested all this time and energy into a path for her, only to watch her reject it all."

I can't speak right away. Her words are too heavy, too honest.

Too wrong.

Finally, I say, "First off, I *hope* my daughter finds her own path in life."

Jordy scoffs, shaking her head. "Like her mom did? How proud do you think Bob and Bec are of Sasha for making her own way?"

"That's not a fair comparison—"

"Isn't it? I'm sure they had dreams for Sasha. Instead, she robs them blind and takes off, making them sell the store just to keep the farm afloat."

I know the gravity of what Sasha did. I've thought the same things. But something about the way Jordy frames it makes me want to defend her. Even more, I want to argue against Jordy's skewed sense of parenting.

"Okay, Sasha made mistakes—mistakes that Bob and Bec never would've wanted for her. But they still keep her room ready for her, in case she comes back. No matter what she's done, or what happens, they'll always welcome her home. That's what good parents do." I look at Lottie, who is still playing with her food. "That's the kind of parent I want to be for Lottie. Yes, I have hopes for her, but they aren't set in stone. I hope she finds what excites her each day and chases that with everything she's got. I hope she fails so that she knows how to pick herself up again. Most of all, I hope she lives a life of her own making, even if that means rejecting my plans for her. All I can do is offer her a foundation of love and support, so she knows she's safe and loved no matter what path she takes."

Jordy's eyes are wide when I finish, and she quickly turns away.

I see it then—she's crying ... or trying not to.

"Hey. What's happening? What's on your mind?"

She waves her hand, trying to brush it off. Then she gets up, picking up her plate to clear it. I know it's her way of escaping.

"Leave it," I say gently. "Come here."

She shakes her head, wiping her eyes. But still, she sits back down, pushing her plate away. I reach for her hand, pulling her closer. The intimacy of the moment hits me like a freight train. Her cheek against my chest. My arm around her shoulders. The warmth of her tears soaking into my skin.

And I don't care if it's too forward, I just want to comfort her.

I stroke her hair softly. "Tell me what you're feeling."

"I'm feeling stupid," she says with a soft laugh, trying to pull away. But I keep my arm around her, just enough pressure to keep her there, but not too much. She relaxes, leaning into me. "I'd like to think I've been a better daughter than Sasha ever was."

"Fair," I say, "I don't doubt that's true."

When she pulls away this time, it's only to wipe at her eyes. She gives me a watery smile, her face still beautiful despite the tear stains.

"I want to tell you that you have no idea what you're talking about," she says softly, her voice breaking, her smile fading. "I want to tell you that she's too young for you to know how you'll act when she comes home drunk for the first time, or starts dating a guy you don't approve of, or when she decides to quit acting and try something else—like designing shops and office buildings."

I stay silent, watching her, learning more about Jordy in these few moments than I have in all the time we've spent together.

"But I know it's not true," she whispers, her sobs becoming more frantic. "I did everything right, and it still wasn't enough."

I want to pull her back into my arms and take away the pain, but I let her speak.

"I did the acting classes, even though the other girls were better than me. I starved myself to a size 0, but my mom still pointed out all my body flaws." Her voice cracks. "And after I—"

She breaks into a sob, and this time I reach for her but she steps back.

"I kept it secret from the rest of the family when I got pregnant," she says, and my chest clenches. "My parents knew, and of course, Brayden and his parents. But no one else." She scoffs. "I had to keep up appearances, you know?" She looks down at her hands, twisting them in front of her as if they can undo the emotional knot in her chest. "I accepted Brayden's proposal, even though I barely knew him. My mom said I'd be a disgrace if I had a baby outside of marriage."

She pauses, eyes glassy as she fights to get the words out.

"And when I lost the baby," she whispers, "I didn't say a word. I held my head high, pretended everything was fine. But I was falling apart."

My heart shatters.

"Oh, honey. I'm so sorry."

Lottie's fussing pulls my attention away, and I feel torn. Jordy is breaking in front of me, but my daughter needs me. As I pick Lottie up from her highchair, Jordy smiles through her tears.

"Lottie is lucky to have a parent like you," she says softly. "You know how to put her first."

And then she walks away.

Floating Down the River

Jordy

It only takes a few days to order everything I need for Timeless. I knew this would be the quick part. Now comes the waiting part. I have workers lined up for the next few weeks to build the partitioned back-office space, paint the walls, install the lighting fixtures, and add in raised flooring. Originally, I balked when Alexander suggested I stay on site while all this work happened. There really wasn't much for me to do except to observe the work, which hardly required my every day presence.

Now, I'm glad.

It's not hard to settle into the easy living lifestyle Lahoma Springs seems to generate. Ashton and I always start our day at Bec and Bob's house for breakfast at way too early o'clock. He drops Lottie off at the Felixes' house before I even wake up, and then we all eat together once I pull myself out of bed and head to their house. I'm aware that the logical thing would be for me to bring Lottie with me later so that Ashton doesn't have to drag her out of the house so early. I mean, it'd be the least I could do. But I can't bring myself to offer, and he never asks. So it just remains this unspoken burden I let mull around my mind.

But on Day Three of no work and nothing to do, I'm going stir crazy.

"I think I'll do a little exploring today," I muse to Ashton while we clean up the dishes. Bec is in the other room playing with Lottie, and Bob headed into town to pick up some feed. Washing dishes with Ashton—him rinsing the plates and me drying them and putting them away—offers a feeling of belonging I can't quite explain. Like this is my home too. Even if it's just for a few more weeks.

"You should see what Michael or Grace are doing," he mentions, and I wrinkle my nose. He tilts his head at me. "What? I thought you liked them."

"I do," I say. We ran into each other a few times over the last couple days, but only in passing. Even though I'd felt a brief connection with them that first day, it never extends beyond that. Just the thought of approaching them makes me want to crawl inside myself and hide. "I just don't think we've reached the point in our friendship where we invite each other to do things together."

"It has to start somewhere," he points out. I breathe in deeply, unspeaking, and he laughs. "Okay, fine. Still, exploring this town alone hardly sounds fun."

He's right. This is so much different than exploring Europe. Back then, I was completely anonymous. Plus, I had all these lists of places I wanted to see and experiences I wanted to try.

I don't know Lahoma at all, other than the Felix farm and the short drive into town. Plus, thanks to my first day appearance, I'm kind of a celebrity here—hardly anonymous. The people in this town no longer shun me, but they don't offer warm welcomes either. Instead, I feel kind of like a tiger pacing its cage. The town watches my every move, but no one speaks to me beyond vague pleasantries.

"I have an idea," Ashton says, rinsing the last plate before handing it to me. "How about I take the rest of the day off and give you the full Lahoma Springs experience?"

For a moment, I stare at him, thrown by the casual generosity of his offer. Then my brain goes straight to the gutter.

The full Lahoma Springs experience.

What will I experience first? The weight of his body? The feel of his hands? The taste of his sweat?

Jesus. Pull it together, Jordy.

"What are you smiling at?" His lips curve, amused, and I smother my grin before shaking my head.

"Nothing," I say, my voice an octave too high. "That sounds fun."

He puts the towel down, then nods at the door. "All right. First things first, you head home and change into a bathing suit and clothes you don't mind getting wet."

"We're going swimming?" I ask. He shakes his head.

"Not intentionally. Something better."

An hour later, we're on the dock of the Lahoma River, each of us getting paired with a stand-up paddle board. I'm wearing shorts and a large sweatshirt over my bathing suit—both of which will NOT get wet if I can help it. The weather is somewhat warm, though not warm enough to go without layers. It's definitely not warm enough to go swimming—not that I want to. The water is brown from sediment, and has a slight mossy smell to it that would likely cling to my hair for weeks. It's no worse than the manure smell of this town, though that odor has thankfully faded with time—that, or I'm just used to it.

Regardless, standing on the dock and looking at the murky water, I'm unsure how I let Ashton convince me this would be fun.

Speaking of Ashton, he's incredibly hard to look away from in his swim trunks and boat shoes. If I think he looks good in a shirt, I'm definitely not prepared for the state of the ab situation he has going on. Holy fuck, the man is ripped. He's seriously built like a linebacker. Everything about him is broad, from his shoulders to his core to the way his ass fills out those damn shorts. I swear I try not to look, but that man is packing. There is no mistaking that when I say broad, I mean *everything*.

But of course, he catches me looking. The way the tip of his tongue slides over his full lips as he catches my gaze, I cannot look away fast enough.

"Uh, I can honestly say I've never done anything like this before." My cheeks burn, and I take a deep breath in. "Paddle boarding, I mean." What the fuck. What else would he think I meant?

"It's as easy as walking," the guy at the dock says and claps Ashton on the shoulder, instantly breaking whatever tension is happening … or not happening. "Dude, where have you been? I feel like I haven't seen you in years."

Ashton's eyes leave mine, and his grin fades into politeness. "Hey Brett," he says, then shrugs. "You know how it is. Lottie is growing like a weed, and the farm isn't going to work itself. Between those two things, it's not like I have a lot of free time to float down the river."

"Man, there's always time to float. You just have to make it a priority. Look at me, I have two girls and Janie is pregnant with our third, and I still find time to go with the river flow."

"Not so hard when it's literally your job."

Brett laughs, clapping Ashton again. "Fair point, my friend. Still, don't be a stranger. Let's grab beers sometime."

Ashton nods, though I notice he never really confirms. He turns to me, and I offer a small smile. *I get you*, I want to say. He nods, just slightly. The impact of it though, just that tiny connection, makes my heart swell.

"Let's get you in the water," he says, but I shake my head.

"You need to go first because I have no idea how to get on this thing without going for a swim."

He laughs, then sets his board down. I do the same, using my paddle to keep it in place while he easily steps on his board and drifts out. Then he nods at me.

"It's that easy," he calls.

"Do it again," I say. "I don't think I caught that."

Ashton laughs from his paddleboard, effortlessly balancing as he drifts ahead.

"Come on, New York. You got this."

I take a deep breath.

"Atta girl," Brett encourages beside me. "Just step forward in one motion. The board's sturdy, it won't flip."

Wanna bet?

I exhale sharply, then force myself to commit, stepping onto the board with my arms out wide, the paddle clenched in my right hand. The second my foot lands, my core tightens, adjusting to the wobble. For a split second, I sway but— miraculously—I catch my balance.

"You did it!" Ashton raises his paddle in the air, grinning. Water droplets fly from the blade, hitting my sleeve.

I narrow my eyes. "Did you just splash me?"

"What? Me? Never."

I point my paddle at him. "You're going to regret that."

He smirks. "We'll see."

I follow his lead as he applies his paddle to the water, and we head downstream with the current. He teaches me how to move the paddle like a C, the arc curving away from each side of the paddle board, to keep the board straight. Once I get the hang of it, I feel sturdier. I realize it really will be hard to fall off, though not impossible. A few times I still feel wobbly. I've never been gifted in the athletic department. Even when I took dance classes, I was always one of the bottom five.

But as we keep going, I marvel at the fact that I—Jordy Gallo—am actually doing something that can be considered sporty, and I am not that bad at it.

I catch up to Ashton, and we match pace as we continue with the current.

"Did you and that guy at the dock used to be friends?" I ask. He glances at me and shrugs.

"Not exactly," he says. "Brett went to school with Sasha, and when we first moved here, she introduced me to all these people she grew up with. But they were all *her* friends, not mine. I just kind of tagged along while she caught up with everyone. When she left..." He shrugs again. "I mean, it's not like I knew them well enough to grab beers with them in real life, you know? It's like, that's just something you say when there isn't anything else to say." He glances at me. "You know what I mean?"

Of course I do. I nod and offer a small smile, plus the same words he used on me, "It has to start somewhere, though. Right?"

He rolls his eyes, but grins. "Okay, fine. I asked for that. I guess I don't really want to hang out with anyone, or get to know them. If it weren't for Sasha, I wouldn't even know any of these people. Now that she's gone, I just don't think they're interested in getting to know me."

"Or, there's a third reason," I say, applying my paddle as my board drifts too close to his. "Maybe you're rejecting them before they can reject you."

He tilts his head at me, raising an eyebrow. "Sounds like you know what you're talking about."

I push the paddle in again, moving slightly faster. "Maybe a little," I say.

We take a break near a bridge, just three miles downstream. Ashton sinks to his knees and I do the same, keeping my balance as he ties our boards together. Then he opens the snack pack he brought and hands me a container. I bite back a smile as I open a mini charcuterie with crackers, cheese, grapes, cured meat, and some olives. He also pops a mini bottle of champagne and hands it to me before doing the same for himself.

"There is nothing like sparkling wine on the river," he says, tapping his glass bottle against mine with a tink.

Side note: I've been off my strict food plan since I landed in Lahoma. I'm usually so disciplined, eating only vegetables and lean proteins to keep myself slim. I've never had a weight problem, but I've also never given myself the chance. Besides Italy, that is. When I was traveling, I enjoyed every food that landed in front of me, and at least two gelatos a day. But when I came home, I was in the gym every single day, banned carbs from my diet, and drank a gallon of water daily until the weight slid off.

Now here in Lahoma, I'm eating things like the crackers and cheese in front of me, Bec's delicious waffles and bacon, and drinking whole milk like calories aren't a thing.

Besides the guilt and my mom's voice in my head, I'm loving it. Everything tastes so good. Probably because most of it comes from a nearby farm. I've never had food like this, where there's a story behind each ingredient. Food has always been a burden to me, something to control and manage. But here? It's not just nourishing for the body, but also for the soul.

"Thank you for doing all of this," I say after taking a sip of bubbles.

"What?" He grins at me, that intoxicating crooked smile of his. "This was nothing."

I shake my head. "This was not nothing. You've been so good to me ever since I got here. Even though I hate depending on you, I'm kind of glad the hotel thing fell through. Otherwise, I'd be spending every night alone in my hotel room and just focusing on work."

"No you wouldn't." He nudges my leg, and even though his hands are cold from the champagne bottle, I feel the warmth of him travel all the way through me. "You probably would have charmed this whole town without me monopolizing all your time."

I scoff, nudging his foot with mine. "That's where you're wrong, buddy. I don't make friends, and with the rocky start I had here, I was definitely not charming anyone. If it weren't for you, this whole project would have felt like a disaster. I probably would have quit halfway through."

"So, that's where I went wrong." He winks, but his grin falls when I don't return his smile. "What?"

I quickly mask my features, smiling to hide my discomfort. But inside I'm beating myself up. God, I'm such an idiot. He's only been hanging out with me to be nice, not because he likes my company. I mean, of course that's the reason. The fact that I'd even think otherwise is so completely stupid. Fuck, this whole paddle boarding trip is so obviously just another one of his nice guy moves, and he's just counting down the days until I leave.

"Sorry, I think I'm just overheated. That sun is unexpected." It's true. I'm sweating through my layers, but I can't let him know I'd relaxed into believing any of this was more than a kind gesture.

"I have my dry bag, if you want to take off your sweatshirt and place it in there," he says, grabbing the bag and handing it to me. I take it, hating that this dark cloud inside me is ruining what had been a perfect day. I slip off my sweatshirt, sliding it into the bag before handing it back to him. His eyes glance down, then quickly to the bag as he takes it back.

We eat in silence for a while, the sound of crunching crackers competing with lapping water and the call of a nearby osprey. Cars drive overhead on the bridge, the sound of their tires echoing along the banks. I do my best to let go of my shame just so I can take in this moment. When was the last time I enjoyed the sounds of nature like this? When have I enjoyed nature, period? I've always loved the fast pace of New York, the constant sound of car horns, the shush of garbage trucks, and the echoes of people calling out on the street. It's like this incredible symphony, a cacophony of sound that is never the same from one moment to the next.

But here, I can think. It's both relieving and terrifying. For the first time, I feel myself take a breath in, and then feel myself exhale. And it's just that. Breathe in. Breathe out. Feel.

"I fucking love this," I murmur, almost involuntarily.

"Me too," Ashton whispers. I turn to him, and he looks back at me. He takes my hand, and my breath catches in my chest. "Lay back," he says.

I lie back on my board, watching the clouds drift across the sky. For the first time in a long time, I let myself just exist. No expectations. No pressure. No deadlines. Just me, a sky full of moving clouds, and Ashton's hand in mine.

His thumb brushes the back of my palm, slow and deliberate. I stay perfectly still, afraid that if I move, I'll give myself away.

"Look at the sky," he murmurs, "and just listen."

I do.

I hear the water. The wind. A far-off radio playing music somewhere down the way. I hear my own breath, and I hear his.

I feel more alive in this moment than I ever have in my life.

Paddling upstream is a lot harder than drifting with the current. I start out on my feet, but exhaustion quickly wins out. Sitting cross-legged, I treat the paddle board like a canoe, dipping my paddle from side to side in slow, steady strokes.

We pass fishermen casting from the banks, each offering a lazy wave as we paddle by. Rowing teams glide past us, their oars slicing clean through the water while the vocal guy in the back—the coxswain, as Ashton calls him—barks encouragement. Riverfront houses come into view, their porches dotted with couples sipping coffee, watching us drift along like it's the most natural thing in the world.

And maybe it is.

Is this what small towns feel like? A rhythm you fall into without even realizing it?

Lahoma Springs is starting to feel like more than just a detour. It's starting to feel like a place I don't want to leave.

And after all I've worked for to get to where I am, this is not a feeling I want to entertain.

12

Lahoma's Resident Artist

Ashton

It's both a brilliant plan to get Jordy out on the water—and a near disaster.

Why?

That fucking bikini.

I've never seen a woman look that good in so little clothing. The way my swim trunks do absolutely nothing to hide my reaction is almost comical, and by the way she glances down toward my cock, she definitely notices.

But come on, a woman like Jordy *has* to know how hot she is. And a guy would have to be dead not to look.

Still, if I have any chance of keeping my dignity, I need to get her out of the water and into a few more layers.

Unfortunately, I'm not ready to be done with her yet.

"Where are we going?" she asks as we climb the ramp back up from the dock.

"You wanted to see Lahoma," I say, "so I'm showing you Lahoma."

"But what does that mean, exactly?"

She grins at me—those long lashes, those brown eyes, that smirk—and I feel like I've just stepped into a puddle of mush.

"You'll have to wait and see."

She swats at me playfully as we cross the bridge to the parking lot. Her hand swings close to her hip, and every muscle in me tenses with the effort not to reach for it. Holding her hand on the river already felt bold enough.

Truth is, I'm not used to this.

Before Sasha, if I liked a girl, I made a move. No hesitation. Just said it like it was; *I like you. You're hot. Want to fuck?*

Sasha flipped that script. She came on fast, took control, and I didn't mind.

But with Jordy, everything feels different. Holding her hand felt *huge*. Like I'm back in high school, trying not to screw up the one shot I might get.

We change at the truck, pulling sweats over our swimsuits. The sky starts to cloud over again, stealing what little warmth we snagged earlier. I catch the last glimpse of her smooth, perfect stomach as she tugs on her sweatshirt and nearly lose the ability to speak.

Perv.

"Okay," she says, hopping into the passenger seat. "Now can you tell me?"

I shake my head, barely hiding a smile. This giddiness is new. My life is usually made up of three things: my daughter, the farm, and the handful of people in my circle. Everything else is black and white.

But with Jordy, it all feels like color. Like maybe there's room for more.

We stop at the corner business on the same street as The Till, or rather, Timeless. On the opposite end is one of my favorite places in town: The Painted Nest, our local art gallery.

"Lahoma Springs isn't just tractors and livestock," I say, stopping her at the door. "We've got a growing community of artists. This place showcases a lot of them."

I open the door.

Jordy steps inside, takes one breath, and freezes. "Oh. Wow."

Her hand brushes my bicep as we enter, and I have to actively focus on *not* reacting to the warmth of her fingers.

In the center of the gallery stands a life-size elephant sculpture made entirely of broken porcelain plates. The thing is stunning—realistic in form, but impossibly intricate in detail. I watch Jordy walk around it, hands behind her back like she's in a museum.

"It's okay to touch," a woman calls from the front desk. She's all red—dress, lips, even her shoes—and her short, dark curls framed her face like a retro painting. "It's part of the experience. A tactile display."

Jordy hesitates, then lifts one finger to brush the tiles. Her palm follows, soft and reverent. I copy her—not because I care about the sculpture, but because watching her touch it makes me wonder what it would feel like if she touched *me* the same way.

We wander the gallery slowly. At each piece, Jordy leans in, quiet and focused, like the wrong breath might disturb the art. Her wonder is contagious. I've seen these pieces several times this past month, but everything feels new through her eyes.

She pauses extra-long at one painting. It's of a young monk in a red robe, standing alone in a narrow boat, drifting across still water while surrounded by the blue of twilight.

"This one's my favorite," I say quietly.

She steps back to take it all in. "The red. The water. The gold in the boat. It's like a meditation."

"How so?" I ask, though I can't stop watching her instead of the canvas.

She turns to me, and her eyes lock on mine.

"Because it reminds me to breathe—even as it takes my breath away."

For a beat, I can't speak. Her face, flushed from the sun. Her lips, parted just slightly. I feel my hand twitch, the need to touch her almost overpowering. I reach for her—

Just as she breaks eye contact and moves on to the next painting, my hand hovering in air with nothing to grasp.

"Jordy!"

We round the corner to see Grace hurrying toward us, her arms wide. She pulls Jordy into a hug, though Jordy's return is stiff at best.

"Well, hello you two!" Grace grins, looking to me, then back at Jordy. "Are you on a date?"

Jordy glances at me. I glance back. Her mouth opens, but no sound comes.

"No," I say. "I'm just showing her the town."

"I'm at a standstill until the construction crew starts on the shop," Jordy adds. "Ashton offered to take me on a tour."

Grace leans in conspiratorially. "Between you and me, Bernie was kind of a bitch about the whole reservation thing."

"Between me and the whole world, Bernie was a *total* bitch." Jordy grins. "Not just kind of."

Grace's eyes go wide, but then she cracks up. "Don't let her hear you say that."

"Why? She going to blackball me? Already been there. I've got the t-shirt to prove it. Actually, *Sasha* does. That girl had the weirdest sense of style."

"Oh my god. Her *t-shirts*?" Grace laughs. "My favorite one of hers is Thicculous Cage."

Jordy blinks at me. I sigh. "It's a thick Nicholas Cage next to a literal cage. You had to be there."

Jordy doubles over laughing. "Okay, that's amazing. I'm officially a fan."

Grace points to a small corner of the gallery. "Anyway, that's why I'm here. Those are my pieces."

"Grace, you paint?" Jordy's eyes widen as she steps closer. "These are incredible."

And they are. I've seen her sketch in her notebook at Lock & Key, and occasionally in ceramics class. But these? These are next level.

Each of the four paintings are unique: a strangely elegant frog with an umbrella, a girl floating in a pond, an old woman with a storm of stories in her eyes, and a yellow umbrella abandoned on a rainy sidewalk.

They're vibrant. Emotional. *Alive.*

"Why aren't you doing this full time?" Jordy asks. "Why work for Bernie?"

"And go to school," Grace adds. "I'm one semester away from a business degree."

Jordy stares at her. "You should be doing an art internship. These belong in a New York gallery."

Grace laughs. "Yeah, and make what, a hundred dollars a month? These took forever to paint. It's not sustainable."

Jordy looks at the price tags. "You have them listed for *seventy-five* dollars?"

Grace shrugs. "And they haven't sold."

"Wrong."

Before either of us can react, Jordy marches to the front desk. "I'd like to purchase all four of the Grace Dalton paintings," she says. "But I'd like to negotiate the price."

The woman at the desk blinks. "Uh, the listed prices are final."

"I'd like to pay *a thousand dollars each,*" Jordy says, pulling out her wallet.

Grace rushes forward. "Jordy, no—"

Jordy holds up a hand. "You're not my charity case. You're my artist."

The gallery woman looks flustered. "We could … arrange that."

Jordy doesn't budge. "And if Grace's work ever shows up here again, it doesn't go in a dark corner, and it doesn't get listed for less than five hundred dollars—or I'll have her pull every piece and we'll go straight to a private collector."

The woman nods, nervously ringing her up.

Jordy turns back to Grace and grins. "See? That wasn't so hard."

Back in the truck, I can't stop hearing how she rattled off her New York address to the gallery manager. It shouldn't have hit me so hard, but it did.

I brush it off though, and give her a side glance.

"So, Miss I-Don't-Have-Any-Friends," I tease. "That was pretty damn friendly, and a hell of a lot of money to shell out on art."

Jordy shrugs. "I have an inheritance from my late grandmother. Most of it is tied up in stocks and savings, but occasionally I use it if it seems like a worthy investment." She gives me a pointed look. "Besides, that wasn't me being friendly, that was me making an investment. Grace Dalton is an untapped talent. Once she's discovered, those paintings will be worth ten times what I just paid."

I nod slowly. "You really believe that?"

"I *know* that. Galleries in New York would kill for work like this. She's just too big for this town. No one here sees it."

I don't argue. But it doesn't sit right with me either. Yeah, small towns have their limits. Boxes people can't escape. Labels that stick longer than they should. But no one gets lost here. People belong to each other, even if they don't always see it.

And while Jordy may be right about Grace and this small town, New York isn't some magic fix either.

Some people are just too big for small towns.

But Jordy? She hasn't just outgrown the box. She's redesigned the whole damn room.

And me? I'm just the guy watching her walk through it, knowing the door is already halfway closed.

13

Paint Night is Just an Excuse to Drink

Jordy

I wake up the next morning feeling sore from my day on the river. But happy.

And a bit confused.

Enough that, as I hear Ashton milling around the kitchen with Lottie, I stay in bed and pretend to be asleep until I hear the front door click and the silence of an empty house.

Spending yesterday with Ashton felt so natural, like we did stuff like this all the time—and let's face it, he's really, really nice to look at. But it also makes me realize that my time in Lahoma is not as long as I originally thought it would be. Even though I have a few weeks left, it's not enough time.

And crushing on him is making this reality so much worse.

I know this is going nowhere. It doesn't even matter if he returns my feelings. My whole world is in New York, and his is here. It's pointless to start something we can't finish.

And yet, I can't shake my feelings of restlessness.

Last night, we arrived back home after dinner to very little conversation. I'd put on the teakettle, thinking we could unwind after Lottie was in bed, but he said goodnight without even looking up from his phone. Somehow, that hurt more than I want to admit. Yesterday morning, we were holding hands on the river. Now it feels like we're strangers in the same house.

The message is crystal clear—this crush is very one-sided, and it's probably for the best.

Now I'm alone in this empty house, lying in bed with my feelings.

Eventually I drag myself out of bed. I pull on a pair of slacks and a silk blouse, followed by my black heels. But when I look at myself in the full-length mirror, it's all wrong. No one around here dresses like this. I love my clothes—I've created a very distinct style for myself—but looking in the mirror, it all feels so stuffy.

I dig around my bag again until I find a pair of workout pants and a sweatshirt. It's not my favorite to wear athleisure as fashion, but it's better than silk and stilettos.

Today's mission: a new wardrobe that's less New York and more Northern California.

And I can't do this alone.

I head into town, stopping first at Lock & Key. My heart sinks when I see the girl at the counter. I recognize her as the single mom with a million kids who'd been picketing outside the store, and I warily back up so she won't see me.

Too late, though. She looks up, her eyes locking with mine. It takes a moment for her to register, and I stand paralyzed as I watch it happen. Her eyes widen, then narrow.

"Grace!" she calls out, and I wince at the shrill tone of her voice.

"Listen, I'm not trying to cause problems," I say, holding up my hands.

That's when Grace emerges from one of the aisles, her face lighting up when she sees me.

"Mabel, this is Jordy! The friend I was talking to you about!"

My heart leaps at the word *friend*. I can't recall any time recently when someone I wasn't related to had referred to me that way. I'm not anyone's friend. I'm not even good at being a friend—judging by the amount of times Nina calls me, but I never call her.

"You are incredible," Mabel says.

I pause, studying the way she said it. Sincere. Not a note of resentment.

"Are you fucking with me?" I ask. She shakes her head.

"No. Thanks to you, Grace covered our whole rent this month, and I'm able to catch up on my bills."

I turn to Grace. "You gave this lady your money?"

Grace and Mabel look at each other, and then Grace starts to laugh.

"I forget that you're not from around here," she says. "Jordy, this is my sister, Mabel."

"Charmed," Mabel says, sticking out her hand. I take it loosely, looking from one to the other. Now that she's said it, I can see it. Mabel's a brunette while Grace's hair is blonde. But their faces are nearly identical, with the same blue eyes and striking features. I didn't get a good look at Mabel before, dismissing her as some country hippy with the paisley dress and yellow hat she wore the first time I saw her. But she's actually really pretty—totally clueless about fashion, but pretty.

"We live together," Grace explains. "So we both contribute to the rent. But school started a month ago and the kids needed new clothes, and money has been really tight. Your help came at the exact right time."

"I didn't help you," I remind her. "I bought a few art pieces for my home, and they just happened to be yours. It wasn't a favor—it was just a sale."

"Whatever," Grace says, rolling her eyes and waving her hand. "Call it what you want. It was the biggest pay day of my life, and I owe you forever."

"You don't," I insist. "But I *could* use your help." I look down at my clothes and then at Grace's. She's wearing a pair of jeans and a loose sweater over the top. It's cute. Casual. Exactly what I'm looking for. "Would you come shopping with me so I can buy something a bit more laid back?" I glance at my athleisure wear. "I mean, classier than this. But something more casual than my pencil skirts and heels."

"Oh my god, really? You want to go shopping with me?" Grace claps her hands together, then looks at Mabel. "Do you mind?"

"Go for it," Mabel agrees. "It's not like we have a line out the door or anything." She gives me a wistful look. "I only wish I could go with you guys. There's this thrift store a few blocks away I just love. It's where I find all my cutest clothes, like the outfit I'm wearing today." She steps out from behind the counter, and I do my best to keep my face blank. Mabel is wearing a pair of corduroy overalls and a grey thermal, plus a pair of heavy utility boots—like she's headed to the garden right after work, and knowing this town, she probably is.

"What a shame," I say, then turn to Grace. "Ready?"

"Just be back before I have to go," Mabel calls after us as we head out the door. "I was late yesterday picking up the kids from school, and Grayston never let me live it down.

"Got it!" Grace calls. To me, "Grayston is her oldest. He's eleven, but he acts like he's forty. Probably because he's the man of the house now. Then there's Alex, she's the middle child, and the baby is Logan."

"And their dad?" I ask as we approach my car. I don't know why I'm asking—it's obvious there's no father in the picture, especially if Grace is helping to pay the bills.

Fucking deadbeat.

"He died a year and a half ago, just before Logan was born."

I didn't expect that. I don't even know what to say, though I feel bad for judging Mabel's fashion choices too hard.

We get in the car, but before I pull from the curb, I look at Grace. "Is she doing okay?"

Grace nods. "It was hard. Sometimes it's still hard, but we're managing. If it weren't for this town though, I don't know." Grace goes on, describing how the town pitched in with meals, helped keep up the yardwork, and even helped Grace move all her things over to Mabel's house so she could help lighten the load.

"There's always someone willing to help with rides for the kids or babysitting when Mabel can't be in three places at once." Her face gets serious then. "I think it's hardest for Grayston, though. He was really sad at first, then angry, and then he kind of went into project mode, making sure all the things his dad used to do were being done. He's out there mowing the lawn every Saturday. He makes sure Alex does her homework. He even helps Mabel clean up after dinner every night. You don't even have to ask him."

"Sounds like this is how he's coping," I say.

Grace nods. "We know. Mabel put him in counseling, and it's helping a little. But he's still not ready to talk about any of this, and throwing himself into all these duties seems to be holding him together, so we aren't pushing."

I nod, and inwardly I promise myself to never judge a person by their paisleys again.

"You know who needs to go with us?" Grace suddenly blurts out. "Michael!"

"Really? You think he'd want to hang with two girls shopping for clothes?"

"Are you kidding? This is the kind of event he lives for."

Sure enough, Michael immediately flips the "Closed" sign as soon as we tell him our plans.

"While I think everyone here could benefit from dressing like you," he says as we head to my car, "the least I can do is help you look two steps ahead of the community instead of ten."

Grace directs me to a cute boutique at the edge of town, one she promises is not the same thrift store Mabel shops at. We head in, and Grace and Michael both immediately abandon me in favor of scouring the racks like pros. I mingle by the nearest rack, thumbing through shirt after shirt. This is so different from any store I shop at, and I'm not sure what I'm looking for.

"Stop that," Michael says, smacking my hand as I pick up a blouse that's similar to the one I had on this morning before I changed. Then he places a pile of clothes in my arms. "Go try these on." He points at the dressing rooms in the back of the store.

The two of them make me do a fashion show for every outfit. They clap at the ones they like, and frown at the ones that don't quite hit the mark. In the end, I walk away with a few t-shirts, some sweaters, a few pairs of non-designer jeans, and even a pair of Vans that tie it all together. All of it for a fraction of what one outfit costs me in New York.

"Damn, I'm going to need another suitcase to bring all this home," I say, then laugh. Grace pretends to wail.

"I keep forgetting you're leaving! How much longer do you have?"

"About three weeks," I say, feeling my heart sink.

"Then we don't have a lot of time," Michael chimes in.

I look at him and then at Grace, but they're too busy looking at each other, grinning.

"For what?"

"Paint night!" they say in unison.

And that's how I find myself sitting in a studio, an apron covering my new casual outfit of a t-shirt and jeans, a very full glass of wine to my right, and a blank canvas in front of me.

I like to think of myself as a creative, crafty person. My job requires me to know how to sketch, and I do a pretty decent job of it.

But painting? Frankly, I suck.

"It's not fair," I hiss at Grace, who is already starting to outline the jellyfish we're supposed to be painting. "You're just making us do this so you can show us up."

"Honey, it's not about the painting," Michael says on my other side. "It's about the wine and the gossip."

"Gossip?" I already feel like I know way too much about everyone in this town. "Don't you all mind your own business?"

Michael shoots me a look. "Hello, are you new here?"

"Yes," I reply, then dip my brush in the purple paint.

"Fine. Well, you have some intel that we don't have, and it's time for you to spill the goods."

I roll my eyes. "All I've done since I got here is dodge insults and protests, and keep my head down while I do my job."

Michael and Grace glance at each other, and I realize I'm not in on whatever they're hinting at. "What are you two eyeing each other about?"

"About the fact that you've done something to make that tall, broody farm boy smile in ways we've never seen him smile before."

I gawk at them. "Are you talking about Ashton?"

Grace bumps me, and I almost skid my paintbrush across my canvas. "Hey!"

"Sorry. But yes, Ashton." She gives me a pointed look. "That guy has been a somber train wreck since Sasha took off, barely even talking to any of us anymore. But you show up, and suddenly he's whistling while he's picking up supplies at the feed store, or smiling and staying to chat when he delivers produce to the restaurants. Everyone is talking about how you two were paddle boarding down the river, and I don't think I've seen him do that since he first showed up around here. Then at the gallery, the way he was looking at you." She fans herself, but I just feel confused.

"What way?" Everything they're saying is sparking hope in my heart that feels both exhilarating and dangerous.

"My god, don't you see it? That man could not take his eyes off you."

I roll my eyes at Grace, then look at Michael. "And how do *you* know anything? It's not like you've seen us together."

"No, but everyone else in this town has, and girl, you're the buzz. Now that people have moved on about the whole store takeover, they're onto bigger and better things. Namely, how you landed the most unavailable bachelor in this town."

Despite myself, I can't help laughing. If Ashton could hear them talk right now. "According to Ashton, everyone here has tied him to Sasha and expects him to remain single for the rest of his life."

"Are you kidding?" Grace shakes her head. "That guy would see he has a line of women begging for him to give them attention if he would just look up."

"Guys too," Michael pipes in.

I give him side eye, and he shrugs. "What? The man is fine. You can't tell me you don't think so."

I bite my lip, dying to cave to the gossip but also not wanting to feed it. "It's not like it matters. I'm leaving in a few weeks, and his whole life is here."

Grace groans and pretends to slither out of her chair. Michael just shakes his head.

"Nothing is so permanent it can't be changed for the right circumstance."

"Or the right person," Grace pipes in. "Come on, tell me you don't feel something whenever you're around him."

I say nothing. Instead, I take a sip of my wine, and my eyes stay on hers—which become saucers—and then she bursts out laughing.

"I knew it! You like him! You might even loooove him."

"I do not," I say, smacking her arm. "I've known him all of ten days."

"Fine, but in those ten days, how many times have you thought about jumping his bones?" she asks.

I bury my face in my hands, then peek at them both. "Way too many times," I groan.

Grace nearly falls to the floor laughing, while Michael offers a smirk and a raised wine glass. I tink my glass to his.

"It's about time, bitch," he says.

"What are you talking about? It's been ten days."

"Ten days of you two eye fucking each other, according to everyone in this town. It's like watching a slow-motion rom-com with no kissing." He looks at Grace, who nods.

"Infuriating," she said. "But also kind of hot."

"You two are the literal worst."

But even as I laugh, it gets me thinking. He hasn't said anything to me. Hasn't even tried to make a move. I haven't seen half of the things Grace and Michael—and apparently the whole town—are saying. But I have seen Ashton's small glances. The way his eyes shift. How he's so careful around me.

What if this really isn't a one-sided crush? What if he feels the same way I do, and is hiding it—just like me?

But do I even want to open that door?

14

The Crooked Jellyfish

Ashton

Jordy walks in the door, wobbling slightly as she closes it behind her. I know that walk all too well, and even though I'm pissed at her for driving when she's obviously had way too much to drink, I'm even more pissed at myself for not thinking of being her designated driver when I knew she was going out with Michael and Grace.

Paint nights are never a sober affair.

"Did you seriously drive home that way?"

She shoots me a sloppy grin, then holds up the painting in her hand. It's a purple blob with strings painted all over it, surrounded by murky blue.

"Look, I painted a jellyfish," she slurs, then stumbles again as she tries to take her shoes off.

"Is that what that is?'

Fuck, it's hard to be mad at her. I get up off the couch, moving to her side so that she has someone to balance on while she slips off her … Vans? I've never seen her in any shoes except for high heels and Sasha's flip flops. Stepping back, I get a good look at her, and fucking hell. Her pencil skirts and stilettos are cute, but they have nothing on Jordy in jeans and a t-shirt. It makes me want to wrap my arms around her and fold her in tight, fitting every one of her curves against me.

"We should hang this," she says, pushing it toward me.

I take it, chuckling lightly. "Seriously, you could have called me. You shouldn't be on the road like this. You could have been hurt."

She scoffs. "I didn't drive, Mabel did. She picked us all up and brought me home."

Relief floods through me, so much that I wrap an arm around Jordy's waist and pull her to me for a hug. Her head rests under my chin, and I have the strongest urge to lean down and kiss the top of it. The yearning takes my breath away. But not before I inhale the scent of her skin, the lilac of her shampoo, the pheromones that rush at me while my defenses are down.

I let go of her, taking two steps back. Then I pretend to be very interested in her painting. "A jellyfish, huh?"

She laughs. "Okay fine, it's not my best work. But that was after two very big glasses of wine. You're lucky the paint even made it on the canvas." She looks around the room then points at the wall in the living room. "It would fit perfectly there."

I don't even argue. She could've painted a giant dick and I'd still hang it, just because she painted it. What that says about me, I don't know. Even if she returns my feelings, it's not like we can do anything about it. I've experienced enough hard goodbyes in my life. I don't need to open myself to another.

Jordy holds the painting while I take a pencil and mark the corners of it on the wall. I pound in the nail, and she—with unsteady hands—moves to hang it. She almost makes it. The painting crashes to the floor, having missed its mark, and Jordy pitches to the side as her hands scramble for purchase. I grab her, pulling her tight against me until she finds her legs. Then we linger there like that for a moment.

Goddamn, she's beautiful—and so fucking close. She's looking at me, her eyes half lids as she keeps glancing at my lips. That subtle move makes me feel insane. Feral. I want to throw away all my inhibitions, every single reason why this shouldn't happen, and show her everything I've thought of doing to her since the day she arrived in this town.

"We keep finding ourselves like this, Oregon," she murmurs.

I close my eyes, breathing in the scent of her wine that mingles with everything feminine about her. I just know this woman would taste better than she smells.

But I know if I give in, there's no going back. Because I won't be able to stop.

"That's what happens when you drink too much," I tease, releasing her with every ounce of strength I have. I turn, but not before I see a flash of disappointment cross her face. I can't take it seriously, though. She's only tipsy, but it's enough. By morning time, we'll just be friends again—temporary roommates until she's back on a plane to New York.

"I was wondering," Jordy says, playing with the hem of her t-shirt. "Tomorrow when you go to work, what if you left Lottie with me?"

I search her face, then shake my head. "You don't have to do that," I say.

"Not because I have to," she says, then sits on the couch. Right near my pillow. Right where I will smell her all night long.

Fuuuuck.

I sit on the other side, and she folds her legs underneath her. "I mean, yes. It would kind of be a way to pay you back for everything you've done for me so far."

I start to interject, but she puts a hand up.

"Let me finish. It's not just that. It's more like, I need to get over this whole fear of kids thing."

"So, you're going to tackle your fears by using my kid as a guinea pig?"

She winces. "Damn, that sounds bad. That's not exactly what I mean, and it's also totally what I mean." She wrinkles her nose, looking at me. "It's just that, I know if it's too overwhelming, Bec is just across the way. So it kind of makes it feel safe. Also, Lottie isn't some helpless baby, she's a tough toddler. And I've watched her. That kid is not going to break easy."

"She's an Elliot," I agree, flexing my bicep. "We're sturdy folk." I meant it as a joke, but her eyes linger on my arm, even after I lower it. She does this slight little tongue thing, just a flick across her lower lip, and my damn dick springs to attention like she's called its name.

"You really want to do this?" I ask, and her eyes immediately move back to mine.

"What? Oh, yes. Lottie. I think it would be fun. I mean, I can't go anywhere since my car is parked downtown. But she and I can hang here, or maybe even take a walk in the field and visit the cows."

Her face turns serious then, and she looks down at her hands. "I know it's irrational," she adds quietly. "But maybe if I can handle one morning, it'll remind me that I'm not broken forever."

I'm not really worried about Jordy watching my kid. She's been around us long enough that Lottie knows her. I've seen my daughter light up when Jordy comes in the room, though Lottie loves anyone she recognizes. And Jordy seems to understand Lottie's stilted language, knowing the difference between "kunchies" (crackers) and cheese, which sounds almost the same when she reaches hyperventilation stage. Jordy still doesn't pick her up or play with her, but she's no longer taking the seat furthest away from her when we eat, either.

And honestly, I get it. I think of the ways I've protected myself from hurt, how I'm still doing that now because I can't go through that kind of pain again. But it's nothing compared to how it must have felt for Jordy to lose her child.

This is a big step for her, and while this is all her and not me, I can't help feeling proud of her.

"I think the two of you will have so much fun together," I say.

The next morning, I awake to Jordy stirring in the kitchen. I peek over the couch, watching as she locates the coffee grounds in the cabinet and sets up the coffeepot. You know what's better than Jordy in jeans and a t-shirt? Jordy in sweats. Her ass fills out those grey sweatpants like they have no business doing. I sit there in the dark of the living room, watching her move, pretty sure I could spend a lifetime doing this.

What. The. Fuck. The girl has been here less than two weeks—not nearly enough time to have forever kind of thoughts.

"Oh, did I wake you?"

I flick my eyes to hers, then shake my head, hoping she didn't catch me checking her out. "No, I need to get up soon, anyway. I should get Lottie ready before I go."

"No, you shouldn't," she says, pulling two cups out of the cupboard while the percolator brews. "I can do all of that. You can even sleep in, if you want to."

"Well, that would be a dream," I say, even though I know I'm not going to fall back asleep. Still, I burrow back under the covers and just listen to Jordy move around my kitchen, wanting to memorize the sound so I'll remember it when she's gone.

I actually do drift off again, long enough that I awake to Jordy placing a cup of black coffee on the table next to me, just as Lottie starts to babble from the bedroom.

"I got her," Jordy warns as I start to get up. "Enjoy your coffee."

I sit back, not even fighting my grin as Jordy eases open the bedroom. I pick up my cup, taking a cautious first sip, reveling in what it's like to wake up with coffee instead of getting a fussy toddler first. I love my daughter, but I also miss the slow pace of childless mornings.

Jordy comes out, holding my sleepy little girl wrapped in a blanket. Lottie's hair is all over the place, and I fight the urge to go wash and oil it before putting it in braids, just so it will be out of her face.

She'll survive one day of messy hair.

Jordy sits in a chair across the room from me, just like I always do with Lottie in the morning. She keeps my daughter on her lap facing away from me, but the little girl twists, trying to find me. When she finally succeeds, she pushes against Jordy, trying to get down.

"Okay, fine," Jordy sighs. She loosens her grip, and Lottie slides out of her lap and runs to me. "I tried."

"She'll warm up once I'm gone," I promise. At least, I hope she will. I've never left her with anyone else besides Bec and Bob, so this will be an experiment for all of us.

Lottie must know something is different this morning, because she clings to me like a sticker weed. As I shave in the bathroom, she plays at my feet while Jordy hovers nearby. When I get dressed, she insists on staying in the bedroom, shutting the door between Jordy and us. And as I move to the door, Lottie flings herself forward until Jordy swoops her up.

"Are you sure you'll be okay?" I ask over Lottie's shrill wails. My daughter is like an octopus in Jordy's arms, her hands stretched out for me while Jordy gets a mouthful of her poofy hair.

"She'll probably stop crying once you leave," she assures me. I don't miss the anxiety on her face.

I also know I cannot get in the way of this huge step for her, even if my daughter screams the whole time.

God, I hope she doesn't do that.

So I give my daughter a quick kiss on the cheek while dodging her flailing arms. Then, I lean in and kiss Jordy's cheek before I can think too hard about it. Her skin is warm against my lips, and I pull away fast—before I give in to the urge to linger.

She doesn't say anything, but her eyes follow me all the way to the door.

And I leave—my gut full of guilt over the sounds of my daughter's muffled cries behind the closed front door, and my heart trailing behind me.

15

What the Hell are Zowies?

Jordy

Lottie goes into full meltdown once Ashton closes the door. Half of me prays he will keep on going. The other half hopes he'll walk back in and relieve me of this stupid, idiotic idea that I'm actually capable of caring for a toddler.

What the fuck was I thinking?

"Come on, Lottie girl. Let's get you some breakfast. Are you hungry?"

She quiets for a moment, then points to the refrigerator.

"Zowies," she whimpers, then sticks her fingers in her mouth.

Well, that's a new one. What the hell are Zowies? I place her in the highchair, and Lottie immediately collapses into shrieks once again.

"Hold on, baby. I'm getting you Zowies."

I open the fridge, peering in there for anything that might look like it could be Zowies, while Lottie flings herself out like roadkill on her tray.

"Um, is it toast?" I ask, pulling out the bread. Lottie looks up, then wails, pointing toward the fridge again. I dive back in, sounding out everything on the shelves to see if it sounds remotely like Zowies. Tortillas. Salami. Yogurt.

Each item I hold up is met with insistent screams, Lottie's finger pointing...

At the cupboards above the fridge. Goddamn it.

I open the cabinet where the cereal is. She immediately calms down.

"Zowies," she mumbles around her fingers.

"You want cereal? You know how to say cereal." I grab the nearest box—Chex.

"No!" Lottie pounds on her tray. "Zowies!"

The only other box is Cheerios. I grab it, and Lottie immediately starts laughing.

"Zowies! Mine!"

I don't realize just how tight my whole body is until it relaxes with the first sound of her laughter. I grin, feeling completely insane, but also very proud of myself for not losing my cool while Lottie lost hers.

"Is this Zowies?" I ask. Lottie grins, her hands reaching out and making *gimme* gestures.

I should have known. The first day I met her, she was all over these damn Cheerios. I pour a bunch on her tray, because why not? And she happily eats her little Zowies while I get myself another cup of coffee and a few moments to breathe.

What I don't expect is for my eyes to well up with tears as I watch Lottie eat. It's not from overwhelm. It's not even because of the baby I lost. No, it's because this is the first time I've ever felt capable around a child. Even if it took me a couple tries.

I manage to get a piece of toast in my belly before Lottie flings the rest of the Zowies on the floor and announces she wants "Up!"

I remove the tray, lift her up, and set her on the ground so I can clean up all the Cheerios. She immediately stomps on the cereal, leaving little trodden land mines all over the floor.

"No, Lottie," I moan, but she just giggles. Well, this is a battle I'll have to lose. I roll my eyes, waiting for her to finish her Godzilla destruction of Zowie town until she grows tired of that and finds a thread to pick at on the floor mat. I take the opportunity to grab the broom off the porch and quickly sweep up every Zowie I can.

It's just enough time for Lottie to completely disappear.

"Lottie, where are you?" I keep my voice sing-song, but inside I'm panicking. I mean, it's not like she can escape far. This house has two bedrooms and a bathroom besides the open concept kitchen and living room. She can only be in one of three—

My thoughts are interrupted by a very distinct SPLASH.

I race to the bathroom, just in time to see her throw the second of my new pair of Vans in the toilet.

"No, Lottie!" I yell, snatching her up just as my shoe lands in the bowl, splashing water everywhere. My sudden movement must have shocked Lottie because she completely loses it in my arms. She screams, pushing against me as she tries to get down.

"Not yet, little girl," I say, trying not to freak out alongside her. So much for small wins—this feels like I'm taking the "L." I sit her on the sink, holding her toilet water hands in mine and get to her level. "It's okay," I soothe, even though I'm certain those shoes are going straight into the trash. It's too bad, I kind of like them. She quiets as I take a soapy washcloth and wash her hands, even laughing as I boop her on the nose with sound effects. Then, I sit her in the playpen, which is what I should have done to begin with. Once she's quietly playing by herself, I clean up the bathroom.

As for my shoes, I really think hard about this one. These aren't just any shoes. They're ones Michael and Grace picked out for me. It's silly, but that means something. It doesn't feel right to throw them away.

I take in a deep breath, then let it out slow. There's one person who will know what to do in this moment.

"Well, that's a face I love to see," Nina says on the other end of the video call. I hold my phone a little further away so that she can get the full view of my messy hair, makeup-free face, and probably a million lines of stress around my eyes. "I think you're trying to prove something," she says, laughing. "But all I see is a beautiful woman."

"You're my favorite cup of coffee," I say. "Can you just wake me up every morning with your positive affirmations?"

"I'd be happy to, if you'd take my calls."

Her tone is teasing, but it still stabs me just the same. She's called at least twice since the last time I talked to her. To be fair, I was totally engrossed with work at the time she called.

Nina's never known for good timing, but I never called her back.

"I'll get better about that," I promise. She waves her hand.

"It's fine. You're just super busy building your empire. I knew you'd call me when you could."

"Well, it's for a reason. So, I'm babysitting right now..." I turn my phone to train it on Lottie, then back to me. Nina's face is one of deer-eyed awe, her mouth scrunched into an aww.

"That has got to be the second cutest baby I've ever seen. What's her name?"

"That's Lottie, short for Charlotte. It's a long story, but I'm watching her and realizing just how inept I am."

"Oh, I doubt that."

"Within the first ten minutes, she tried to flush my shoes down the toilet."

"Ouch. It wasn't the Manolo Blahniks, was it?"

I shake my head. "No, thank god. But it was a pair of Vans."

Nina coughs then moves closer to the phone camera. "Uh, Vans? Who are you and what have you done with my cousin?"

"Hey, I wear casual shoes too." Like when I'm at the gym. "At any rate, I don't want to throw them away, but I don't know how to clean them. You have Vans. Do you know what to do? Should I throw them in the wash?"

"Whatever you do, don't do that. I did that with my first pair, and they not only shrunk, but they also melted a little."

"Oh shoot. No, I won't do that. But what do I do?"

"First, how bad was it? Was there anything left in the toilet?"

"No," I say. "It was clean, except for all the bacteria living in there, waiting to jump on anything a toddler may toss their way."

"Well, that's good. What you can do is just fill a bowl with hot, soapy water. Not boiling, but hot tap water. Then let the shoes soak in there for a while. Afterwards, you can take a washcloth with soap and rub at them to get anything it might have missed. Rinse them again, then set them out to dry. They should be good as new."

"So, I don't need to throw them away?"

Nina laughs. "I mean, you'll probably never forget they're poo shoes."

"Ugh, gross!" But I'm laughing too. "Okay, I think I can live with that."

I settle onto the couch, watching Lottie play. She's engrossed with some blocks, fitting them together, or just banging them on top of each other. "Tell me, what kinds of things do you do with June?"

"Well, she loves when I sing to her. I tend to sing about everything I'm doing when she's in the room, and she gets the biggest kick out of it." She then launches into a song to the tune of "Zombies" by the Cranberries: "What's in your hamper, your hamper? Laundry, laundry, laundry-y-y."

"Okay, okay, I get it," I laugh.

"Hey, you gotta start the kids young if you want to introduce better music than Baby Shark or that damn Gummy Bear song Brayden thinks is so funny."

"I'm not familiar," I say.

"Count yourself lucky."

I do, in more ways than one. Even if it still sucks to know he has his perfect little family, and I just have me.

But then I look at Lottie, and looking at Lottie makes me think of Ashton. Suddenly, I don't feel sorry for myself. Even if there's nothing between us, I still feel more of a spark with him than I've ever felt with anyone else.

Just knowing that makes me believe I can find this feeling again … but with someone who makes more sense.

Ashton makes the most sense.

"We also play peek-a-boo," Nina says, and I realize she's still rattling off ideas while I'm drifting into daydreams.

By the time we get off the phone, I have a small list of things I can do to occupy Lottie until it's warm enough to go outside.

We start with getting her dressed and changed. I realize quickly just how full a diaper can get, because this one is like a big wet balloon spilling out of her pajama bottoms.

"Okay, Lottie. Let's do this together." I lay her on the bedroom floor like I've seen Ashton do, a pad under her body. Then I strip off her wet clothes and full diaper, turning my head when I catch a whiff of strong urine.

"Plan B, baby girl. Let's get you in the bath."

Lottie has no problems taking a bath. I stay right there at the edge, my eyes never leaving her, so afraid that she'll slip under the water if I even blink. She doesn't though. She splashes and plays in the water, and even lets me wash her hair.

I've never seen hair quite like hers. I recognize the afro-texture she's inherited from her father, but the color is this amazing dark red that I know she got from Sasha, as I remember from the photos.

I also know that hair like hers requires different care than mine does. So, once her hair is washed with her baby shampoo, I dare a peek at Google on my phone about how to care for her hair.

Oil, comb, leave-in conditioner. Got it.

Lottie is easy to get out of the bath. Even snuggly. She burrows into her towel, feeling like a sweet squishy package in my arms as I carry her to the bathroom countertop. My god, she feels so good in my arms. I hold her for a moment, looking at the two of us in the mirror. I'm a total mess. My hair is all over the place and my face definitely looks tired. I don't think I've even had a drop of water to drink today, and my skin will let me know tomorrow.

But holding Lottie, I like the way we look together. I squeeze her closer, and she fits into me like she's returning the embrace—even swaddled as she is.

"I love you, baby girl," I murmur. For the second time today, tears spring to my eyes. It feels like I'm not just saying it to her, but to the baby I lost—and to the girl I'd been in that hospital room, to the girl I was when my engagement ended, when I booked a flight to Italy, and when I opened the door to my New York apartment for the first time.

Even to the girl I was when I stood on Main Street in Lahoma Springs, wondering how the hell I was going to cross that picket line.

"We can do hard things," I say, this time to Lottie as I sit her down. But then I look at my reflection in the mirror again, look myself right in the eye, and nod.

We can do hard things.

I watch about a half dozen TikToks on textured hair until I feel confident. Lottie doesn't act like I'm doing anything wrong as I comb through her hair. It's so much longer than I expected, but once the curls take shape in my hands, it shortens up into these sweet little spirals.

The sun is shining bright through the windows, so I dress us both in shorts and t-shirts, plus sweatshirts to make up for the lingering fog.

My shoes are soaking in soapy water, but I find a pair of women's shoes in Ashton's closet that are only a half size too small.

"Thank you, Sasha," I whisper.

We head outdoors just as Bec is walking up with a plate of cookies.

"There's my girls," she coos. Lottie reaches for her in my arms, and I trade Bec for the cookies. "How'd the morning go," she asks.

I shrug, not sure I want to reveal all the disasters. But one look at Bec, and I know I can't keep it from her.

"Well, she screamed for half the morning. Then tossed Cheerios, which I discovered are actually Zowies, all over the floor. She also threw my shoes in the toilet."

"Oh no, poor you," Bec says, landing a hand on my arm.

"But we turned it around. I gave her a bath, and now that it's warmer, we're headed out to see the cows."

"Well, that sounds about standard," Bec says with a laugh.

"She's thrown your shoes in the toilet?"

"No," Bec says. "But she tried to flush the cat. She's lucky she didn't get scratched."

"Oh no, that's terrible!"

I put the cookies in the house, and the three of us walk towards the fenced in field where the cows are grazing. Halfway there, Lottie turns in her grandma's arms and reaches for me. I widen my eyes with surprise.

"Well, someone has good taste," Bec says, handing her off to me. Lottie curls under my chin, and my heart nearly explodes at the preciousness of it all.

Bec stays with us for a short while, but when she sees Ashton heading our way, she says something about needing to check something in the oven. She greets Ashton on her way back to the house, touching his arm, and then looking back at me with a smile before taking the path to her front porch.

"Well, this doesn't look so scary," he teases. He starts to reach for Lottie, but she burrows deeper into my arms. Both of us catch eyes, and I laugh.

"If you knew the morning we had, you'd recognize what a miracle this is." I look down at her, then kiss the top of her curly head.

"I can imagine. Looks like you won her over."

There's something in his smile, though. In his eyes. Something that says so much more than his words. Something like maybe I won *him* over.

I dismiss the thought—the wish—as soon as it comes.

"Her hair looks great. Have you done this before?"

"Never," I laugh, peering down again at my handiwork. I'm proud of what I did. "Not bad for a first timer, huh?"

"Not bad at all. How many YouTube tutorials did you watch?"

I laugh. "None."

He raises an eyebrow.

"TikTok videos," I say.

"Brilliant." He looks at the house, then back at me. "I'm heading back to the house for an early lunch. Is it all right if I hang out for a while?"

"It's your house, silly. And we've only had toast and Zowies."

"Ah, the famous Zowies."

"Yeah, that one took a while to figure out. Thank god she's patient."

He raises an eyebrow. "Is she though?"

I shake my head. "Not at all."

Back at the house, Ashton fixes sandwiches for both of us, and for Lottie, some cut up cheese, turkey, and bread. I'm really loving this whole carb thing. Who knew bread could taste this good?

When Lottie starts to drift in her highchair, I wave Ashton off and carry her to the bedroom. She doesn't even fuss as I kiss her little cheek then lay her in the crib. I linger for a moment, watching the way her lashes brush the tops of her cheeks, how her lips purse into tiny petals, how her hands curl in fists above her head.

She's so damn precious. Once again, I'm bursting.

I leave the room, closing the door behind me. When I turn to Ashton, there's a soft look on his face.

"What?"

The corner of his mouth turns up. "You know."

Yeah, I know.

I didn't think I had it in me to love a child, not after what happened. But here I am, my heart out of my chest for this little girl. Even with our rough morning, I know I'd do anything for her.

Maybe kids aren't so scary after all.

16

Broody Silent Farm Boy Thing

Ashton

You know.

No, she doesn't know. She has no fucking clue.

But I do.

Watching Jordy fall in love with my child has shattered me in the most unexpected way. Honestly, it's like I'd been blasted apart, and I have no idea how to put myself back together. I'm falling for her, fast and hard. It's safe to say I've never felt this way before. Not for Sasha. Not for anyone.

But for Jordy, I suddenly have this image of her in *our* home, *our* bed, her stuff in *our* closet. Fucking her slowly every night, and waking up to her every morning.

I want it all.

It's not just about wanting her body—though god knows I do. It was the way Lottie nestled under her chin as we stood near the cows, how Jordy brushed her hand over my daughter's back, protecting her from the world, how carefully she carried her to her room at naptime.

And the look on her face as she closed the door.

Pure love.

Fuck, if I don't feel it too.

I think about this the whole drive into town. I wanted nothing more than to stay back at the house with Jordy. But I knew if I did, there was nothing stopping me from rushing across that room and pressing her against a wall as I tasted every inch of her.

I had to leave.

And here in my truck, I feel every single breath in my lungs as I try to stop obsessing about her.

And fail.

Is it real? Or am I just grateful to her?

No, it's so much deeper, and I'm running out of reasons to put on the brakes.

I manage to pull myself together once I reach the feed store. Jordy is still on my mind—that woman is always on my mind—but I'm able to at least put one foot in front of the other as I order the supplements we're running low on.

"How's that little girl of yours," Paul asks as he fills the order. "You should bring her by next week. We have some eggs about to hatch, and I think she'd get a kick out of all the chicks."

"Oh, I know she would," I say. But in my head, I'm thinking how Jordy would love that too. Has she ever held a baby chick before? It might freak her out, but maybe she'd get a kick out of it.

Pull it together, Ashton.

"Next week, you say? I'll bring her by."

I put the supplies in the truck, but I don't want to go home yet. I don't trust myself, not yet at least. Besides, Jordy probably wants a little more time with Lottie before I take over.

At least, that's what I tell myself. My head feels screwed on sideways, and I'm unsure what the fuck I'm supposed to be doing right now.

Figuring coffee might help, I slip into Java Joe's and order a drip. Then I find a table in the back away from the noise, just so I can sit in silence and wait until my mind feels clear again.

"You're doing that broody-silent-farm-boy thing again."

I look up, and there's Michael, who sets his coffee on the table and takes the seat across from me. I'm in no mood to visit, but I nod at him anyway.

"Good morning to you too."

"Oh man, you've got it bad."

I level a look at him. "I have no idea what you're talking about."

"Really? Because she's written all over your face."

Jordy. Fuck.

I look out the window again, neither confirming nor denying. But then I realize Michael spent a whole evening with Jordy. Knowing his prying nature, I'm dying to know what they talked about.

"You're going to have to be more specific," I say, praying he'll stop with the riddles and just spell out whatever he's hinting at.

"Nice try." He takes a sip from his mocha, then eyes me. "Why don't you tell me what's putting you in such a foul mood. You'd think you'd be happy."

I tilt my head. "And why would I be happy?"

Michael purses his lips, then raises his eyebrows. Then he says NOTHING.

Fuck, this game is getting old.

We both sit in silence for a while, just sipping our coffee and staring out the window. I'm ready to cave, to tell him everything. He knows something and isn't telling me.

I hold my breath as I swallow every word that bubbles into my throat.

Finally, I blurt out, "She's driving me crazy" at the same time that he says, "You know she has a thing for you."

"Wait." I gape at him. "What?"

"She's driving you crazy?" He appears wounded, his hand at his chest like I've stabbed him.

"No, not like that." I shake my head. "I can't stop thinking about her. She's in my house, and it's like I miss her when she's right in front of me. And today, she was holding my child and all I could think of was how I wanted this in my life forever. Her. Me. My daughter. The three of us as a family. Even as I feel like I'm falling apart, I'm also very aware that this is not real. She's been in my house for not even two weeks. I don't know her favorite color, her mother's name, or what her middle name is."

"Her mom's name is Lillian, and Jordy's middle name is Danielle, which I assume is for her father Dan. Her favorite color ... no clue."

"How the fuck do you know that?"

Michael peers at me. "Dude, Google is your friend. You should cyber stalk anyone you take in like a stray."

I roll my eyes, even as I know he has a point.

"So, are you going to let her know how you feel so you can stop the brooding?"

I shake my head. "What's the point? She's almost done with this job. In a couple weeks, she's headed back to New York. My whole life is here, and hers is there. There's no way I can make a long-distance thing work, not with Lottie and the farm."

"And you've discussed this with her?"

I huff. "Come on, man. You of all people know I can't."

Michael sits back in his chair. "Me of all people. And why is that?"

I can see I've offended him, but I'm not willing to back down. "Yes, you of all people. I don't see you out there on the dating scene anymore, not after Dominic fucked you over the way he did."

He looks out the window, his usual self-righteousness stripped from his face, a somber expression in its place. "Fucking asshole exes," he mutters. Then he looks at me with a small smile. "Okay. So you're being cautious so you don't get hurt. But what if you're missing out on what could be the best thing in your life? You don't even know where her head is at."

"And I suppose you do?"

He winks. "I've already said too much. You need to figure this one out on your own. But here's a hint: If you wait too long, you're going to regret it for the rest of your life."

"And you know this because…"

He sighs. "Because I am a student of people, and I know my subject."

"Meaning you're a busybody who's up in everyone's business." I raise my eyebrows, and he grins.

"Same diff."

My mind goes a million miles a minute as I make the drive home, and not all of it is from the caffeine. I keep going back and forth on what to do. Tell Jordy how I feel and make the most of what little time we had left? Hope that she considers a permanent residence in Lahoma Springs? Or just remain quiet and let her go, hoping I can eventually forget her?

By the time I reach the gravel drive, my heart is pounding with my decision.

I have to tell her. I have to at least let her be a part of the conversation I keep having in my head. If what Michael said was true, that she actually likes me, it's not fair for me to shut things down without giving her the chance to choose.

I open the door and am about to call out to her, but I can hear her in the bedroom on the phone, and I don't want to disturb her in case it's her work. I peek in on Lottie, but she's not in the crib. It's way past her naptime anyway. She's probably with Jordy. I head toward the back room to relieve Jordy of babysitting duties. But as I approach the door, the conversation leaps out at me.

"We're from two different worlds. It would never work."

I step back, knowing I should leave, but unable to move my feet.

"You're not listening, Mom, I'm not even interested in him."

It can't be me she's talking about. But could it? I don't actually know about her day-to-day life. Could she be talking about someone else?

"Yeah, I've been here two weeks now. He's been really generous, and it might be because he wants more. But I don't think of him that way." She laughs. "It's actually kind of annoying, if I'm being honest. He keeps hinting, and I have to keep dodging, but politely so I can keep a roof over my head." Another pause, and my heart is pounding. "Yeah, the money is an issue. We're completely unmatched."

I think back to the gallery. How she moved away when I reached for her hand. How she bought all four of Grace's paintings for a total of $4,000, as if it was nothing to her.

Meanwhile, I'm paying less than market rate for this tiny house, living on my ex's property, and staying frugal just so I can save for Lottie's future. I don't have $4,000 to drop on art, let alone anything else.

I don't want to hear the rest of the conversation. I start to leave, but then I hear Lottie squeal, "Daddy!" through the crack in the door. I can see her straining in Jordy's arms. Jordy turns, a look of surprise on her face.

"Mom, I have to go."

I ease the door open, and the look on her face is pure guilt. But I smile, pretending I heard nothing.

"There's my girl," I say, scooping Lottie up as she giggles. "Thanks for watching her."

"Anytime." Jordy gets up, smoothing her shirt out. It's obvious she's uncomfortable. "Hey, you want to grab dinner or something? We could see if Bec and Bob can watch Lottie so that we can get out, or she can even come with us."

"Nah." I head to the door. "I think Lottie and I are going to hang with Trash Truck on TV, then have some mac and cheese for dinner. But you're free to go out if you want. I'm sure Grace or Michael would love to spend time with you."

I try not to look at her as I leave the room, but she follows, and I can't help glancing in her direction. Her face looks confused. Disappointed.

"I can't," she says. "My car is still downtown."

Fuck. I forgot.

"Borrow the truck," I say, pulling the keys from my pocket. I aim to toss them to her, but she shakes her head.

"No, it's fine. I'll just..." She looks back at the bedroom. "I guess I'll just hang in the bedroom and read."

She stalls for a little longer, lingering as I sit on the couch and picked up the remote. I can't fend off the guilt that settles in my belly.

"Should I save you some macaroni?" I finally ask, looking over my shoulder.

"Nah." She hesitates, then says, "I've been eating too many carbs anyway. Just because I'm stuck here doesn't mean I need to let myself go."

The bedroom door clicks shut.

And the sound of it echoes through me like a roll of thunder. Like the moment a storm is no longer coming—it's already here.

I stare at the wall where her jellyfish painting hangs crooked, and this time, I can't laugh at it. All I see is the moment it slipped from her hands. Almost like it had been trying to tell me something.

It's never going to hold.

Not the painting. Not us.

One-Sided Crush

Jordy

The house is quiet. *Too* quiet. I'd holed up in my bedroom all evening, not wanting to intrude on Ashton's time with Lottie because … well, because I know when I'm not wanted. It was apparent by the cold shoulder Ashton gave me this evening.

I'm not sure what I did or didn't do for him to act so distant. Or maybe I'm reading too much into all of this. I don't know. I feel like a crazy woman trying to make sense of the senseless. Everything in me is screaming to tell him how I feel about him. Well, almost everything. My sensible side keeps reminding me that my time here is running out, and starting something with Ashton will only cause heartache for the both of us.

For all three of us, really. There's Lottie to think about too.

Ashton is already asleep on the couch when I venture out of the room to brush my teeth. I can hear the soft hum of his breathing, and it makes my heart ache a little more. I pause, listening to him for just a moment as a form of self-torture. But that's when my stomach noisily reminds me that I haven't eaten dinner yet.

I make a detour to the kitchen to peek in the fridge. Score. A bowl of leftover mac and cheese sits on the top shelf, almost like he'd been saving it for me. I nab it, not even bothering to warm the bowl so I won't wake Ashton. Then I sit quietly in the dark, eating the cold noodles.

Talking with my mom earlier today has triggered my food issues. I can just hear her voice telling me to stop stuffing myself, how no guy wants to marry a woman who bloats. But goddamn, even cold, this mac and cheese hits the spot. Bloat be damned.

I think back to my conversation with my mom. In her downtime—which is often since she doesn't work, clean, or do anything beyond Pilates on Tuesday nights—she Googled my boss and then immediately called me.

"Why can't you land a guy like this? He's not only rich as sin, he's a babe. Any company policies against dating him?"

Stupidly, I told her I was an independent contractor—free to date whoever I wanted to, even if they gave me a paycheck. Even worse, I told her that we *did* date for a moment.

That's when I got the whole lecture on how money could make anyone fall in love.

"Not me," I'd said. I detailed the one date I went on with him, where he wouldn't shut up about his golf game or his investments. "We're from two different worlds, Mom. It would never work."

Of course, that wasn't good enough for her.

"Jordy, you're a good-looking girl, even if your crow's feet are starting to show. You're still younger than Alexander—young enough to snatch him up and never have to work a day in your life. He probably won't care that you can't have kids anymore. It might even be preferable, so he can just spoil his hot, young wife." My mom sighed. "His bankroll should be a bonus, not an issue."

Crow's feet. Childless.

I'd closed my eyes, tried to shut out her barbs. But her words had already gotten in, like they always did. She always found a way to bring up the kids thing. When I lost my daughter, I also lost my ability to have kids. While it had never been my intention to have children, it still stung that the decision was no longer mine.

Apparently, my mom was also reeling from it. But telling her to stop only makes it worse, so I pretended she never said it.

"Yeah, the money is an issue," I'd muttered. "We're completely unmatched."

Luckily, Ashton had showed up just as she was getting started, giving me the perfect excuse to get off the phone.

Of course, I'd felt totally guilty that he even caught me on the phone. I was there to hang with Lottie, not ignore her while gabbing away. But honest truth, I'd rather gab with Lottie than my mom any day. I'd rather hang with Ashton, who had taken Lottie from my arms while I failed at the small job I'd been requested to do.

I glance again at the couch, listening for Ashton's soft breathing in the dark. I'd been waiting all day for us to hang out. I'd wanted to brag about how quickly Lottie warmed to me, and to show how capable I was of caring for a toddler.

Me! Jordy Gallo! A kids person!

But as soon as work was done, Aston took off for the feed store as if he couldn't get out of there quick enough. He didn't even ask if we wanted to go with him.

Jesus, Jordy. Codependent much? I wonder how many times he's noticed my stupid puppy dog eyes. Is he counting down the days until I'm out of here?

I'm crushing on him hardcore. Meanwhile, he's likely wondering when he'll get his house back. It's probably why he didn't say more than two words to me when he did get home, didn't even want to hang out.

I feel like I have whiplash. Two days ago, we were on the river holding hands. Last night, I thought we almost kissed. This morning, he smiled at me like I was someone special.

Tonight, he didn't even look my way.

Have I imagined everything?

I get up and put my bowl in the sink, running a little water in it so it can soak overnight. In the bathroom, I brush my teeth while staring at myself in the mirror. I look tired, still flushed from our river day in the sun.

What does he see when he looks at me? And why, when I'm leaving in two short weeks, do I even care?

"Pull yourself together, Jordy," I whisper, looking myself right in the eye. This is not the time for some inappropriate crush. I have a job to do. The workmen will be finished with construction by the end of the week, and then I'll be busy with pulling in every fixture I've purchased for the place in preparation for the grand opening. The last thing I need is a distraction, and definitely not one that will end in heartbreak.

I turn off the light then head back into the hall. For just a moment, I linger near the living room. Not close enough to see Ashton, but I have a clear view of the back of the couch. I catch a glimpse of the jellyfish painting on the wall—still crooked, and completely ridiculous.

I'd laughed when we hung it, now it just looks like a bad joke. A mess of strings floating in confusion.

"My god, don't you see it? That man could not take his eyes off you."

Grace's voice rings in my head. But she's wrong, and I'm wrong for still being here.

Ashton stirs on the couch, and I turn and tiptoe back to the bedroom. *His* bedroom. I turn on the light and look around, taking in all my clothes in piles on the floor, a chair, and the end of the bed. God, he's on the couch while I take over his room.

Even though it's late, I start putting everything in neat piles. I tell myself I'm just picking up. Just folding a few clothes. But then the suitcase comes out, and one pile turns into two, then more.

And suddenly, I'm not just tidying—I'm preparing. For what, I'm not sure. But I need a plan B, a softer place to land when it all falls apart.

Someplace far from here.

18

Strong Opinions

Ashton

I didn't sleep. I just laid there on the couch all night, listening to the soft creaks of the house and trying not to think about Jordy—about how much I still want her, even after everything she said in that phone conversation. I heard her come out once, probably to brush her teeth. I pretended to be asleep—coward move, maybe—but I wasn't ready to face what I'd heard last night.

Or how I feel.

I rub a hand over my face, trying to will the memory out of my head. But her voice won't leave me.

He's been really generous, and it might be because he wants more.

I don't think of him that way.

It's actually kind of annoying.

He keeps hinting.

I keep dodging, but politely so I can keep a roof over my head.

Obviously, I'm just a pity project to her, something she's putting up with. I think back to our day on the river, about holding her hand and then later taking her to the art gallery. I thought there'd been a connection. I'd seen the way she looked at me, felt the tug of that thread between us.

Did I misread everything?

After Jordy went to bed, I'd stayed up a little longer. She had too, apparently. Her light had been on for at least another hour, and it took everything in me to not knock on her door and demand to know what was going on. But I didn't. The thought of her rejecting me again when the phone call had done the job so flawlessly ... it would be more than I could take.

And I had two more weeks of putting up a good front.

I stretch, taking the last few moments of alone time before I have to get moving on my day. All I want to do is burrow under the covers and forget the world exists.

The sound of wheels on the linoleum floor gives me pause. I peek my head over the couch, and there's Jordy, rolling two suitcases—one in front of her, and the other behind. She winces when she sees me.

"I thought I'd ask you for one more favor. My car is in town, so…"

I sit up. "So you need your suitcases?" I shake my head, looking from them to her. "What are you doing?"

"Getting out of your hair. I figured it was time." She takes a deep breath, then offers a shaky smile. "You've been so generous," she says.

Generous. That fucking word.

"Is that what you think this is? I'm just being generous?"

I get up from the couch, and her eyes widen. But I'm pissed.

"I'm not trying to get in your pants by letting you stay here," I say. Her jaw drops.

"Um, okay?"

"In fact, I don't expect anything from you just for staying here. Did it ever occur to you that I was just being nice? That I saw you in a hard spot, and I let you stay here because I have the room?"

"Well, I thought you did it because you felt guilty for getting me drunk," she says. She laughs a little, but I note the hurt in her eyes, which pisses me off even more. She doesn't get to feel hurt, not after playing fucking games and then gossiping to her mom about what a clueless idiot I've been.

"I heard you on the phone last night."

She looks confused for a moment, tilting her head. "When I was talking with my mom?"

"Yeah, and I heard everything. How you don't think of me that way. How it's annoying. How you're just being nice to keep a roof over your head. Well, let me tell you something … you don't have to worry about me. I might be attracted to you, but you don't need to pretend to be interested just so you can stay here. You don't even need to leave now, even though I'm livid you think that of me. There are no strings for you staying here, Jordy. I would have kept my mouth shut until the day you left, if that made you happy."

She inhales sharply, then lets it out in a slow, unsteady breath. "You're … attracted to me?"

I open my mouth to answer, but Lottie chooses that moment to let her presence be known. Her wail sounds loudly on the other side of her door. I move to it, but I point to Jordy's suitcases.

"I'll drive you to get your car, but your shit is staying here."

Then I turn to my daughter's room, trying not to let my anger affect the way I open her door.

On the other side, I pause to catch my breath. Lottie quiets as soon as she sees me, watching me with wide eyes.

Fuck. I can't believe I actually admitted I liked her, even knowing that she found it "annoying." I said the unspoken thing aloud. Now what am I supposed to do? Walk out of this room and pretend nothing is wrong?

I gather Lottie in my arms, who seems to understand that her daddy is in a strange state. She pats my cheek, almost as if to comfort me.

That's the thing about my daughter, I could be having the worst day of my life, and one sweet little gesture from her can make it all go away.

"You're my girl, you know that?" I kiss her forehead, then lean back to look at her. My beautiful girl. She grins, then moves her head toward me again for another forehead kiss. It's our game, to see how many kisses she can take. I give them all to her, peppering her face with kisses while she squeals.

By the time I leave the room, the ice is broken. I'm still mortified by my admission, but I said what I said. Even if Jordy doesn't return my feelings, I no longer have to hide behind them.

"Want coffee?" Jordy asks. She's seated at the end of the counter, almost like she's waiting for me. Her suitcases are no longer in view, which feels kind of like a message—she's staying. I don't know whether to feel relieved or panicked.

"Sure." I strap Lottie into her highchair then turn. Jordy is next to me, holding the cup of coffee.

"You're attracted to me?" she asks again as I take the cup from her hands.

I narrow my eyes as I take my first sip. "That's all you got from what I said? What, you want to rub it in my face?"

"Ashton, when have I ever been that horrible to you?"

I take a deep breath, looking up at the ceiling. "Maybe not *to* me," I say, "but you seem to have a very strong opinion *about* me."

"You're right," she says, stepping closer. She takes the coffee from my hands and puts it on the counter. She moves even closer, placing one hand on my hip and the other at my chest.

"Come on," I murmur, looking down at her. I want to move away, but my feet are firmly planted on the ground. I feel dizzy from her proximity, completely consumed by her. It's cruel. "What are you doing?"

"Showing you my opinion," she says, her voice husky. Then she brushes her mouth across mine with the softest of kisses. Barely a whisper. Testing. Tasting.

And I break.

I grab her hips, pulling her against me like I've been waiting a lifetime. Her hands slide around my neck, and my mouth claims hers. It isn't sweet—it's *hungry*. It's all the conversations we haven't had, all the tension finally snapping.

I can't get close enough.

"Zowies?" Lottie asks.

I break away from Jordy, laughing even as the confusion sets in. What the fuck just happened?

"I don't understand," I say, reaching for the Cheerios and pouring a small hill on Lottie's tray. "You said all those things to your mother."

"And I bet you thought that call was about you," she teases.

"Huh?"

"I was talking about my boss." Her hand lands on her hip, and she gives me a pointed look.

It takes a few beats for me to register what she's saying. "You mean, Alexander Winslow?"

"Yes," she says, rolling her eyes. "We dated for a minute, before I started working for him. I realized quickly that we weren't compatible."

Just the thought of that man's hand on her … I want to pop his fucking head off his body. I still remember that too wide grin he had as we went over the paperwork with Bob to sell The Till. Just knowing he aimed that slimy smile at Jordy makes me feel like I could commit murder.

"What's his deal? Is he still fucking with you? I mean, unless you want him to. But aren't there laws against that?" I clench my fists at my side, and she glanced at them, her face looking amused as her eyes flicked back to my face.

"I'm an independent contractor," she says. "And did you not hear what I just said? No, I don't want him. That's what I was trying to tell my mom."

I scroll back the mental tapes, trying to remember what I heard.

"You said I'm generous and putting a roof over your head."

She shakes her head. "No, I said *he's* putting the roof over my head. I'm paid well for what I do, and I get to keep my New York apartment thanks largely to that paycheck."

"You said the money was an issue." Even as I say it though, I realize what a fool I'd been.

"It is," she says. "He's made of money. He lives completely different than me. If I were interested in a relationship with him, it would mean giving up my autonomy and bending to his world. Money is nice and all, but it's not everything." She touches my arm, sliding it down until our hands clasp. "It didn't matter if he bled money, I knew I'd never love him."

There's something in the way she says it—*love*—how she's touching me when she says it. It makes me feel hopeful. We're nowhere near the meaning of that word, but fuck, it feels like a possibility.

One that I want.

"And you?" I ask, turning toward her, loving the way her fingers feel laced with mine. "Are we unmatched?"

The corner of her mouth quirks up, and she shakes her head.

I lift her chin with my finger so that she's looking up at me. "Are you attracted to me?"

She bites her lip, then nods.

"Even though we're from different worlds?"

She moves closer still, her face inches from mine. "Not all that different."

But we are. She's in my arms now, but soon she'll be on a plane, heading thousands of miles away.

"In two weeks, you leave for New York, and I'll still be here in Lahoma Springs."

She takes a deep breath, her smile faltering for a moment, then she looks back up at me. Her eyes are so beautiful, a deep, dark brown I could get lost in. I want to smother myself in her, to consume and be consumed. I feel complete, and I also feel like I can't get close enough.

"I can't keep stuffing these feelings," she admits, and it makes me take a quick breath. Because I can't either, and the relief of this moment is almost overwhelming. I have her. But the ache in my heart can't stop telling me that I'm going to lose her.

"What do we do?" I ask.

Her eyes sparkle with unshed tears, but she smiles through them. I brush a thumb over her lashes, catching them before they fall. She closes her eyes briefly, leaning into my hand. When she looks at me again, it's with renewed determination.

"We make the most of our time," she whispers, then presses her lips to mine.

19

Petunia

Jordy

Ashton leaves to feed the animals soon after, letting Lottie stay with me at my insistence. All I'm doing today is coordinating the deliveries coming in at the end of the week, and they can be scheduled from my laptop while she plays ... in her playpen, that is. My newly clean Vans are on my feet, and I'm not willing to sacrifice any of my other shoes to the porcelain god.

More than ever, I feel the limits of my time here. That kiss ... I pause from my work to touch my lips, feeling breathless as I recall the way he tasted, how his soft, full lips felt against mine.

I don't want to think about what happens when it's time to go home. I want to savor every moment, every experience before I leave Lahoma. That means spending as much time with Ashton as possible. I don't want to get too deep into whatever this is between us … but I know it's too late for that. Kissing him made it way harder to think about leaving.

I have no regrets.

Ashton is gone for just over an hour. When he returns, he's sweaty, his dusty t-shirt clinging to his bronze skin in ways that leave me breathless. Only, this time I don't have to hide noticing. He catches my stare, flexing slightly with a chuckle. I groan.

"You're killing me, Oregon." Now that we've lowered our walls, I want more. I want all of him.

But Lottie wants her daddy, which she makes known with a loud whine, arms outstretched in her playpen.

"All right, princess," he says with a laugh, winking at me before crossing the room to reach her. She brushes her springy hair out of her face once she's in his arms, and he leans back to get a good look at her. "Let's get that 'do under control, what do you say?" He looks at me. "Could you wet her hair while I get the supplies?"

I nod, feeling a little apprehensive. Lottie's hair is so thick and textured, it's hard to know what to do. Even though I'd figured it out before, I worry I'll do it wrong.

Amazingly, Lottie sits still while I work at her hair. I spray it, then work a comb through it carefully. Even when I yank, she doesn't seem to mind.

"You'll be at it for hours at that pace." Ashton grins, bumping my hip so I scoot to the side, then he takes over. It's like a dance. I watch his fingers move deftly as he uses oil to work her hair into little braids at the crown of her head, securing it so that the rest of her hair is natural. When he's done, she looks like a little queen, her red hair fanning out in back like a royal flush.

"I never learned how to braid," I muse, running my hand over Lottie's gorgeous hair.

"I think that's so sad," he says, laughing as he dodges the rubber band I fling at him. "How did you wear your hair when you were younger?"

I shrug. "Just long or in ponytails. In buns when I went to dance class. But my mom didn't know how to braid, so I never learned."

Ducking my head, I feel shy all of a sudden. But the question hovers at the surface until it finally bursts from my mouth.

"Would you teach me?"

Ashton grins, then motions for us to move to the living room. He places Lottie back in the playpen, then has me sit in front of the chair. He sits behind me, his legs on each side of my shoulders, and he tilts my head back.

"I'll try to be gentle," he says, and then he starts.

Holy hell, I'm not prepared. His fingers run through my hair, stroking my scalp as he combs out any tangles with his fingers. I moan slightly, and he stills.

"Jesus," he breathes, then gives a low chuckle. "If this is how you sound when I touch your hair…" he trails off.

I look up and grin.

"What?" I ask, biting my lip.

His answer is a low growl and a slight tug of my hair that is both demanding and suggestive. The braid is the last thing on my mind as I think about how he could pull my hair in other ways.

"Damn, Ashton," I exhale. He leans down, his breath hot against the shell of my ear.

"You like that, huh?" Then he tugs again, his mouth brushing against my skin before he goes back to finger combing my hair. "I think you and I might have the same appetite."

I'm thinking the same thing. It's been ages since I've been with anyone, and fuck if I'm not hungry—and not for anything soft or sensual. I want a good, hard fuck, and I have a feeling Ashton could take care of that for me.

But right now, we have to keep things fairly G-rated. Lottie is doing her own thing in the playpen, but the things I want to do to this man are not suitable for little eyes. It's taking all my restraint not to turn around and straddle him so I can see what else he could manipulate with his hands.

I hold it together. While he parts my hair into three strands, I do my best not to melt under his touch. When he gives me a mirror and shows me how to grab more strands to weave into the braid, I hold my breath to keep from moaning. As he keeps tugging at my hair, mostly unintentional, I manage to keep my hands to myself.

But my god, I'm coming apart at the seams as he ties off my hair with a rubber band and gives it one last tug.

"I swear to god," I say, turning to face him. "If that's the only hair pulling I get today, I'm going to explode."

He licks his lips as I stand, looking me up and down.

"I bet Lottie would love a sleepover at Mimi and Papa's house tonight. What do you think?"

What do I think? I'm already wet, that's what I think.

"I think it should start sooner rather than later."

He's about to speak, but there's a loud banging at the door. We both turn, and there's Bob. He's smiling, but I recognize the urgency in his face.

"Petunia is close. She should be calving any moment," he says when Ashton opens the door. Ashton whoops, and grabs his jacket. He then strides to Lottie's playpen and swoops her up.

"Grab her jacket off the hook," he says, pointing. I do, then hand it to him. "I've been waiting for this. Lottie still hasn't seen a cow give birth, and I thought this would be the perfect opportunity. Want to come?"

I nod, though inside I'm nervous as hell. I've only seen animal births on nature shows, and they're pretty gross. Can I handle it up close like that?

But this isn't the biggest issue. My gut is working overtime because, even though this is a damn cow, my mind is totally consumed by my own experience with birth.

One that ended with holding a dead baby—one I didn't even know I wanted until I held her.

Would I ever get over this? I'm not sure. But I'm not about to show how much this is affecting me. So I race out with them, keeping close as Bob leads the way to the barns.

Petunia is by herself in the corner of the pen, her stomach broad, her tail up in the air as she restlessly moves her head, braying every few moments.

"Oh man, she's close," Ashton says, handing me Lottie as he gets a better view of the large protrusion from her backside. My eyes widen, and he must have noticed the shock on my face. "It's her water bag," he explains, taking a few steps back. "The amniotic sac. The calf should come in the next hour or two."

There isn't much to do while Petunia is preparing to calf, so we sit on the other side of the pen and wait. Ashton picks flowers with Lottie to keep her from getting bored. But I'm gripped by the cow's obvious discomfort. I can't tear my eyes away, completely consumed as she paces, stopping every now and then to hit her head against her side as if to make the pain go away.

I keep glancing at Ashton, afraid he'll notice the deep breaths I keep having to take so that I don't panic. But he's thankfully preoccupied, keeping Lottie entertained and glancing up now and then to check the cow's progress. Occasionally he offers me a wink with an excited grin, and I must do a pretty good acting job because he never notices how completely overwhelmed I feel.

Petunia eventually moves to her knees, then to her side, and I sit up straighter as I see the water bag bulge even more, and then burst.

"Ashton!"

He's up in a second, holding Lottie as they lean over the fence. Bob is right there beside the cow, not touching but closely monitoring, as the calf's head emerges. It all happens so quickly, that little body slipping through the canal and sliding with a gooey rush to the ground.

For a moment, it's like time stands still. The calf is like a rag doll in the dirt, unmoving and lifeless. My breath hitches, tears stinging my eyes, and a suffocating tightness grips my chest.

And then it lifts its head, scrambling to its feet while struggling to stand.

"You see that, Lottie? See the baby?" Ashton is all smiles, and Lottie is pointing, her words coming out in bell-like babbles.

But I'm fighting to catch my breath, trying to hold back the sob that is trapped in my throat.

I will not ruin this for them. I can't. They're so fucking happy, but I'm consumed by death. For a moment, that calf was Violet, my lost child. When the calf came to life, it reminded me that my baby never would, that she's bones and ash in the cold ground, invisible to everyone but the mother who dared to wish she never existed—and then got her wish.

"I can't believe I missed it," Bec says, walking up beside me.

Every part of me is shaking, to the point I'm not even sure I can keep standing. I can't let them see me this way, let them know that I'm falling apart while they celebrate this fucking miracle.

"Dear, are you okay?" Bec's voice is soft and low, and my sob is involuntary. Once it escapes my lips, I'm on my knees, holding my head in my hands, and losing the fight against my tears. I crumble in the middle of everyone. I ruin everything, just like I always do. I fall into the darkness, and I can't bring myself out.

I feel arms around me, but I'm too far gone. Then we're moving, my eyes closed, my head against a broad, warm chest. I'm barely there. My screams are the only thing I can hear, my panic the only thing I can feel. The whole world caves in on me, and all I can do is hope I'll die before it rips me apart.

20

Triggered

Ashton

She's hysterical. I hold her tight, forgetting anything but her as I carry her back to the house and away from everyone. Jordy's breath comes out in gasps as she cries uncontrollably, her hands clutching my shirt as if she needs an anchor to keep from floating away. I reach the porch and set her down on the bench, her legs draped over mine as she clings to me.

"Breathe, baby," I murmur, and she tries to pull in a shaky breath. Her eyes are wild, frantically looking around without focusing on any one thing. I realize she's having a panic attack, the way she doesn't seem rooted in reality. "You're safe," I whisper. "Take a breath."

She tries again, this time quieting as her forehead presses against mine, her body still shaking as she struggles to breathe. I take her hands in mine, and she squeezes them hard.

"You're here with me," I whisper. I keep telling her she's safe, that I'm not leaving her. I remind her to breathe.

Eventually she stills.

"Breathe in," I coax, then take a deep breath at the same time she does. We hold at the top, her eyes finding mine. They appear larger than life, brimming in tears, her face streaked with dirt. She looks so fragile, so unlike the Jordy I've gotten to know these past few weeks.

We release our breath together.

I coach her through another few breaths until her grasp on my hands loosens and her body relaxes. She falls into me, resting her head on my chest as I softly stroke her braided hair.

"Thank you," she murmurs.

My phone vibrates in my pocket, but I ignore it as I continue to hold her. We stay that way for a little while, until she finally sits up, pushing against my chest gently until she's sitting beside me. I see her mask shift into place, and I shake my head.

"Don't stuff this," I warn her. "It's okay to be vulnerable." She inhales with hitched breath, looking away quickly, but not before I see her eyes fill with tears again.

"I have no idea where that came from," she says, offering a shaky laugh.

Liar.

It could have been the shock of seeing a cow give birth. Maybe it's exhaustion from watching my kid. All I know is that her reaction came from somewhere deep.

And she's not talking.

A part of me says to leave it alone. It's not my business, whatever happened out there. But that's what I did with Sasha. She didn't talk, I didn't press—look where it left us.

"I think you do," I say softly. She doesn't look at me as she stands, wiping at her face. "Do you want to talk about it?"

She nods, then stops. Then shakes her head.

"Can I go take a shower?" she asks, still not looking at me.

I'm at a loss. She's pushing me away, trying to lock up anything she hasn't released yet. I feel desperate to keep her here, to make her feel whatever she's repressing.

"You don't have to..." I start, but then stop myself. She needs space. I can see it in every cell of her body. As much as I want to barrel my way in, to make her talk so I can fix it for her, I realize I can't. Even with Sasha in mind, how we just brushed everything under the damn carpet, I know I can't push Jordy.

So I stand and open the door for her, then follow her inside. She disappears into the bathroom, closing the door behind her.

My chest tightens, feeling like I'm losing her even though she's just behind that door. I have no idea what to do, what to say.

It's like Sasha all over again.

My phone vibrates again, and this time I pull it out and look at the screen.

Bec.

Fuck. My kid.

"I'm sorry," I say as my greeting. "I can't believe I abandoned Lottie. I'll come get..."

"Lottie is fine," Bec says. "She's with Bob, completely fascinated by that calf. It's Jordy I'm worried about. How is she?"

"Okay, I think." I look toward the bathroom door, hearing the quiet rush of water on the other side. I breathed out heavily. "She had a panic attack. I helped her breathe through it, now she's in the shower." I sit on the couch, collapsing against the back of it. "I don't know what to do. She won't talk about it, and I don't even know what happened. I feel like the biggest idiot. She's probably never seen a cow give birth before, and I just gave her a front row seat to the horror show. I can't believe I didn't check with her first."

"I don't know," Bec says slowly. "I know we've just met Jordy, but she's a strong woman. I can't see something like the birth of a cow sending her into a panic like that." She's quiet for a moment. "Tell me what you remember happening."

I do, though my focus had been on Petunia and her calf, plus Lottie in my arms. Not Jordy. I detail how Petunia had been pacing until she finally laid down, and how the calf came out quickly after that.

"It didn't move at first," I say. "For a moment, I thought we lost the calf. But it was only like that for a few seconds tops before it started kicking its legs."

Bec makes a sympathetic noise in her throat. "And Jordy has never seen an animal birth?" she asks.

"I mean, anything is possible. But it's not like there are a lot of opportunities in New York."

"Okay, maybe it's not about animals. Maybe something else? Could the calf appearing stillborn have affected her?"

The word hits me like a sledgehammer. Stillborn.

"I'm such a fucking idiot." I look at the door again, the water still running. "I need to go. Can you watch Lottie for me for a while?"

"Honey, you know you don't have to ask. We treasure our time with Lottie, and I haven't seen her in a few days."

"So you'd keep her overnight?"

That was already the plan, but the reason changed. I know Jordy needs the quiet, and anything could be a trigger— even my daughter. The least I can do is provide her space to recover.

"It would be our pleasure. Now, go tend to our girl."

Our girl. I love the way it sounds, like Bec already knows something is brewing, and she's accepting Jordy like a daughter.

Even though she isn't Sasha.

I head to my bedroom, noting Jordy's still-packed suitcases sitting in the corner. The room is spotless, not a sign of her except for those suitcases. I furrow my brow at the sign of her attempted getaway. Thank god I'd stopped her. We only have two weeks left, but it's still time. I'll take what I can get.

I unzip the suitcase and choose some new clothes, finding the comfier ones buried below the rolled-up silk blouses and linen dress pants. Even in her haste, I marvel at the way she packs things so that nothing is wrinkled. It goes to show how careful Jordy is at keeping everything neat and tidy.

Just like her life.

She told me about the loss of her baby in the first few days of knowing her. It had slipped out in a brief, emotional moment before she tucked it away again. So brief, barely a mention for something that had obviously affected her.

And like a dumbass, I hadn't thought of it since.

When I was young, my mom had a miscarriage. The pregnancy had been unexpected, and my dad blamed my mom for not taking her birth control, even though the fucker could have used a condom.

"It's not like we can afford the kids we have," he'd screamed at her. "How are you going to support another mouth to feed?"

My mom had been the only one working at the time, cleaning houses while he lay on the couch drinking. I think we all knew we were screwed if she had to take time off to have a baby. So when she lost it, none of us mourned. Thinking back, I'm not sure how my mom actually felt after losing the baby. We never talked about it, and it was like the baby never happened.

But it did, and it was likely that my mom felt a whole lot for that baby, even as inconvenient as it was. She loved her kids with all her heart, another baby would have been no different.

I gather Jordy's clothes plus a fresh towel, then I knock on the bathroom door.

"I'm almost done," she calls. I can tell she's masking, pretending everything's okay. I crack the door open.

"No rush," I say. "I brought you some fresh clothes and a towel. I'll just place them on the counter. Take your time."

"Thanks." Her voice cracks slightly. I ease the door closed again.

Needing to distract myself, I water the plants around the side of the house and organize the tools in the shed. I know if I wait inside, I'll just hover. And as much as I hate it, I know Jordy needs time to process alone. But when I can't stand it any longer, I head back in the house to find her sitting on the couch. She's scrolling her phone, but puts it down as soon as I approach, scooting over to make room for me. The screen is face up, showing off an Instagram page full of baby photos. I look at Jordy, who shift her eyes from me to the phone, then back at me again. She quickly turns the phone off, then places it face down.

"It's my cousin, Nina," she explains. "Her whole page is dedicated to her daughter, Juniper." She gives a light laugh. "I've never even seen her in real life. It's mainly through Facetime, when Nina springs it on me, and on Instagram, when I scroll through the photos as a form of punishment."

I note the emphasis she places on that word. *Punishment.* As if she needs atonement for something that wasn't her fault.

"How so?"

She looks at me then, her eyes welling with tears. Then she laughs, looking up at the ceiling. "God, I'm a fucking mess."

I take her hand away from her face, wiping her tears with my sleeve. She presses her face against my hand, shuddering slightly as she leans into me.

"You know who Juniper's father is?" she asks. I nod.

"Your ex-fiancé, right?"

She looks at her hands, nodding. "It's not like this is new or anything. I mean, June's nine months old now."

"And seeing her is like seeing the baby you couldn't have, right?"

I say it cautiously. Gently. And when her face crumples, I pull her to me.

"Oh sweetheart, I'm so sorry."

She shudders as she leans in, but holds herself together. I feel her breathe a heavy sigh as she relaxes into me.

"I didn't even think of that when I invited you to see the cow give birth," I say, stroking her hair. "I thought it would be something cool, but I never even considered how that might make you feel, even knowing you lost your child. Were you far along?"

She nods. "About seven months," she says, and my breath stills.

I remember Sasha at that point in her pregnancy. That was around the time we showed up at Bob and Bec's front door. Sasha was wearing my clothes because she couldn't fit into her own. Bec had taken her shopping that first week we arrived, getting her proper maternity clothes. She'd also set up prenatal appointments, and we'd found out we were having a girl. Lottie was born six weeks later.

Jordy's baby didn't survive.

"Are you okay?"

She nods. "I'm fine."

I look down at her, and she gives me a weak smile.

"I am," she insists. "I mean, I'm raw right now. Most days, I don't even think about it. It's been so long since it happened, enough time that I can go about my daily life without even thinking about…" She hesitates, takes a deep breath, "about her."

She says this, but I see it differently—especially now that her trauma is becoming clearer.

"Honey, you avoided my daughter like she was some scary creature when you first arrived here."

"I'm not a kids person," she says weakly. I raise an eyebrow at her. "What? I'm not!"

"Right. Which is why you've been so fantastic with her once you gave her a chance."

"Okay, fine," she says, bumping me with her shoulder. "But that doesn't mean anything."

"You're stalking your cousin's Instagram immediately after having a panic attack over seeing a cow give birth."

At this, she pulls her knees into her chest, making herself a tight ball against me. I squeeze her shoulders, then kiss the top of her head.

"I thought the calf was dead," she whispers, then wipes her eyes against my shirt.

"I know, sweetheart."

She's quiet for a moment. I listen to her breathe, inhaling the scent of her freshly washed hair, feeling the warmth of her skin as my heart breaks for everything she's feeling.

She looks up at me then, her eyes glassy. "You know the worst part about losing a baby like I did?"

"All of it, I'm sure." I kiss her temple, waiting for her to continue.

"Well yeah, all of it. The loss. Everything. But I guess what makes it all feel worse is that you can't talk about it. I'm like the plague. When people think about babies, they think happy things, like sweet smells and soft skin and tiny little feet and hands. Babies are innocent and precious and vulnerable.

Then there's me, the mom of a dead baby, and I feel like a bull in a China shop. If I so much as mention the fact that my daughter died, it's like I'm ruining it for everyone." She laughs, but the sound is full of ire. "You should have seen me at Nina's baby shower. There was pink everywhere, and all these precious little cupcakes and gifts. Everyone was fawning all over her, guessing who the baby would look like more, and I felt like this giant toad in the middle of all this sweet baby stuff."

"That must have been terrible," I say, stroking her shoulder.

"The worst," she agrees. "But I had to go, you know? First, my mom insisted. But second, if I didn't go, everyone would think I was just bitter about Brayden having a baby with another woman."

"What's wrong with that? He left you for her, and he *did* have a baby with her. Any person in the world would be bitter over that."

"But not me," she says, then gives another harsh laugh. "It's not that I want Brayden. I don't. The honest truth is, once the dust of my broken engagement settled, I felt relieved. I just wasn't prepared to care this much when Nina got pregnant. I was fine when I found out, but once she started to show..." Jordy trails off.

"You were triggered."

Jordy nods. "I didn't even want kids. When I found out I was pregnant, I was pissed. Brayden and I barely knew each other, but he proposed anyway. We were a terrible match, and I felt caged into a relationship with someone I didn't love. I spent most of that pregnancy trying to pretend I was excited.

But really, I was scared shitless. I had plans for my life that didn't include being tied down or having a baby. When I lost her, I was so devastated, but there was also a small part of me that felt relieved." She looks at me. "You probably think I'm a terrible person for even saying that."

"I don't," I say. "It's not like Lottie was a planned baby. We were young and poor, working on a pot farm. My family isn't exactly roses, as you know. I haven't even talked to my mom in years. When Sasha got pregnant, I was sure I was going to mess this kid up."

"But did you ever…" She pauses, wincing.

"Hope that maybe the pregnancy would end? I had moments, especially in the beginning when it was all new. I don't think that makes you a bad person, though. I think it makes you human."

She wraps her arms around me, shifting closer. I tighten my hold on her as she breathes.

"My life would look so different now if she'd survived," she murmured. Then she looks at me. "I'm not sure it would have been a good thing. I never wanted to be a mom. I mean, I can't anymore. When I lost Violet, I had to have a hysterectomy. So the choice was taken from me, but it's whatever, you know?" She heaves a heavy sigh. "Even if I didn't want a baby, I wish she hadn't died. Like, maybe she could have been born to a different mother or something. I guess I wish we'd been more careful and never gotten pregnant in the first place." She rolls her eyes. "But, it's like that saying—what doesn't kill you, makes you stronger."

"Well, I don't think we have to wade through shit to become strong people, Jordy." I kiss her forehead. "I think you were already strong and had a shitty thing happen to you."

I look down at her then, and she doesn't break eye contact. She inches a little closer, and I lean down, pressing my lips to hers in a soft, lingering kiss. Her lips part slightly, and the tip of my tongue touches hers. She tastes like an invitation, like the sweetest meal I've ever had. I pull her on top of me, my hands finding her hair in that damn braid, still slightly damp from her shower. I make quick work of it, pulling off the rubber band and tangling my hands into the waves of her hair. She grinds against my already hard cock, which is straining against my jeans to reach the furthest depths of her.

But I can't. My body wants her so bad, wants to fix everything by fucking it out of her. It's like this carnal need, to feel her skin against mine and protect her with every part of me.

I feel so fucking selfish. I can't focus on my needs when she's so much more important.

"We don't have to do anything," I whisper against her mouth. She kisses me quiet, pausing just long enough to pull my shirt over my head.

"I want to," she says in between kisses, her hands pawing at my back. I break away, even though it nearly kills me.

"Seriously. I can hold you. We can just kiss. I have no expectations."

"Ashton."

I stop kissing her, pulling away as she looks down at me. Her hair hangs in waves around her face, the lights from the room casting this glow about her. She's so damn beautiful, it takes my breath away.

"I want this." She places a hand at my cheek. "I want you. I need to feel you against me. Everywhere. Inside of me."

I search her face, looking for the cracks, looking for anything that will make me believe she's doing this for me.

All I see is the same fire I feel mirrored in her eyes.

"Are you sure?"

She answers by lowering her mouth to mine again. Her tongue moves against mine, her mouth seeking something deeper. More.

I want—need—more.

I stand, her legs wrapped around me, our mouths hungrily seeking as I walk toward the bedroom. Her body feels like the missing part of me, like a completion of sorts. I cannot believe I existed this long without her.

We land on the bed, a tangle of arms and legs. My hands thread into her hair as I consume her. She consumes me. She tears at my clothes, and I pause long enough to strip my shirt off, to help her with hers, to…

Fuck, her body is so perfect. So tight. So ready for me. I take in her olive skin, the way every part of her seems molded for my hands. I want to taste the salt of her skin, find out how her tight nipples feel between my teeth, cup the firm slope of her ass while driving into her.

I want to heal her and wreck her, all at once.

"I don't think I have it in me to be gentle," I growl, pulling at her underwear as she fumbles with my button.

"I don't want you to be gentle." She unzips my pants, pulling them down my hips. I land on her with the motion, both of us laughing at the absurdity, our mouths finding each other again. She's right there, and I still can't get close enough.

I pause long enough to retrieve a condom from my dresser drawer. Thank god I thought to get some. When was the last time I needed one? Far too fucking long. But for her, I'd wait forever.

I pull my pants completely off, standing before her as her eyes take me in. She looks at me like I'm a meal, her gaze raking over me while her tongue flicks across her bottom lip.

And her. She's a goddamn vision. Her hair is wild from my hands. Her skin already reddening from the places my mouth has been. Her lips swollen and parted. Her breath coming out in rushes of air.

"You can stop me at any time," I say, ripping the condom open. "Even now. Tell me to stop, and it stops."

"Ashton, if you stop, I'll die. I don't want you to stop."

A gentleman would have asked again. Would have checked to make sure she was okay. That she wouldn't regret this later.

I was not a gentleman.

I slide that condom on so fast, my cock straining in my hands, ready to annihilate that beautiful cunt of hers—and fuck, it's a gorgeous cunt. Glistening and ready. I can't wait to bury myself in her. But goddamn, I need to taste her.

I dip my head, my hands holding down her writhing hips as I swipe my tongue across her slick center. She tastes like heaven, a burst of earthy sweetness. This is my new obsession. Her taste. Her smell. I could devour her and still not get enough.

Her clit is at a peak when I wrap my lips around it, and I feel her body arch into me as I suck. My fingers enter her, feeling the plush softness of her inner walls wrap around me, grabbing me. Her hands reach for my head, fingers raking against me as I feel her swell in my mouth.

She cries out, her body bucking as her sex spasms around my fingers. I pump them inside her, feeling her body give way and fully submit to me.

Open for me.

And I can't wait any longer.

I land on her and she greedily kisses me, tasting herself on me in a way that makes my cock tense with anticipation. I nudge at her entrance, sure that this is the part where I check in with her but not wanting to, for fear that she'll say no.

"Can I—"

"Fuck me, Ashton," she breathes into my mouth.

It's all the permission I need. I press into her, feeling her gasp as I cross the barrier. She's warm and soft, but like a vice grip around my dick.

Jesus, this woman. She's made for me.

I hold her body to me, so tight. Every part of her is wrapped around me. Her legs. Her arms. Her slick pussy. I push deeper, then pull back. Gently at first, trying to be conscious enough to stop if she even breathes hesitancy.

She must sense my caution because she suddenly pulls a move that has me on my back, my cock still inside her as she straddles me.

"Well, fuck me," I laugh.

"Oh, I plan to," she says, bracing a hand on the wall as she grinds against me.

And holy hell, I'm not ready. The way I feel her shift around me, her thigh muscles gripping me as she moves with intention. Her eyes are laser focused on mine, and it's so goddamn sexy to see her take control. To see her body, every muscle working as she rocks her hips.

My thumb finds her swollen clit. I don't move, but let her slide over my thumb as she fucks me, feeling her tighten as she throws her head back, letting out a guttural moan.

Fuck, she's sexy as hell. The way she lets loose. No inhibitions. No hesitancy. This is not like a first-time fuck. There's nothing polite about this, nothing reserved. It's like our bodies have known each other all along.

I hold her hips as she rides out the wave, feeling her goosebumps erupt across her skin. When she comes down, she's half here, half gone. Her lazy smile spreads over her glowing face, and she bites her lip.

"Your turn," she says.

"As if you're done," I laugh, flipping her onto her back. But this time, I don't hold back. The vision of her riding me will be with me forever, but seeing her splayed out below me— her hair wild, her eyes half lidded as I drive into her.

This is everything.

I thrust into her, driving deep as she throws her head back. She takes all of me, clutching at me as if she can take more. Fuck, I want to give it all to her. She feels so goddamn good. My hand finds her throat, and she lifts her head while I squeeze with the lightest pressure. It's enough to make her tighten around me, pulsing as she cries out. I lower my head, grazing my teeth against her nipple, sending her into oblivion as she writhes below me.

I can't hold back any longer. I could fuck her all day and through the night. But there is no way to last through this. I fucking explode, my whole body spasming as she continues her climax. Her skin is salty sweet, and I clamp down on her neck and taste her, bite her, cling to her.

I feel the soft shudder of her body as I slow. It's slight, and I look down at her, seeing the crumple of her face.

Holy shit, I fucked up. I should have stopped.

"I'm so sorry. I didn't…" I hold her as she succumbs to sobs, her arms clinging to me as I remain inside her. I start to move away, but she pulls me closer.

"No, don't leave me," she whispers, her breath shaky. "You did everything right. I just … I can't…"

I realize she's letting down. All her defenses are cast aside, and this is what's left.

I hold her close, rocking her body as she sobs into me. I wrap myself around her, constricting her tightly. Like swaddling a baby, the way I held my daughter when she was in the throes of panic. I feel Jordy relax completely, her body growing limp as she molds to my embrace.

I slip out of her, keeping my hold tight. I feel her soften. Her breath slows, one shaky inhale at a time until she falls asleep in my arms.

And when I close my eyes, I drift off easily, lulled by the rhythm of her breathing.

21

Blue's Clues is the Best Medicine

Jordy

It's evening when I wake up, the sky outside dusky and deep blue. Everything feels still, except for the soft thrum of satisfaction pulsing through my body. I feel like clay—molded, pliable, and completely undone in the best possible way. Every ache is a delicious memory.

I turn my head and find Ashton watching me. His eyes are soft, but the heat is still there, simmering just beneath the surface.

"Hello, sleepyhead," he murmurs.

I smile and scoot closer, pressing my cheek against his warm chest, my leg sliding over his. His arm wraps around me, pulling me tight. God, his body feels good, solid, grounding, familiar in a way that surprises me. A shiver ripples through me at the flash of what we've done, how we finally gave in to what's been brewing for a while. I grin into his skin, breathing in the scent of him—earthy, masculine, with a hint of soap and sex.

"If I'd known it was going to be like that, I would've made a move a long time ago." I look up at him, biting my lip as I take in his dark eyes, the sharp edge of his jaw, the invitation of his mouth. I could lose myself in this man.

He chuckles, his eyes shining as he reaches to brush a strand of hair from my face and kisses me soft, like we have all the time in the world.

"I guess this whole roommate thing has its benefits," he says, then ducks when I nudge him. His face takes a serious turn then. "How are you feeling? Are you okay?"

I nod, and genuinely, I am. I still feel the raw edges of grief, though I suspect that's normal, given that this is the first time in years that I've actually faced my complicated emotions about Violet, Brayden … all of it.

But I also feel cleansed. It's like I spent the day swimming in the waves. My lungs hurt, my body weighs heavy, every muscle is sore. But I'm rested and spent. Deliriously happy.

And a little embarrassed.

"I didn't mean to totally lose it out there," I say. "Bec and Bob probably think I'm some lunatic."

"First off, you had a trauma response." Ashton lifts my chin so that I'm looking at him. "And not only does Bec *not* think you're a lunatic, she recognized what was happening. She called to ask how you were doing while you were in the shower." He kisses my forehead, then pulls me close. "They adore you, Jordy. We all do." He peers into my eyes. "I do."

He kisses me slow, his lips lingering on mine as he strokes my back. I feel so good against his body, enjoying the warmth of him, our legs tangled up in each other under his weighted blankets.

His kiss deepens, and he pulls me closer to him until I'm on top. I can feel how hard he is already, and I'm all for round two. But that's when my stomach gives a loud growl—loud enough that he pulls back, laughing as he helps me off him.

"I'm going to have to feed you if we're going to do that again," he says. I groan when he whips the covers off of us.

"Get dressed up," he orders, already grabbing a pair of boxer briefs. "I'm taking you on a proper date."

A proper date means dinner at Charred. Of course it does.

As soon as we pull up, I give Ashton a look. "Seriously? I've had their burgers and Manhattans. Not impressed."

"I don't know," he says, cutting me a sidelong glance. "You had three Manhattans last time. Seemed like a fan to me."

He winks and jumps out of the truck, circling around to open my door like a gentleman. When I hold out my hand, he takes it slowly, his gaze raking down the length of me.

"Jordy," he says, voice low, "I can't tell you enough, you're breathtaking."

I inwardly roll my eyes, though I'm thrilled he likes the way I look. My silk mauve dress hugs all the right curves and hits mid-thigh, and the strappy gold stilettos give me just the right amount of height. My wrap hangs loosely around my elbows, more for style than warmth.

But the way he looks at me? Like he's never seen anything more beautiful? Yeah, I feel it.

"You clean up nice yourself," I say, stepping out and letting my eyes sweep over him. Black suit pants, black silk shirt slightly unbuttoned to reveal just a peek of tattooed chest. And the stubble on his jaw? Dangerous. Especially as I think about that stubble raking along my inner thigh.

I step in close and breathe him in—a mixture of aftershave and his own personal scent that makes my insides melt. "I swear, I could bottle you."

"Mmm." His lips brush the edge of my ear. "But for now, let's get some food in you. We've got plans later."

I bite my lip, then glance toward the restaurant. Just remembering the last time I was here elicits a dramatic groan. "Fine, let's get this over with."

We approach the restaurant hand-in-hand, and then his palm meets the small of my back as he holds the door open.

"Ashton!" Griffin's voice booms from behind the bar. His grin grows wider when he spots me, and his gaze lingers on the way Ashton's hand stays right where it is. "Well, well. Miss New York returns. Ready for another Manhattan tasting, I see?"

"Yeah, no thanks." I give him a sweet smile, refusing to rise to his teasing. "Think I'll stick to something less tamper-friendly. Like a bottle of wine—opened at the table, where I can see it. And maybe, just maybe, you can try serving us like an actual professional. Think you can manage that, Griff? Or should I send you a customer service manual?"

Griffin's smile doesn't even flicker. He glances at Ashton, offering a wink. "You have a feisty one, huh?"

"Oh, I don't have anything," Ashton says, his voice calm but firm. "Jordy's her own woman, and I suggest you listen to her."

Griff mock-salutes. "Noted." He nods toward the hostess. "Seat them by the window. Roasted oysters on the house."

Dinner at Charred is a whole different experience this time. No side-eyes, no shenanigans—just warm lighting, cozy window seating, and Griffin doing his best impression of a competent server.

The food arrives hot and unburnt, unlike the last time, and the conversation flows as easily as the wine.

"What's a guilty pleasure you'll never give up?" I ask, pushing a mushroom around my plate.

He thinks for a beat. "What qualifies as a guilty pleasure, exactly?"

"Something you love but feel vaguely embarrassed admitting. Like it's indulgent or weird or something you'd never bring up in polite company."

"What's your answer?"

I narrow my eyes at him, but with a playful smile. "Nice try, I asked you first."

His eyes crinkle at the edges, and he tilts his head in thought. "Oh, I know. So I get these fruit snacks for Lottie. There's like maybe five or six to a package, and they're super soft, and easy to chew. I cannot stay out of them. I give her a package, then I take a package, or I'll eat one after she's gone to bed. One day I had like five of them, one right after another. Like, I could seriously get more refined snacks, even fruit snacks meant for older kids or adults that have way more in each package. Instead, I'm eating these little jelly treats like candy. And they're not cheap! I buy them in bulk, and I'm still having to replenish them every week because I can't keep my mitts off them."

I laugh at this, though I know damn well I'd be doing the same thing if my house had a box of fruit snacks in it.

"All right, I told you mine. Now tell me your deep, dirty, guilty pleasure, and make sure you spare no details." He grins, waggling his eyebrows. Then he grows serious. "And not your guilty pleasure of stalking your baby cousin and never visiting her."

"Hardy har har." I think for a moment, then recall one that I can't possibly tell him.

He notices. "That face. Whatever you just thought of, that's the one."

I sigh dramatically. "Fine. On days off, when I'm completely burnt out, I stay in my sweats all day with the blackout curtains drawn. No sunlight. No responsibility."

"So far, that just sounds like a healthy boundary."

"I'm not finished." I smirk. "I dig out a secret box of Lucky Charms I keep hidden from myself, pour a giant bowl, and park it on the couch. Then I binge old cartoons, like Rugrats, Kim Possible, Blue's Clues—but the Steve version, not that Joe dude."

His brows lift. "You go full nostalgia hermit?" He looks at me like I'm unreal. I duck my head.

"See? I told you it was weird."

"Actually, it sounds awesome.

"Wait, really?"

He waves down the server. "Can we get the check when you get a sec?"

She raises an eyebrow. "Not interested in dessert?"

He smiles, then looks at me, a wicked look in his eyes. "We've got dessert at home."

When she walks away, he mouths, *Lucky Charms*, and I swear it's the second sexiest moment of our day.

An hour later, we're in sweats, curled up on the living room floor in a nest of pillows and blankets, and we're each holding a big bowl of Lucky Charms drowning in milk.

And on the screen? Blue's Clues with Steve. Obviously.

"I forgot how calming this show is," Ashton says between bites. "Why is it still so good?"

I shrug, transfixed by Steve chatting with Mr. Salt and Mrs. Pepper. "I used to imagine Steve was my older brother."

Ashton looks at me, curious but not judgmental. "Really?"

"Yeah. I didn't have siblings growing up, but I didn't want to be the oldest. So I made one up." I smile, a little sheepish. "Steve was always there in my imagination, cheering me on when I tried new things, telling me it was okay to mess up."

He doesn't say anything, just watches me as I talk. I take a deep breath and keep going.

"My mom could be…" I sigh. "Well, she was harsh. She'd criticize my clothes or my weight, sometimes in front of her friends. If I spoke up, she'd say I was too sensitive. Steve was my buffer. In my head, he'd defend me, tell her to back off."

I glance at the screen, blinking at the cartoon dog wagging her tail.

"One time, I didn't just imagine it—I said it out loud. She was picking at me again, and I snapped: 'You must feel really powerful, picking on a ten-year-old.'"

Ashton let out a low whistle.

"I'd heard my dad say something like it once. She didn't respond in front of her friends, just gave me a tight smile. But after they left, she stormed into my room, slapped me across the face, and washed my mouth out with soap until I gagged."

I pause. "After that, I stopped pretending Steve was there."

Ashton reaches over and gently places his hand on my back, running his palm slowly up and down.

"I'm sorry," he says softly.

I shake my head, forcing a smile. "Hey, no sadness allowed. We're eating Lucky Charms."

"And watching Blue's Clues," he adds, nodding toward the screen. "There's no crying in Blue's Clues."

"Actually, I think Blue has cried."

"Okay, but it's still a happy show. Steve is a damn hero. I mean, best imaginary brother ever."

"The absolute best." I lean into his shoulder.

There's a quiet moment between us, warm and easy. Then I nudge him.

"Okay, your turn. What's your trauma?"

He raises a brow. "Oh, you mean the obvious one? That I'm raising a kid on property owned by my ex's parents, trying to rebuild after she completely ghosted us?"

"Sure, but that's present-day trauma. I'm talking origin story—parents, siblings, where you came from."

He sighs, then takes a long sip of wine. "Okay fine. I had two brothers and a mom and dad. My parents were good to us, but they weren't good for each other. My dad was an alcoholic and my mom battled depression, though as kids we just saw it as Dad was always angry and Mom was always crying."

I stay quiet, letting him tell it.

"Then my dad lost his job. Things got worse. Mom, despite everything, pulled herself together. She packed us up and left." He shakes his head. "He didn't even come after us. We moved in with my aunt, and my mom cleaned houses, putting away money until we could get our own place. But it wasn't enough."

His eyes cloud a bit, but he keeps going.

"I started stealing food … eggs, veggies, even a chicken once. We lived next to a farm, and the food seemed ripe for the picking. But I got sloppy, because one night, the farmer met me with a shotgun."

My eyes widen. "What happened?"

"I froze, dropped everything, and begged him not to shoot. Well, he didn't shoot. Instead, he fed me. Then he loaded his truck with food and drove me home, told me to show up the next morning to work off the debt. That farmer was Mr. Agers. He taught me how to work the land, and basically changed my life."

"Is that what brought you to Oregon?"

He nods. "Eventually. I had to get out of Louisiana, too many ghosts. I found my cousin's farm up there. Cody. Our dads were brothers, though I found out mine had passed a few years before."

He pauses, then chuckles softly. "Before Sasha, there was another girl."

I raise an eyebrow. "God, do you ever stop charming women?"

He laughs. "It wasn't like that. She had a kid and a bad boyfriend, a real piece of shit—beat her, disappeared for days, cheated constantly. Cody told me to leave it alone, but all I could see was my mom, stuck with my dad. So one day, I took her and her daughter out for lunch, bought her groceries. I barely had anything to my name, but I spent about four hundred bucks just so they could eat."

"That's incredible. She probably thought you were her hero."

He scoffs. "I wasn't though. If I'd acted the hero, I would've broken that guy's damn arms."

His jaw is tight. I reach for his arm, running my fingers over the tense muscle. "Are you talking about her boyfriend? Or your dad?"

He freezes, then blows out a breath. "Whoa." He looks at me, his eyes serious. "I never wanted to be like him. I still don't."

I lean in and kiss him. Slow. Certain. His hands find my waist, then my back. I press my forehead to his, breath mingling with his.

"You're a good man," I breathe.

He snorts. "So good the mother of my child bailed and never looked back."

"She was an idiot," I say gently.

He laughs and shakes his head.

"She wasn't. She was overwhelmed. I know it wasn't about me, but it feels that way sometimes."

"Just like it feels like I'm totally unlovable because my fiancé left barren old me to have a baby with my cousin."

"God, you make it sound so Jerry Springer."

I laugh at this. "What would this episode be called?"

He thinks for a moment, then kisses the tip of my nose. "The Jilted Lovers Club." He gives a mock salute. "I'm proud to be a card-carrying member."

I curl into him, kissing him again. "I'll join your club."

"Darlin', you're the co-president. Our exes have no idea what they're missing."

I look at him, the playful spark between us turning into something quiet and electric. My heart aches—not in a bad way, but in that warm, terrifying, I-could-fall-for-you kind of way.

I don't want to think about the flight back to New York, or the expiration date stamped across this moment.

I just want this.

"I think it's time for bed," I murmur, my gaze locked on his, "and I don't want to sleep alone."

22

Just a Massage

Jordy

Time passes faster than I want it to. Ashton no longer sleeps on the couch, but next to me in his bed every night. We don't talk about the limited time we have left—pretending we have forever feels easier than facing what's coming. We stop eating at Bob and Bec's house for dinner, just so we can have our own time together. If they're hurt by this, they don't mention it, and Bec still kisses me goodbye every morning when I drop Lottie off before heading to the shop.

The work at Timeless is just about done. Construction was completed last week, and all of the fixtures are in place. I've spent the past few days incorporating the finishing touches, but I'm in no rush. I'm afraid that if I move too fast, the job will be done, and I'll have to leave early. So I spend most of my days arranging and re-arranging, taking photos and videos for Alexander's approval and social media, and wishing I could stop time.

That my life here could be just as timeless.

But, this is not my home, and Ashton is not my boyfriend. My life is in New York, and I'll be back there in just a few days. His life is obviously here, and that isn't going to change.

Eventually, I have to call the job done though. I place the final item, then step back to check out my handiwork. The shop looks exquisite. A mix of modern and vintage, with the chandeliers, the minimalist displays, and the pieces and plants I purchased from surrounding shops. There is still one spot left for Bernie's armoire, which I haven't completely lost hope for, but still can't find it in me to ask Alexander ... or Bernie. Other than that, I'm done. Timeless has become a place I'd be proud to shop at, and one I hope the people in town will love too.

Ashton is setting up Lottie in the highchair when I walk in the door, chicken Alfredo simmering in the cast iron pan on the stove. I inhale, smiling.

"Man, that's what I like. Coming home to a home-cooked meal." For just a second, I forget about the time limit. In the moment, it feels almost like forever, like eating together as a family is just something we do every single night.

"Is the shop done?" he asks, moving to me and kissing me on the cheek.

Just like that, our limited time hits me square in the face, obliterating any good feelings I had. But I hide my troubled mind as I nod.

"It is. Just finished before I came home. All I have left to do is be there for the deliveries on Saturday morning when they hold the Grand Opening."

It's to be an exclusive event for the stakeholders and some out-of-town guests. I'd asked Alexander early on if he was opening it to the public, and the way he laughed let me know that the answer was *no*.

"I can't believe we're already here," Ashton says, setting a plate in front of me at the counter, then one for himself. Lottie has a small bowl of chicken and pasta, which she happily paws with her hands.

"Me either. Time passed quickly."

"Not timeless at all," Ashton jokes.

It's the closest we've come to discussing this time limit we have. A week ago, when we first admitted our feelings, it became this unspoken rule that we didn't talk about the end. We both know it's coming, but to talk about it means facing the facts that we have an expiration date.

But the lack of discussion messes with my head.

What if this is just a way to pass the time for him? We've made good use of every night, sometimes wild and intense, sometimes so gentle it makes me want to cry. But I'm starting to like him in a way that clouds reality. It's possible we'll reach the end, and he'll be fine while I'm an absolute wreck.

I want so badly to ask where Ashton's head is at, if he's as devastated by my pending departure as I am. I mean, I only have a few more days and he's just sitting here, eating his chicken Alfredo, talking about the new calf as if the world isn't ending.

"We finally came up with a name," he says.

I force myself to be present, feigning interest on my face. "Oh yeah? What did you decide."

"Sunflower. You know, because her mom is Petunia. All of Petunia's babies are named after flowers. We had Morning Glory, Sweet Pea, and the twins, Dahlia and Daisy."

Despite myself, I burst out laughing. Ashton looks confused.

"I'm sorry, but it's so funny that you do that." I shake my head. "Not because it's weird, but because my family did that too. My grandmother named her daughters Poppy and Lillian, or Lily for short. She had this whole flower thing going on, which she fully expected her daughter to take on, and they rebelled against, since my name is Jordan and my cousin's real name is Antonina. But Nina brought back the tradition with her daughter, Juniper. And I…" I pause, taking a deep breath. "Well, Violet would have been a part of it too."

He reaches over and squeezes my hand. No words are needed, but his smile reaches me in a million warm ways. Then he pulls out his phone, and after a few moments, he grins.

"Apparently, your mom doesn't know her flowers."

He hands me the phone and I look at it. "Jordan" is the name of a particular fig-bearing Ficus. And then he shows me another called Monardella Antonina.

"You've got to be shitting me." I laugh. "Nina is going to be thrilled when she hears about this."

"You'll have to invite Nina and Juniper to the farm so they can meet Sunflower and…"

He trails off, his face appearing frozen for a moment. He inhales sharply, then closes his eyes. When he looks back at me, it's everything and nothing.

Because there won't be time to invite any of my family to meet him, the cows, any of this.

There wouldn't be a point.

That evening, we both put Lottie to bed. She kept asking us to read one more story, and even though I was tired, and I could see in Ashton's face that he felt the same, neither one of us argued. We read until she couldn't keep her eyes open any longer.

I brush my teeth first, watching myself in the mirror as my doubts play ping pong in my head. I can hear Ashton moving around on the other side of the door, shutting off lights and setting up the coffee for tomorrow morning. It's all so routine, the predictability something I once would have considered mundane. Now, I find it comforting. In just these few short weeks, Ashton's home, his routine, everything—it all makes me feel safe, like I'm finally home.

I wish more than anything I lived closer, at least close enough where Ashton and I could have a chance. But staying doesn't make sense, Ashton isn't a career plan. He's a whisper of something that could be—if I'm willing to risk everything else. While I wish that was enough, it won't pay my bills. It won't fulfill the dreams I've worked so damn hard for.

My whole life is in New York. All the opportunities I'd hoped to achieve. All the connections I'm still courting. The chance to actually make something of myself.

Here in Lahoma Springs, I just don't see how that can happen. If I stay...

I pause my brushing, just to linger on that thought for a moment.

If I stay...

"What are you thinking about?" Ashton slips behind me, looking at me in the mirror before kissing the nape of my neck. I feel the shiver go through me. The goosebumps. The electricity of his touch.

"I don't know." I rinse the toothbrush, suddenly too tired to play this game of pretend any longer. But I can't voice what I'm thinking—mostly because I can't make sense of what I want. Any changes I make have a flavor of forever, and I can't tell if I'm thinking with a clear head, or from the impulse of a smitten heart. "Now that the shop is done, there's just a lot to think about with the Grand Opening."

Lies. Most of it is being handled by Alexander's team. If it weren't for that party, I'd be heading home now.

Ashton turns me around, his hands at my shoulders as he searches my eyes. "Is that all?"

"Is that all?" I repeat, stepping away from him, feeling my defenses well up in me. "As if that isn't enough? This isn't kid's play, Ashton. It's my job. I take it very seriously."

A flash of surprise crosses his expression. "That's not what I meant. I just thought..." He shakes his head. "Never mind. You're right. I'm sorry."

I close my eyes, feeling like the biggest idiot.

"No, I'm sorry." I open my eyes again, looking at him, willing myself to not tear up or show any more emotion than I already have with him. "You know when you've been going so hard, and when you finally sit down, you realize how damn tired you are? I think my body is just letting down."

"Yeah," he says, "I know something about that." He reaches out and takes my hand, squeezing it. When I don't move away, he moves to my shoulders, then my neck. I moan, stretching my neck to give him better access.

"Okay, maybe not that tired." I lean into his hands, and he gives a low chuckle.

"Come on, let me rub out some of that tension. No ulterior motives, I promise."

I look over my shoulder and pout. "None?"

"Well, I won't stop your motives," he says. "But if you just want a massage, I can just give you a massage."

"I definitely won't turn it down."

We head to the bedroom, and I strip down in front of him. I love the way he watches me, how his eyes grow hungry even though he's keeping his distance. I lie on the bed, and I hear him rummaging around in a drawer. I nearly jump when I feel a few drops of something land on my back.

"Sorry," he says, smoothing his hand over my skin. I immediately smell lavender. "It's infused oil," he explains.

I soften under his touch, my body relaxing immediately as he begins to knead my muscles. He starts at my shoulders and neck, moves to my back, then down to my ass. Every section of my body he treats with the utmost care, taking his time.

And fuck, it's doing two things: One, I'm like putty in his hands—seriously, he could do anything to me and I wouldn't protest—and two...

I want to fuck him so badly. The more he touches me, the more I need. He moves to my inner thigh, his finger grazing the edge of my sensitive folds, and I nearly go feral.

"Sorry," he murmurs. But *is* he sorry? Because I'm not.

But I also don't want to cave first. Even though he's driving me crazy, I remain still as he works his magic, his hands covering every inch of my body.

"You like that, love?" he murmurs, and I moan in response. I spread my legs a little wider, and hear his breath hitch. "Fuck, baby."

I grin into the blankets, waggling my ass a little. He smacks it, and I yelp.

"Hey, you're supposed to be relaxing me." I look over my shoulder, liking the way his eyes are on my sex, not on me. His cock is straining in his shorts, looking like a snack.

"Are you not relaxed?" he asks, moving his eyes to mine, a sly smirk on his face. "Turn over."

I do as he commands, arching my back slightly just for his benefit. He sucks in a breath and shakes his head. Oiling his hands, he starts at my temples and face, smoothing over muscles I didn't even know held stress. I let out another moan, closing my eyes as he continues, and I hear the low growl in his throat.

He moves to my chest, and his hands smooth over my tits before squeezing them. He keeps at this, sometimes including my nipples between his thumb and forefinger, pinching them slightly before letting go.

"Fucking asshole," I breathe, but there is no way I want him to stop.

Thank fuck he doesn't. He keeps going, moving his hands over my stomach then my thighs. His upper body drapes over mine until my face is near his groin. I lean up, putting my mouth over his pants and blowing hot air on his straining bulge. This time, his growl is more like a moan.

"You'll pay for that," he says, low and deep. In a flash, my hands are secured by his knees holding them to the bed. His own hot breath cascades over my pussy, and I squirm in anxious delight, my face inches from his cock.

"No ulterior motives?" I ask, laughing.

"Quiet, you."

Then his mouth is on me. I gasp as he swipes his tongue across me, before finding my most sensitive part and clamping on.

"Ashton," I breathe, throwing my head back. I wish his pants were off. I want his cock in my mouth so bad. But in this position, I'm completely at his mercy, unable to reciprocate. So I close my eyes and welcome every sensation.

And goddamn, does he know what he's doing. That man sucks and caresses with expert precision, tugging and pulling, nipping and licking. He makes a feast out of me, his mouth sliding over me like I'm his dessert and he refuses to waste one drop.

His finger finds my entrance, then another finger. All while his mouth clamps over my clit and he sucks in and out with featherlike touches. I dig my heels into the bed as he adds one more finger, his mouth increasing its suction as I feel my clit pulse and engorge.

The orgasm starts slow, tingling over my head, cascading over my body, making me lose my goddamn mind as he refuses to let go. The whole room vanishes as I lose all my senses. All I know is his mouth on my cunt and his body holding me in place, all while I unravel completely.

When I can't take any more, he lifts off me, going for his dresser drawer. I'm spent, but not so much that I don't crave his cock. I need his hardness between my legs, need to feel him drive into me. No mercy.

"Are you ready for this?" he murmurs, his lips brushing against my ear as he lines himself up. "Because I don't have it in me to be gentle."

I tug at his back, pulling him toward me in response. The head of his cock presses against my entrance, sliding over my juices as if to tease me.

And just when I'm about to protest, he pushes all the way in, filling me as I gasp. I feel every inch of him, the way he hits my inner walls, how he throbs with each breath he takes.

Ashton clutches my body to his, wrapping himself around me so that I'm immobile. It's a new kind of sensation, one that makes everything about this that much more intense. I wind my legs around him, clamping my knees shut against his ribs until he groans.

"Fuck, baby. I'm not going to keep this up with you squeezing me that way."

"Don't stop," I beg, but unwilling to loosen my grip. It's like we're knotted together, connected beyond our limbs. If I could hold on to him forever, I would.

Forever.

Just for a second, intrusive thoughts threaten to steal my joy, rob me of this moment. I bat them away immediately, squeezing my eyes shut. But not before the tears escape, grabbing hold of my lashes.

Ashton tenses on top of me, his face buried in my neck as I will myself to stay with this. When he comes, my own orgasm joins his. We breathe into each other for a moment, and when he looks down at me, I swipe at my eyes quickly then smile. His expression softens, and he pulls me into him. We say nothing about what we just did. How we're running out of time. I'm not even sure what he's feeling.

All I know is that lying in his arms as his breathing slows, I'll probably miss this moment most of all. Not just his touch. Not even the way he makes me come undone. But the silence after, the way we fit in it.

The way it feels like maybe, for just one second, I belong to him … and he belongs to me.

23

A Corporate Town

Jordy

Two more days.

The thought drifts in as I wake to the warmth of Ashton's body pressed against mine. Today and part of tomorrow. That's all I have left before Alexander flies in. Then I'll be tied up with whatever he needs me to do until I board the plane on Sunday to head back home.

But how can New York be home to me anymore? I've changed too much in the time I've been here. Do I even fit there anymore?

I open my eyes and catch Ashton watching me. Just like he always does when he wakes up first. Despite myself, I can't help the giddiness in the pit of my belly, or the smile on my face.

"How long have you been awake?" I ask.

"Not long," he says. He wraps an arm between my legs and the other under me, and in one swift motion, scoots me closer to him. I squeal at the strength of him, my body already responding. Every part of me fits within his embrace, molding against his firm torso. "Long enough to see you overthink everything that just happened before you opened your eyes."

I laugh. "Am I that transparent?"

"If you ruminated much longer, you'd probably be packed and halfway to the airport by now."

I lean forward and kiss his nose, and then his mouth. "No way. I'd at least wait long enough for one of your famous omelets."

I have this intense urge to wrap myself around him. I look into his eyes, and his gaze is warm—soft—like someone I could fall into and never recover.

And it scares me to death.

What if I feel more than he does? A memory flashes in my mind of the moment my ex told me he was seeing someone else, before I knew that *someone else* was my cousin. I didn't see it coming. I'd been planning our wedding, and Brayden had been off fucking Nina.

I can't fall for Ashton. Even if he feels the same way, this just doesn't make sense. If I don't pull the reins now, we'll be facing a messy goodbye full of heartache and broken promises.

"I can't begin to thank you for these past few weeks," I say, leaning up to playfully bite his lip. "You've definitely been the highlight of this trip. Honestly, you might be the part I'll miss most."

He pulls back, looking me over. "A highlight? What, like a stop on your tour of Lahoma Springs?"

The look on his face is enough to make me regret saying anything. But I can't keep this thing between us—whatever it is—going.

I swallow hard, then force a smile. "We're just having fun, right?"

He doesn't say anything for a moment, but he also doesn't pull away. He seems to ponder my words, and the pause confuses me.

"I mean, we live on separate coasts," I continue. "Your whole life is here, and mine is in New York." I sit up on my elbows, pull the covers over my chest. "It's not that I don't care for you, I do. If we lived closer, this would make a lot more sense, but—"

"Stop," he laughs. He squeezes me closer, bringing my face to his chest as he kisses the top of my head. "You don't need to explain yourself. Yes, we're having fun. I mean, it's not like I'm going to propose marriage or anything."

As crazy as it is, these words offer me little relief. In fact, it makes me feel disappointed.

"Right," I say, looking up. He leans down and kisses my lips softly.

"You're here right now, though," he says, then kisses me again. "And I'm here with you."

My mouth quirks into a small smile. "It would be a shame to waste such an opportunity just because we don't have a future."

His eyes shift as he looks into mine, and he takes a deep breath before smiling. He smooths my hair from my face, then rests his hand under my chin.

"A damn shame." Then he kisses me long and deep, drawing me closer until I'm on top of him. "Why don't we make use of this opportunity now before Lottie wakes up, and before I go to work?"

An hour later, fully sated, we both enjoy our first sips of coffee over the center island. Lottie is already at Bec's house, which I know Ashton did so we could have more time alone together. I love that little girl, but I'll take every moment I can with her father.

He makes the requested omelet, along with toast and sausages rolled up in crepes. It's still so early, the sky is still dark, but I'm getting used to these rancher hours.

"Can I come with you to feed the animals?" I ask.

He takes one look at me in my silk robe.

"In that?"

I throw a piece of toast at him, and he laughs as he dodges it.

"I have all those thrift store clothes Michael and Grace got me."

He tilts his head. "Yeah, but this is a dirty job, I don't want you to ruin your clothes."

"I can wear something of yours."

He laughs at this, then stands so he's towering over me. He has almost half a foot on me, and his body is twice as broad as mine. "You'll drown in any of my clothes, but you can wear something of Sasha's. I might have something left here."

I roll my eyes, then look out the window.

I don't really want to. I've already had to borrow clothes from his ex too many times, and I've never met the woman—

236 — *Crissi Langwell*

nor do I want to. But I also don't want to ruin any of my clothes, even the secondhand ones.

So I agree, and he goes off to his bedroom to rummage through his closet.

My phone pings while he's gone, and I look down to see Alexander calling me.

"Hey stranger," he says when I pick up. "Are you going out of your mind there, or what?"

"No, it's been nice," I say. That's an understatement. It has been so much more than nice. "Lahoma Springs is a really cute town. I can't believe you ever left it."

"Believe it," he grunts. "The moment I left that place, I never looked back. I think I'm just too sophisticated for a behind-the-times cow town like Lahoma. New York is way more my speed. I bet you can't want to get back."

"Yeah, I guess."

Ashton comes in at that moment, holding a pair of overalls and a thermal. "There's some boots that will fit you in the porch bin where I keep the shoes," he says. Then he sees the phone in my hand, and makes a quiet motion. He leans forward and kisses my cheek. "I'll go shower," he whispers, then leaves for the bathroom.

"Are you there with someone?" Alexander asks.

A million thoughts run through my head in all of a few seconds. I have no idea how Alexander will react if he knows I'm sleeping with someone while on a work assignment. I'm still so new to this line of work, still trying to build my business. What if he considers this unprofessional, and this is the last job he gives me? He has so many connections, what if he spreads the word that I'm unreliable?

As far as he knows, I'm at the hotel, all by myself.

"It's the housekeeper," I say, keeping my voice low. "They came early."

"Got it. So, is everything on track for the store?"

"It's all in place." I share about the work that was done in the store, plus the last of the displays he hasn't seen yet. "All we need now is the product, and it will be ready for this Saturday's Grand Opening."

"Good, good," he says. "I got your earlier photos of the interior, and I have to hand it to you, the place looks amazing. I had my doubts about mixing vintage and modern, but it really embraces the whole look of Timeless. I know this company will flourish because of your creative direction. In fact, I was thinking you could stay in Lahoma for a little longer. There are a few other businesses I've been talking with, and one is really close to selling, which is going to be a game changer for our future plans."

"Which business?" I ask. "And what future plans."

"I can't say anything until the papers are signed, but it's a big one," he says. "As for the future, I'm in the works to make Lahoma Springs a corporate town."

"What does that mean, exactly?"

"It means we'll turn the town into a tourist shopping destination. The location is perfect—right there on the river. We could cruise people in from San Francisco, offer them the whole small-town experience. Think boutique hotels, farm-to-table restaurants, curated experiences. It's Lahoma, elevated."

He sounds so sure of himself, like he's pitching the next great idea.

"I'm bringing opportunity to that town. It's stagnant, Jordy. I'm giving it a future."

"That's the opposite of charming," I say. "What will you do with all the family-owned businesses here? How will they fit into this?"

"Are you not listening? They'll be set up really well when I buy their businesses. It's a drop in the bucket for me. When I bought that seed shop, it was for a wing and a prayer—though they acted like I gave them the moon. It showed me I could keep doing this and eventually own the town."

I take a few deep breaths, feeling lightheaded from everything he's saying. I'm not well-versed in business dealings, but this one sounds completely rotten and all bad news.

"I don't understand, you grew up here. You left because you hated it. But now you're buying it out? Do you have any idea what this will do to the people here?"

"Jordy, this is business, nothing more." He pauses, and I hear him give a heavy sigh. "Look, I'm not forcing anyone to sell. But if they do, I'll compensate them generously. I'm investing in my childhood hometown. This is a good thing. Why can't you see that?"

I'm silent for a moment, anger simmering just beneath the surface.

I think of Michael—how he clawed his way back from cancer and heartbreak, pouring himself into that lush, green shop full of plants and second chances. I think of Grace, on the cusp of becoming Lahoma Springs' most celebrated artist, and of Griffin, who creates culinary masterpieces with local beef and garden-grown vegetables, feeding his community with care.

I even think of Bernie, how she protected her town's legacy and the people in it.

I think of every person I've met over the past few weeks—how they showed up for one another, how they picketed the Felix's shop when it changed hands to corporate interests. How they believed *small* didn't mean insignificant.

"You're suggesting something really awful," I say, my voice low but steady. "You have no idea how special Lahoma Springs is."

Alexander laughs. "Did they brainwash you with a tractor ride and a barn dance or something? You haven't even been there a month. I lived there for years. Don't act like you know more about that town than I do."

I let out an unsteady breath, my hands shaking with anger.

"Look, nothing's set in stone," he says, his tone shifting. "This is just an idea I'm floating. I'm putting out feelers, seeing what's possible. It doesn't mean anything yet, and I'd prefer if you didn't say anything to anyone while you're there."

"That's not fa—"

"Fair?" he cuts in. "Yes, it is. You signed an NDA when you started working with me. That includes discussions about anything related to Winslow & Associates. We'll talk more about this when I get there tomorrow."

Stay in the Present

Ashton

It's the housekeeper.

I shouldn't have eavesdropped, but I did. Then she said that, and I didn't want to hear the rest. It's pretty clear who Jordy was talking with—Alexander. I could hear her talking about the shop before I turned on the shower water, and she obviously did not want him to know she's here with me.

We're just having fun, right?

Right.

I wait for the water to warm. I don't have time to waste, but once the room steams up, I take a few extra minutes to just let the water run over me.

The truth is, I have no right to be upset. Did I really expect more out of this?

I groan into the water, because of course I did. The first girl I've been with since Sasha, and I didn't even consider the implications. I've been so careful this far, so what changed?

Everything.

I'm not the same person I was before Jordy came around—and she isn't either. Both of us leaped over some pretty high hurdles, and we couldn't have done it without the other.

But we also made no promises to each other. We both knew this time was coming. My only regret is that we didn't talk about it before, and now here we are, and she's already moving out of my grasp.

"Pull it together, Ashton," I growl. If this really is just us having fun, I don't want to ruin it with melancholy bullshit. It's time I get over my damn sensitive heart and just live in the moment.

Jordy is in overalls and a thermal by the time I'm dressed and back in the kitchen, and fuck, she looks cute as hell.

"Is this all right?" she asks, fiddling with one of the buckles. I brush aside all my hurt feelings to close the distance between us.

"It is going to be extra hard to work today while you're looking like this." I kiss her nose, then pat her behind. Because, damn, those overalls.

She gives me a hopeful look. "Think you could braid my hair again? It's not pulling back right, and I just need it out of my face." She holds up the rubber bands and brush.

"Sit," I command, taking my place in the chair. She positions herself between my legs. I inhale, smelling the scent of her shampoo, feeling a pang of wistfulness. Two more days...

I make quick work of her hair. Partially to keep from buckling, and partially because I know these animals aren't going to wait much longer. When I'm done, her hair is back in a long braid, and there are minimal flyaways to get in her way.

"You still have to teach me how to do that," she reminds me.

"I will," I promise. But when? She's almost out of my life. "Maybe tonight you can practice on Lottie. She's a great hair model."

The sky is just starting to turn a purplish pink as we emerge from the house. Across the field, I can see Bob tossing scraps into the chicken yard. He spots us and gives a light wave. We wave back, and when I look at Jordy, she's grinning.

"I'm going to miss this place," she says, then looks quickly at me. Her mouth clamps shut. I smile, weaving my fingers through hers.

"This place will miss you," I say.

It's the perfect moment to ask her the impossible.

Stay.

But that damn phone call keeps replaying in my head. Her words, brushing off everything that's happened between us.

"Can we visit Sunflower?" she asks. When I glance at her, she holds a shy, hopeful smile on her face.

"Sure we can."

She keeps her hand in mine as we cross the field to the fenced in yard. I open the gate for her, then close it behind both of us. Jordy gasps when she sees the calf nursing off her mother.

"Is that the same baby?" she asks. I nod.

"She grew fast, didn't she?"

"She doesn't even look like the calf I saw last time." She looks at me, her hand slipping from mine. "Can I pet her?" She peers at Petunia. "Will her mother get mad?"

I shake my head, letting loose a small laugh. "Nah, she's about as tame as they come. She trusts all of us. Just move slow and don't be afraid."

Jordy nods, then approaches the two cows. With a cautious hand, she reaches out and smooths it over the calf's reddish coat.

"She's so soft!" She continues petting her, losing her apprehension as she also gives Petunia a scratch on her forehead.

"She'll lose that in the spring, and will have a rougher coat by summer," I say.

She's quiet for a moment, her hand continuously running over the soft calf. But I can tell her mind is a million miles away.

Mine is a bit closer—about two weeks ago, bringing her out of a panic attack and ending up in my bedroom. The way we turned a corner without even trying.

"This isn't just for fun," I blurt out before I can stop myself. She turns, confusion flickering across her face, then something softer like understanding.

"Ashton, I—"

"No, let me speak. I know you leave the day after tomorrow, but I don't know if I'm ready for this to be over."

She sighs, stepping away from the cow to join me at the fence. "I have to go," she says. "My home is there, my work, everything I've built."

"I'm not asking you to stay," I say, then I shake my head. "Actually, I'd ask you if I thought you would. But that's not what I'm asking. I'm asking if we can make this work." I take her hand in mine, bring it to my chest. "We should be together, even long distance. I don't care, I just want you however I can have you."

She slides her hand out of mine and takes a step back. It's like putting miles between us already.

"I've done the long-distance thing before," she says.

I know she's referring to Brayden, and it feels like a gut punch that she'd even compare what we have to that relationship. "This is different. You know that, Jordy. Don't you feel it?"

She looks away and doesn't say anything for a moment. Her eyes lift to the sky, and I see a flash of emotion cross her face. Just a flash, because when she faces me again, her mask is firmly in place.

"I can't," she says.

"Can't what? Can't feel it? Can't try to make this work?"

She breathes out, then shakes her head. "I don't know what you want me to say."

"The truth!" My voice raises enough that Petunia startles just across the pen. "Do you really believe what we have is casual? Because from where I stand, it's been everything."

The pained look on Jordy's face makes me realize I'm just putting myself through hell. It's obvious this is one-sided. "I'm such an idiot."

I stride past her, pushing through the gate, only lingering long enough to latch it behind her. Then I stalk back toward the house.

"Ashton, wait." She grabs my hand, but I pull away and keep moving. "Wait!"

She catches up to me, jogging to match my pace. "Yes, there is something here."

I slow my step but keep walking.

"I feel it," she says "and it's killing me every day we get closer to my leaving. The truth is, I don't want to leave."

"Then don't." I turn, capturing her face in my hands. As pissed as I am, I can't get past how badly I want to pull her into me, to taste her lips, to find another excuse to make love to her.

"I have to," she whispers.

I close my eyes, letting out a slow exhale. Then her mouth is on mine, and damn if I don't feel so hungry for her. I pull her in, clutching at her as I kiss her deeper. It feels like holding on, and it feels like saying goodbye. All I know is that I can't get close enough. I can't stand the thought of letting her go. I don't want to stop kissing her because when I do, she'll be that much closer to leaving me for good.

We sink to the ground, tangled in each other. I drop to my knees, needing to be closer, needing to hold her like I'll never have to let go. She straddles me, her hands running over the back of my head as our mouths search each other. When she breathes, I breathe. Soon we still, soft breaths shared between us, every curve of her body folded into mine. When we finally find the strength to break apart, she rests her forehead against mine.

"I don't want this to end," she says, "but it has to. I can't stay, and I can't stand the thought of a whole country between us while I fall in love with you. I can't be on hold like that. Because what happens next? Either I give up my dream, or you give up yours, and we can't ask that of each other. It's not fair."

"I could figure it out," I say, even knowing it will be near impossible. "Maybe Lottie and I could try out New York, and—"

"And what? Keep Bec and Bob from her?" Jordy slips off my lap, then sits next to me.

"We'll arrange visits. When she gets older, she can stay summers here…" I trail off.

"Is that really what you'd want?" she asks softly. "To give up this farm, the Felixes, all of Lahoma Springs in favor of car horns and crowded streets?"

I want to say yes. God, I want to. But when she puts it like that, I know I can't. As much as I want to be with Jordy, I know I can't leave this place.

I hang my head. "It's funny. Two years ago, I was the stranger here. Now, I don't think I've ever known any place that felt more like home." I peek at her. "I get it. I hate it, but I get it."

She folds her hands into mine. "I've been avoiding this conversation for a while now."

I smirk, squeezing her hand. "Me too." Taking a deep breath in and stand, pulling her to her feet with me.

"Now what?"

"Now? We stop stalling on this ranch work, and then go see what Bec's fixed us for lunch."

I roll my eyes, then tug her to my side. "No, I mean about us."

"There's now," she says. "Let's not think about tomorrow or the next day. Let's just live in the present moment as if it won't ever end."

Lottie is thrilled to see us both when we enter the house. She drops her toys and runs at me, barreling into my legs. Then she does the same to Jordy, which makes her laugh as she sets down the basket of eggs we collected so she can catch my rambunctious daughter.

"She's been a bundle of energy all morning," Bec says from the kitchen.

"Sorry. I should take her out to run a few laps."

We all enter the kitchen, where Bec is already plating BLTs for each of us. Bob sits at the kitchen island, a half eaten sandwich in one hand and the newspaper in front of him. He nods at us, then looks at me.

"A fox got one of the hens last night," he says.

I groan. I repaired a breach in the fence just yesterday, which means they're finding a new way in.

"Just one?"

He nods. "This time, yeah. I think I found the entry point on the south end of the fencing. One of the hens must not have gotten in before the coop doors shut—served up a nice snack for that fox."

"How awful!" Jordy covers her mouth. When we gathered eggs earlier, she'd been so taken by the chickens who followed us everywhere. The rooster watched us with wary eyes, but the hens had eagerly chased us down, hoping for treats we didn't have.

"It happens," Bob says simply.

"God, farm life is brutal." Jordy sips the coffee Bec placed in front of her. "Mmm. Thanks, Bec."

"Well, luckily you've only got a few more days of this brutal country life, right?"

Jordy catches my eye, and I immediately regret my words. I'd meant it as a joke—but it landed like a jab.

"That's not … I mean…"

"It's fine," she says.

It's not. Not for either of us, and now I've probably pissed her off.

"So, there's a grand opening tomorrow night at The Till." Bec catches herself, shaking her head. "Sorry, I meant Timeless. I'll eventually get it right."

"Yeah, Alexander planned this whole fancy party for the investors. He's even having food delivered from out of the area, even though I told him there were local options."

Bec and Bob exchange a look—their ability to be subtle is one of their finer qualities.

"So he's not wasting any time fucking over this town, is he?" Subtlety is not one of mine.

"Ashton, please."

Jordy shoots me a look, and I go back to eating my breakfast.

"You're being an a—" She stops, glancing at Lottie, then at Bec. "Do you have something you want to say, Ashton?"

I have a lot to say. Jordy and I may have made up, but that doesn't mean I'm not still upset about her leaving. Just the mention of that asshole Winslow has me on edge. All I can think of is that phone call this morning—how she hid the fact that she was with me. It doesn't sit well, no matter what the reason is. But I can't bring myself to say anything to her about it.

"Well, we'd love to help in any way we can," Bec cuts in, her eyes flicking to me. *Behave yourself,* her look says. I give a small nod and go back to my food.

"I wish I could accept your help, but Alexander has it pretty well dialed. Besides, he was adamant that this was a party for the investors and a few out-of-town guests, so I'm not sure…" She trails off.

"Ah, an exclusive shindig," Bec says. She laughs, patting Jordy's hand. "I'm sure it's much fancier than anything I could come up with anyway. Everyone in town can just go in and see the shop once it's officially opened. We don't need some wine-and-cheese event to appreciate everything you've done."

"Well, actually … I think we do," Jordy says.

I glance at her, liking the way she said *we*—including herself with the rest of the town.

"Well, I mean *all* of you," she corrects, glancing at me. "But me too. When you all get a chance to see it, I won't be here to see it with you. But I've already been thinking about plans for our own little soiree before Alexander arrives tomorrow morning. Thing is, it's so last minute, and I kept talking myself out of it until now."

Jordy lays out her vision—local food and wine, a guest list that only includes locals. "I think we owe it to this town to include them in a party like this. The place is full of things from the other shops, and it feels like Timeless belongs to all of us. At least right now, before the official open date."

"So it has to be tonight, right?" Bec says, already pulling out her phone and starting to text.

"If we want to do this. Or we could forget it. I mean, it's not like the town wanted this place to begin with." Jordy looks at her hands.

Bec pauses what she's doing, then takes Jordy's hand in hers.

"Sweetheart, this town was dead set on hating you the moment you crossed city limits. But somehow, you charmed all these people into contributing items for the store they were picketing."

"I gave them money, Bec. They didn't donate their stuff."

Bec waves a hand, dismissing her words. "Regardless, no one's picketing now, and people keep trying to peek through those paper-covered windows. They're excited to see something new. Sure, sometimes they don't like change—but it can also be a breath of fresh air in a town that can often feel the same."

She looks at me and gives a wink.

We all carried the weight of selling The Till on our shoulders, but I'd felt it most. Maybe it really is time to move on.

"Can we get everything done by then?" Jordy asks. "We only have a few hours to pull it all together."

"You leave that to me." Bec picks up her phone again. "Just give me your wish list, and I'll make the rest happen." She turns to me. "We should have Griffin cater the event, and he *has* to include those pancetta-wrapped figs I love."

"I'll pay," Jordy says. "I have an investment fund of my own for things like this. I don't want to put anyone out."

"Nonsense, dear," Bec says. "This is what our town does. We support each other."

25

Throw the Town a Party

Jordy

Bec doesn't fool around. Once I give her a list of my ideas for the perfect party, she runs with it. She's on the phone for another hour while I remain close by. Ashton and Bob go back out to finish work while we remain at the house in party planning mode. I overhear Bec talking to at least a dozen people, plus she starts an email chain with her Bridge group to spread the word to everyone in town. By mid-afternoon, we have a solid plan. All I have to do is get dressed.

When Ashton returns, we leave Lottie with Bec, who insisted on caring for her throughout the evening so we could mingle with guests. I finish my makeup in the bathroom while Ashton takes over the bedroom.

"Are you ready for this?" he asks, walking down the hall, focused on the buttons of his white dress shirt. Freshly shaven, fitted slacks, black leather dress shoes—he looks like something I can't keep my hands off of. But I keep them to myself. Even though we made up, there's still an icy edge between us that doesn't feel right.

He finally looks up and stops in his tracks. His eyes sweep over me.

"Hot damn, you're a vision."

Well, icy edge be damned. The look in his eyes could thaw glaciers.

"This old thing?" I do a little spin, showing off what cost me several months' paychecks. It's a golden-toned sequined Eleri gown by Retrofête, with a plunging neckline, fitted waist, and a side slit that goes all the way to my thigh. The straps gather into a draped panel of material from each shoulder. Thick gold bracelets adorn my wrists, delicate gold drop earrings graze my shoulders, and I wear nothing on my neck, letting the gown speak for itself. My hair is swept into a curled cascade, a waterfall of glamour. Every penny spent is worth it, just for the way he's looking at me.

"I changed my mind," he says. "We're not going out. We're staying in and I'm about to lick every inch of gold off your body." He cages me in his arms, and I pretend to struggle to get free, laughing the whole time. His mouth finds my neck, and even though it sends chills straight to my core, I gently push him back.

"Oh no, you don't," I say. "I don't need you leaving red marks all over my body like you're staking a claim."

"You and I both know there's no claim to be staked," he says, then kisses me on the cheek.

The words burn, as does the imprint of his kiss. He smiles as if he doesn't mean anything by the words, even winking at me before he helps me with my wrap. But I feel it just the same—that frozen wall forming block by block between us.

Maybe it's for the best.

We arrive at Timeless a little early, though Bec and Bob are already there managing vendors. Apparently she also has a key, which she sheepishly hands me while exclaiming over my dress.

"My god, you're stunning," she says, lifting the fabric of my sleeve so that it shimmers in the spotlights. She holds Lottie, who also reaches for the dress.

"Oh no, baby. We don't need anything to tarnish this golden angel."

All three of them are visions as well. Bec is wearing a pale blue chiffon dress that gathers at her waist and accentuates her figure. Lottie is in a navy-blue Christmas dress, even though the holiday is almost two months away, and Bob is in a suit very much like Ashton's, but in black instead of dark grey.

"Well, you all look incredible."

I take a moment to absorb the beauty of the room, mesmerized by everything I see. Not much extra has been done to spiff the place up, but there's no need. The dramatic lighting against the architecture and fixtures creates an ethereal look within the building, and the streetlights outside are like our own personal stars. I can't believe I won't see this space again. It's so beautiful on its own, and honestly didn't need much help from me. Yet, seeing the plants from Leaf, the French country motifs from Lock & Key, and every other item I'd found at the shops surrounding this one, I can feel the heart of this place—and of this town.

I feel a surge of pride as each person files in, their eyes wide as they point at items within this shop. We still don't have the watches yet; those will arrive with Alexander tomorrow. But right now, Timeless feels like a gathering place for neighbors, young and old. My heart is near bursting as the party grows, the drinks flow, the music starts, and smiles are directed at everyone in this room, including me.

"Look what you did," Ashton says, slipping an arm around my waist and kissing my cheek.

Even though things are weird between us, I welcome the warmth of his embrace, leaning into it. I look up at him, taking in his amber eyes, the plushness of his delicious mouth, the way he looks at me now in front of everyone. God, I'm going to miss this man.

"We all did this," I murmur. "You, me, this whole town." I press my lips against his, forgetting in the moment who's watching. That is, until I hear a familiar hoot within the crowd. I grin against Ashton's mouth, then turn to see Grace weaving her way through the crowd, followed by Michael.

"Finally!" she says, holding her hand up for a high five. I roll my eyes, but return the gesture with a grin. She's draped in a flowy green chiffon gown, reminding me of a woodland fairy. Michael is wearing a suit with pants that hang just above his ankles and loafers on his feet. On anyone else, it's questionable. On him, it's high fashion.

"You both look stunning," I tell them, "and it's not like you didn't know this was going to happen." I raise an eyebrow.

"Oh honey, we knew before you knew it was going to happen." Michael leans forward and plants a kiss on my cheek, then one for Ashton, who doesn't even flinch. I have to admit, it only makes me want him more. "You two look like the queen and king of this soiree. It's about time you two made it official."

"So, are you two going to do a cross-country thing?" Grace asks. She appears hopeful, glancing between the two of us. "Or maybe one of you is moving?" She looks pointedly at me with this, and I feel my face flush. I look at my feet, unsure of what to say. Thankfully, we're interrupted when Griffin steps up with a tray of food.

"Guess you're going public, huh?" He claps Ashton on the back, then leans forward to kiss me on the cheek. "Ms. Gallo, you sure clean up well when you're not getting wasted at my bar."

I roll my eyes. "That was one time, and you already saw me dressed up since then. And enough with the … well, whatever you think is going on with us." I glance at Ashton quickly, then flick my eyes away when I realize he's looking at me. Fuck, this is awkward. "Do none of you mind your business?"

"No," they all say at once.

"Hello, have you ever lived in a small town?" Griffin asks, holding out a tray of wrapped figs toward me without even waiting for my answer. My eyes widen.

"Oh wow, Bec wasn't lying. Those look incredible." I take one then bite into it carefully. The flavor of salted meat, goat cheese, honey, and fig bursts in my mouth. "That's sinful," I moan.

"Wait till you try everything else," he says.

"Who's minding the restaurant while you're here?"

He shakes his head. "Are you kidding? The whole town is here. We closed down shop and my servers are here instead." He waves his hand toward the already larger crowd in the building, and I see several people in white shirts and black pants weaving through groups of people with large trays of food. A buffet table is off to the side, artfully arranged with charcuterie, fresh bread, desserts, and glasses full of champagne. The band starts up, a bluegrass group that everyone seems to know, judging by the way the crowd cheers upon the first notes.

I'm pretty sure this is going to cost me a fortune. I must have said so because Griffin shakes his head. "It's not going to cost you a thing," he assures me.

"I'm sorry, I didn't mean to say that out loud," I say, completely embarrassed. "Of course I'll pay, and I'll tip."

"We have it covered," he insists. "Come on."

He takes my arm, and I look back at Ashton, who grins and nods me forward before he goes in search of Bec and his daughter. Griffin shows me the huge, empty water jug at the entrance. On it is a sign that reads "Donations for Local Staff," and inside is a growing pile of money, getting larger with every person that enters through the door. "We take care of our own," Griffin tells me. "That's what it means to be in a small town."

He leaves me standing there by the bottle, feeling the floor drop out from under me.

Corporate town.

Alexander's plans for this place tear at my gut. These people have no idea what's in store for them. I don't even know, but I have a pretty good idea.

And I can't say a thing.

Alexander doesn't deserve this shop. He doesn't deserve this town. If he gets away with his plans, he'll make a ruin of all the people here and force them out of town.

I take in the smiles of everyone around me, watching as they greet each other like family. Many of them offer me the same warm looks, some touching my arm to thank me for bringing us all together, to exclaim over the use of this space, or to mention how they recognize some of the items from stores they love.

I smile back, though I'm starting to feel a little weak in my stomach. I grab a glass of champagne from a passing tray and down it before grabbing another.

"This is some party," a voice says next to me. I turn, my breath catching at the sight of Bernie beside me.

We've avoided each other this whole time. Our first interaction soured me, though Ashton's stories of her kindness softened the bitterness. Still, I'm sore about the armoire she wouldn't sell. It shouldn't matter—I'm leaving soon—but I can't stop thinking about it.

"Hello Bernie," I say coolly. I glance at her, then gawk. She looks completely different than the last time I saw her. Gone is the hotel uniform. She's wearing a black evening gown, her silver hair in waves as it cascades around her shoulders, her face done up with light makeup. Frankly, she's lovely.

"You look beautiful," I breathe. She smiles, a stunning move. I don't think I've ever seen her smile that way before, at least not in my direction. It softens her features, makes her look pretty even.

"You don't look so bad yourself," she says. I laugh, soliciting a wider grin from her. "I have to say, I had my doubts about you, but this place looks magnificent. It's missing something, though."

I peer around us, trying to spot anything that's out of place. "What?"

"That armoire you fell in love with," she says.

I feel a prickle of disappointment in my gut. She's fucking with me, I just know it.

"Listen, if you came here to throw it in my—"

"No," she says, holding her hands up, "I'm offering it to you. For sale, of course. I know how much you wanted it. Look, we got off on the wrong foot, and I'm afraid I wasn't my best self." She looks around, then gestures at the whole of the room. "I mean, look at what you've done, how you've brought us all together." A sad look crosses her expression as she looks around again. "This is what this town is all about," she says softly.

Oh man, how I want that piece. But knowing I'm leaving in two days, it seems even less important to have. I mean, Alexander won't see the value in it, even with the high price tag. He likes new and modern, but this is a piece with history.

No, it belongs with someone who understands the stories within the piece.

"Bernie, I can't. I know how much you love that piece, and honestly, you shouldn't ever sell it. It was a part of your family's history, and it belongs with you."

She shakes her head. "Things are meant to be parted with. It's the people you can't replace. And what am I going to do with a silly old armoire? Especially since I have no place to put it."

"What do you mean? You have Lock & Key, it belongs there."

"That's no longer her store," a voice says behind me.

The air shifts, and I turn.

And there, in the doorway, is Alexander.

26

The Outsider

Jordy

Alexander is a hard man to miss in a crowd. Everything about him screams money, from his Tom Ford suit to his slicked back hair, and the flashy watch on his wrist. He turns heads wherever he goes, and not just because he's handsome, but because his presence commands an audience.

Usually, I'm a little breathless around him. No, I don't want him. But I can't help being in awe of the power he exudes.

Right now, though? It feels like he's sucked all the air out of the room.

He stuffs a wad of cash in the bottle, then saunters in toward Bernie and me. I glance at Bernie, who appears flushed in the face, and probably the meekest I've ever seen her since I met her. Alexander takes a champagne glass from one of the passing trays, then raps at it with the huge gold ring on his finger. People turn toward him as the conversation dies down, but the band keeps playing. He makes his way to the makeshift stage where the band is, and as he does, I lean toward Bernie.

"Please tell me you didn't sell your business to him."

"I'll explain later," she says, though her eyes stay glued to the floor as the band quiets and gives Alexander the floor.

She doesn't need to tell me anything; I already know. He gave her an offer she couldn't refuse, probably more money than the place pulls in each year. If she's been struggling in the least to make ends meet, of course she'd take an offer like that. But I'm starting to understand that Alexander is a shark, and his tactic is to make little kills until he owns the whole ocean. Getting Bernie to sign is an early blow to the heart of this town.

"I'd like to thank all of you for attending tonight's celebration," Alexander's voice booms over the microphone, as if he is the one who planned everything.

I scan the crowd and find Bec, whose expression appears as confused as I felt just a few moments ago. I find Ashton, who's looking right at me. He narrows his eyes as he glances at Alexander, then back at me.

"I didn't know he was coming," I mouth to him. He just looks away, and I have no idea what he's thinking, if he's mad at me, or how to mend what's already breaking.

"I grew up in Lahoma Springs. It was years ago, but I have never forgotten what it was like to live here, from floating down the river to spending all my allowance at Frank's

Friendly on the corner. Does anyone remember Frank's Friendly?"

There's murmurings and light laughter as half the room raises their hands.

"I was really sad to see that Frank's didn't survive. I hear it's been a rough couple of years here in Lahoma Springs, and it would break my heart to see any more stores fold under economic pressure. It's why I was so glad to hear from the Felix family when they had to make the difficult decision to sell their beloved store. I understand that the heart of this town is keeping small businesses small, and I agree … to a point. It's good to keep the shops around here locally owned, but it's not good to keep them so small that you starve trying to keep them afloat."

No one speaks. The room is dead silent as Alexander keeps going, everyone waiting to hear the punch line.

"Come with me," I hiss to Bernie, grabbing her arm and making my way across the room toward Ashton.

"Wait there, sweetheart," Alexander calls, and I freeze, knowing he's talking to me as everyone's gaze shifts in my direction.

"You all, let's give a hand to this gorgeous creature who helped create a beautiful space for our new local store, Timeless, and who'll be making even more stores around town this lovely. Jordy Gallo, everyone."

I feel my face flush as only a few people clap. Inside, I'm a wreck. All the work I've done, all the connections I made … Alexander is undoing everything with just a few words.

"When Jordy told me she wanted to throw a party for the people of this town, I couldn't agree more. It's the people who make up the heart of Lahoma Springs, and what better way to show our appreciation than to treat you all to the first of many gatherings in a space like this. Jordy, thank you for making this happen so we could show Lahoma how special they are to us."

I can't even correct him, to tell him that I had so little to do with this party, that Bec and every vendor she called upon are the true heroes. It doesn't matter because the party is ruined. I look around to see confused faces as everyone around us whispers to each other. No one dares to leave, not yet at least. This is too much of a shit show to turn away now. By tomorrow, I'll be back to being the scourge of this town and lose every friend I've made.

Worst of all, I'll lose Ashton.

"And now, I'm pleased to announce the next client who has joined the Felixes in taking a step into the future. But this woman sold, not one, but two of her businesses so that she can retire a very wealthy woman."

"Oh Bernie, please tell me you didn't."

"I had no choice," she hisses. But I can see regret all over her face.

"Bernice Lahoma, come on up here."

Bernie shakes her head, and I hold on to her for moral support.

"Aw, she's just shy, but she had plenty to say this morning. Did you all know that Lahoma Hotel has been in Bernie's family for close to two centuries? But every person deserves a comfortable retirement, wouldn't you agree?"

He waits for a response, but gets none. Then he smiles. "That's right, and Bernie is no less deserving. She couldn't sell to just anyone, it had to be someone who knows the heart of this town. Which is why she chose to work with me to make her retirement dreams come true while still honoring our beloved small town."

"Listen to me," I hiss. "He is not a good man. He doesn't care about Lahoma. All he cares about is—"

"Jordy, could you join me on the stage for a moment?"

I whip my head towards him as he mouths the words "NDA." Every eye is on me, which means I'm the only one who saw what he said to me. Head down, I abandon Bernie and make my way towards him. Once I get there, he takes my hand and pulls me close, wrapping an arm around my waist.

"I don't want to take up too much more of your time folks, but I couldn't end this without expressing my complete admiration and gratitude for this gorgeous woman beside me. If you couldn't tell just by looking at her, she has an eye for design. I mean, this dress she had me buy for her…" He does a chef's kiss. "Exquisite, and worth every penny, though there were about tens of thousands of those pennies."

I burn with rage, knowing just how long it took for me to save. Why he's taking credit, I don't know. I open my mouth to say something, but he places a finger on my lips.

"You, babe, have expensive taste," he continues, a smile in his eyes. "Which is why I can't wait for you to start designing the hotel across the way. I know you're going to bring this town into the future."

He leans down and kisses me, right on the mouth, right in front of everyone. I freeze up, completely unable to move until he releases me.

"A toast," he says, lifting his glass as I stumble a few steps back. The people in the crowd look at each other, then back at us, reluctantly lifting their own glasses. "To Lahoma Springs, our heart and soul."

There's a quiet rumble of voices followed by a few clinks. Alexander turns back to the band, telling them they can play. I see my chance and race down the steps, looking frantically for Ashton. I finally happen upon Bec, whose face looks ashen as she clings to Bob.

"Where's Ashton," I ask.

"He left," she says, and my heart sinks at the words. "Lottie was fussing, and he said he was getting tired too, so he took her home."

I feel winded, like I can't catch my breath. "I'll just call a cab, I guess." Then I look around, realizing I can't just leave, not while people are still here. "Maybe he'll be awake when I get home."

"Honey." Bec lays a hand on my arm. "I don't think…" She looks at Bob, who steps forward.

"Ashton would prefer if you didn't go to his house tonight. We've agreed to let you stay with us, but just for tonight since it's so late. He said he'll pack up your things and leave them for us to gather when we get home."

"You don't believe…" I look at both of them. "I didn't know Alexander would be here," I say. Bec looks away quickly, and I realize how that sounds. "No, not like that. I'm not romantically involved with Alexander, and I didn't know he was buying up…" I stop, worried about what I can and cannot say legally. "I was hired to work on this shop only. I didn't know there would be others. I never even told

Alexander we were having a gathering tonight. I just wanted to…" I feel like I'm grasping at straws, especially with how drawn both of their faces look. "This was supposed to be so different. You put all this work into making it happen, and so many people pulled together to create a wonderful party." I trail off, unsure what else I can say.

"It's what we do," Bob says, his voice low and gruff. "We stand by each other and pull together. It's why we don't let outsiders in."

He looks at me pointedly, and I shrink under his gaze. I'm the outsider, just as much as Alexander is. In fact, I'm even more of an outsider since I have no stake in this town whatsoever.

The Felixes offered to take me in because that's the kind of people they are, but they don't want me there.

"Got it," I say, looking away so I don't give away my distress. "You don't need to worry about me. I'll find my own place to stay tonight."

Neither Bob nor Bec try to stop me when I turn away, not that I expect them to. The party feels like an afterthought at this point, especially as I see people starting to clean up. Everyone is pitching in to gather trays and take the linens from the tables, and I just stand there in everyone's way. All I want to do is leave, though to do what, I don't know. I have no place to go, all my things are likely in a pile on Ashton's porch, and I feel like this dress is suffocating me.

But I can't just leave, so I slip off my shoes and begin picking up pieces of trash off the ground to deposit them in the garbage can by the front.

"We got this." A sweet-faced elderly woman picks the trash from my hand. "You've done enough, dear. Don't worry about this, we'll make sure it's back to how it started."

"Thank you," I say. "But I can't leave, not until everything is in order. It's not fair to leave you all with the mess."

"You've done enough," the woman repeats, but this time I note the stern look on her face.

"Oh." I back up, looking around. No one is looking directly at me, just a few side glances here and there, plus some quiet talking on the perimeter of the building.

I feel the hot tears stinging my eyes, but I refuse to let them fall. I see Alexander standing in the corner, keeping an eye on the clean-up that's happening in between him reading something off his phone. My devastation turns to anger, and I stalk over to him in my bare feet.

"You have a lot of nerve showing up here like you own the place," I hiss.

A look of amusement crosses his expression. "I do own the place," he says, his mouth twisted in a smirk. "And what's going on? You and I are a team, but you're acting like I'm the enemy here. I don't understand. Back in New York you were enthusiastic about this project. I'd think you'd be excited to have some guaranteed income coming your way. What changed?"

Everything. But how do I explain that to him? And why would I want to?

I saw a quote somewhere once: "From the inside looking out you can't explain it, from the outside looking in you can't understand it."

This was that. Even though the town sees me as an outsider, Lahoma Springs has burrowed its way under my skin, changing me forever. There's no way to explain this to Alexander—a man who's lived here and was still able to walk away—who's now plotting to tear this town apart, brick by brick, so that he can rebuild it into every other cookie cutter town in the country.

I know that once I leave Lahoma, I'll feel a part of me missing. Even though everyone here hates me, I love this town The fact that I'm a part of this scheme, even as an unknowing participant, it kills me.

Bernie is going to lose her family's history, and I'm partially to blame.

"What changed?" I stare down Alexander. "Nothing. I was just blind. I am not taking part in any of your fucking schemes when it comes to this town."

"Careful, Jordy." Alexander glances around, and I do too, recognizing that we're being listened to. "Perhaps we should take this to my room. You know, in my new hotel." He pauses, sniffing slightly. "Have you noticed this town smells like shit? It's like you can't escape it."

I narrow my eyes. "It's called Lahoma Aroma, asshole." The honest truth is, I stopped smelling it weeks ago. I thought the smell had gone, turns out I'm just used to it. "And no, I will not be alone with you anywhere, least of all a hotel room." I huff out a breath. "Mark my words, Alexander, I will find a way to get Bernie out of that sale. She is not selling her family's historic businesses to you."

Alexander laughs, then he leans close. "That's precious of you," he whispers in my ear, "but it's a done deal. We signed papers this morning with my lawyer in a quick sale, and tomorrow I am changing the name to Winslow Hotel." He looks around again. People are lingering, but get back to work as soon as he looks up. "All right folks, thanks for all your help getting this place cleaned up. The cleaning crew can get the rest tomorrow." He glances at the bottle of cash. "I'll divvy up the money and cut checks tomorrow."

"No," I say, stepping to the bottle and turning as I guard it. "This belongs to everyone who worked here tonight."

Someone clears their throat behind me, and then I feel a body side up to me. "You heard the lady," Griffin says, his arm brushing against mine, almost like a protection of sorts— or at least a form of solidarity. "We will make sure everyone is compensated."

Alexander shrugs, then turns, dismissing us.

"Come on, help me get this to the restaurant," Griffin says, picking up the bottle as if it weighs nothing. I follow him across the street, still barefoot but not caring. My mother would have a conniption if she saw me walking on the dirty asphalt, risking blackened feet and bacteria.

Once Griffin locks us inside Charred, I breathe a sigh of relief. He places the bottle on the ground near a table, then turns to face me. The look on his face is much like everyone else's in this town, and I hold my hands up.

"I swear, Griffin, I knew nothing about any of this. I'm just as pissed as you are."

"Somehow, I doubt that."

I close my eyes and take a deep breath. He's right. His mother was just swindled out of her two businesses, one of them being the heart of this town. I've only been used as a pawn in this sham. He lost his family's business.

"I'm so sorry. When I took this job, I honestly thought it was simply redecorating a new business. I never expected that this was a town takeover." I clamp a hand over my mouth.

He turns to me, his eyes blazing. "What do you know?"

I know I just violated the NDA. I don't want to care, but I have to think of my family. If I break the contract, Alexander won't come just for me, he'll come after anything with my name on it. That includes my cousin's shop, Polka Dots, which I own a twenty-five percent stake in—along with Nina, her mom, and mine. If it was just me, I wouldn't care. But I can't put them at risk too.

"I can't tell you."

Griffin scoffs, a disbelieving sneer on his face before he kicks at one of the tables. "This is my family he's going after," he roars.

"And my family will be next if I break the NDA I signed when I first took this job," I hiss.

He glares at me, then shakes his head. "This is fucking nuts. So, am I to understand that he's just buying random businesses for the hell of it? What's his end game?"

I feel so frustrated that I can't say a thing. I'm dying to tell Griffin everything I know, along with the hypotheses I've come up with. But how?

"What if I ask you a bunch of questions, completely unrelated to what's going on with the owner from across the street. Just a random conversation, you know?"

Griffin stops pacing and peers at me. He sits down and gestures to the seat across from him. I take it and retrieve my phone from my purse. I start Googling "corporate towns," then find one in Wisconsin, right on the river. This one is full of boutique hotels, trendy shops, and fancy restaurants. There are a few dwellings, but most of them are apartment located in multi-use buildings. I set my phone down, then look up at him.

"Have you ever visited the town of Maisieville, Wisconsin?"

He shakes his head, and I hold up my phone and nod at him. He gets the hint and pulls out his own phone to look it up. He starts reading, at first appearing bored, but then his eyes widen.

"Just a few years ago, they were a town like ours," he says. He looks at his screen again. "But now they're just … luxury shops and such." He glances at me. "Is this what you're telling me?"

"I'm not telling you anything," I say.

He places the phone down, narrowing his eyes. "You know, if this is true, I can do what I want with this information. I can say that you told me everything."

"And then what? I don't actually know that much about Alexander's plans. But the little I do know…" I trail off. "Just keep reading."

He looks down again. "A corporate town." He takes a deep breath. "So, this big shot asshole is going to buy out our town, one business at a time, until he owns everything. We'll lose our farms, our family businesses, our schools, everything that makes this town Lahoma Springs."

"One could guess that," I say.

He nods. "I need to get my mom over here." He juts his chin at me. "And you're probably freezing. I'll let you go back home."

I utter a sharp laugh. "Home, that'd be something of a miracle."

"I mean the Felix place. I'm surprised Ashton isn't still here with you."

"Yeah well, when Alexander got up there and spouted all that crap, dragging me into it like I'd been an accomplice this whole time, everyone believed him—even the Felixes, even Ashton." I nod at him. "Even you."

"Fuck. Okay, let me call my mom, and then we're heading over to the farm. It's time we put a plan in place."

27

Keep Lahoma Small

Ashton

The house feels unnervingly still when I open the front door, Lottie passed out in my arms. She doesn't even wake up as I carefully lower her into her crib—probably the only person in the whole town who's going to get a good night's sleep tonight.

With her door closed, the silence of the house envelopes me with its chilly breath, like a ghost bent on haunting me. I'm so used to Jordy being here that her absence is almost louder than the thoughts barreling through my head—and yet, she's everywhere. Her sweatshirt lying over the back of the chair at the center island. Her Vans cast beside the couch. A scarf lying on a side table, and the book she was reading a few days ago. Each item mocks me, casting a spotlight on moments I thought were real.

Floating down the river. Soothing her trauma. Worshipping her body.

I was so stupid.

Grabbing her suitcases and a paper bag, I start tossing everything of Jordy's inside. It takes about a half hour, though every time I think I'm done, I find something else. I'm meticulous in my search, wanting to guarantee that once I drop her belongings on my front porch, no part of Jordy will enter this house again.

But even that's a stupid lie. The air in this house is now made up of her perfume. My hands still remember the softness of her skin. My mouth has memorized her taste, and I crave her all the same, despite the shock of tonight.

I can't believe I was so stupid. I invited a woman I didn't know into my house, around my daughter, fully trusting she was who she said she was. I should have listened to the rest of the town when they blackballed her. Instead, like a trusting fool, I took pity on her, brought her home to my chosen family, and let her care for my daughter unaccompanied. I'd been there for her when she cried.

Was any of it real, or had it all been a part of drawing me in and lowering my defenses? Am I just one huge joke to her, starting with selling The Till to that asshole, Alexander Winslow?

I can't forget the way he kissed her on stage. It was a gut-wrenching moment, one that twists my insides just thinking about it. I thought I knew everything I could about Jordy, even in such a short amount of time. But when he kissed her, it was like seeing her take off her mask. The moment stole everything I felt for her these past few weeks. It explains the chill between us these last few days. It explains the phone call and the way she pretended I was no one.

As if everything we've been through was nothing. I mean, she didn't even push him away when he kissed her in front of everyone.

I feel like a total idiot, and not just with Jordy, but with everything. Alexander Winslow basically spelled out how he's performing a takeover of this town, and it all started with The Till. Now he has Lock & Key and the Lahoma Hotel.

If he can charm Bernie, the fiercest defender of this town, then no one else is safe. What other businesses is he after?

How much did Jordy know while she warmed my bed? Is this just a fucking game to her?

I drop Jordy's things on the front porch and pause as I breathe in the cool night air. It's cool enough that I know tomorrow will be frosty, though it doesn't snow in these parts. Not like it did in Oregon. I don't miss living in the snow, not with the amount of shoveling I had to do, or the way it killed off the crops if we didn't cover them in time. But I do miss the blanket of white that seemed to wash everything clean, allowing for a blank slate to start again.

I need that now.

Why am I always the last to know when it comes to women? Because it isn't just Jordy who blindsided me.

I wish I could go back in time, back before Sasha left, so I could recognize the signs. Maybe if I'd been a better partner, things would have been different. If I'd noticed that she was unhappy, that she was falling apart. Her moving into her parents' house should have been a wake-up call. The way she could barely look at Lottie? That should have been the alarm.

If I'd only talked with her about it, maybe she would have revealed her struggle. Maybe I could have helped her through it.

Instead, I pushed her away. Once I realized she wanted nothing to do with our daughter, I wanted nothing to do with her. I mean, what kind of person hates children?

One who's experiencing trauma, that's who.

Now I'm watching the same pattern play out all over again—with Jordy.

As much as I want to believe everything about this woman is a lie, I can't let go of that moment when Jordy's walls came down. She was falling, and she let me catch her. Even if everything else is a lie, the pain in her eyes was real. I felt her fear. It explained everything up to that moment—how she eyed my daughter, the wall she put up between her and a toddler—and when she mentioned all her feelings about losing her child, it clicked into place. Then to see her overcome her fears…

Would Sasha have moved past her own fears had she been given the chance to heal? If I'd only paid attention and gotten over my resentments, maybe The Till would still be ours. Maybe Sasha would still be here, and Jordy Gallo would have been no more than a stranger passing through Lahoma Springs.

Two figures cut across the field in the moonlight, headed straight for my porch. I stand, recognizing Bob and Bec by their gait—the way Bob ambles due to an arthritic knee, and how Bec still rushes to keep up with his long legs.

"Griffin called," Bob explains when they reach the porch. He glances down, eyeing Jordy's suitcase and bag of her stuff, then back at me. "He and Bernie wanted to talk with us about that Winslow fellow, I presume."

"Makes sense," I say. "Though I wish they'd talked to us before she signed papers."

"And what would you have said?" Bec asks, leading the way inside. "Bernie had to have been desperate before selling that hotel and her beloved antique shop, just like we were. You can't talk someone out of something that seems like the only lifeline."

"We can't assume that's what happened." I open the fridge and grab a six-pack of beers, handing one to each of them before popping open one for myself.

"Come on, Ashton, that hotel is the heart of Lahoma Springs. Bernie's great-great-grandfather helped build it stone by stone. Her handprints are in the garden path, her grandmother's quilts hang on the lobby walls. She's made cookies every day for guests, and she still works the front desk even though she owns the place. Bernie lives for that hotel. You really think she'd give it up unless she had no choice?"

Bec's right, she has to be. It's an echo of what happened to us, and the only reason Bernie would have folded.

"I still wish she'd come to us."

Bec opens her mouth to argue, but is interrupted by a knock at the door. Bob crosses the room and opens it, revealing Griffin and his mom. But when they cross the threshold, Jordy is behind them, standing in the doorway, her eyes at the floor.

"What the fuck?" I turn to Griffin, and he shrugs.

"I think you should listen to her," he says, and I shake my head.

"I've been the only one listening to her," I say. Then I sweep my hand toward Bob and Bec. "We all have. We took her in when the rest of the town shunned her, and apparently, we're the idiots because we trusted her." I look to Jordy, who at least has the decency to look sorry.

Weeks ago, she was a stranger to our town, tripping over her heels on the cobblestone road. Now, she's a stranger again, wearing the face of someone I thought I could love.

"I wish I'd let you fall," I hiss.

I feel Griffin's hand on my shoulder, and I shake it off. Jordy never looks up, but she doesn't leave either.

"Come in," Bob says. "You're letting all the cold in."

I glare at him, but I don't argue. I may be the one living here, but it's still their house.

Jordy eyes her things on the porch, but leaves them there as she steps forward and Bob closes the door behind her. She gingerly sits at the far end of the kitchen island. Griffin helps himself to one of the three remaining beers, then hands one to his mom, and finally one to Jordy, who politely refuses. I snatch the bottle and crack it open, setting it down hard next to the unfinished beer in front of me. She's not going to drink my beer. Not this night. Not ever.

"We've been doing some research, and we believe Alexander Winslow has some long-term goals for Lahoma Springs." Griffin unlocks his phone, then shows me the screen. On it is a website for a town in Wisconsin called Maisieville. I'm confused at first, but then start reading the description.

Nestled in the heart of southern Wisconsin, Maisieville was founded in 1670 by early settler John Corgan Green and named in honor of his mother, Maisie. Originally a thriving agricultural community, Maisieville built its legacy on dairy farming, with local producers using the nearby Corgan Green River to transport milk and cheese to surrounding regions, earning the town its title as the unofficial cheese capital of the world.

Today, Maisieville blends its rich heritage with modern charm, evolving from a quiet farming town into a vibrant luxury shopping destination. While the roots of its farming legacy remain, Maisieville now welcomes visitors from near and far to experience its boutique shops, curated experiences, and timeless appeal.

I feel my heart seize as I read, then lurch as I scroll through the website. Luxury shop after luxury shop, so unlike anything a farming community would embrace. It's almost like a mini mall, but with very expensive taste. Each photo shows shoppers wearing high end fashion, carrying tons of bags, or eating fancy food at one of the restaurants. All I can think is how none of these people look like they belong to a small agricultural town.

I open a new tab and search for Maisieville real estate, surprised to find nothing but high-priced rentals in sleek, mixed-use buildings. No farms. No properties with any significant land. Just a handful of homes scattered among what's mostly a sea of businesses—cruise companies ferrying in shoppers, boutique hotels, upscale restaurants, and a luxury outlet mall.

I also find a Reddit article about Maisieville. After clicking on it, I read the headline, then look up at everyone.

"Listen to this guy," I say, then read it aloud.

u/formerfarmkid94 • 2 years ago

Title: We were chased out of a corporate town, AMA

I used to live in this town called Maisieville when I was a kid. We had a huge farming community, and the town was so small that we all attended the same school, kindergarten through senior year.

But in my sophomore year, this company, Jacob & Sons, started buying out family businesses. At first, it seemed like a good thing— our community didn't have much money, and a lot of us were just scraping by. Jacob & Sons presented themselves as another small-town family business that had experienced some windfalls.

When they bought my parents' butcher shop, they said it was to help struggling businesses retire with dignity. My parents were never going to retire. There was no savings, and college was out of the question for me. But with this sale, they were finally able to stop working and even put some money aside for my education.

Then prices in town started going up. Pretty soon, Jacob & Sons owned everything, and people like us couldn't afford to shop for food or basic necessities. They wouldn't hire locals either—they used a ferry system to bring in outside workers.

Eventually, we had to sell our farm. Jacob & Sons offered tens of thousands more than the next highest bid. We later found out they were doing this all over town until they owned nearly everything. I've heard there are still a few holdouts, but the company just built around them to make life as miserable as possible.

I put the phone down, having read enough. "Is this what you all planned? To buy out Lahoma Springs and make it your personal shopping destination?"

"She wasn't a part of this," Griffin says, and I turn to him, barking a laugh.

"What, she got to you too? Figures."

"Ashton, it's true." Jordy's eyes plead with mine, but I shake my head.

"Right, just like you weren't a part of it when you coerced me to take you home and share my bed, only to kiss Alexander in front of everyone." I glance at Bob and Bec. "Sorry," I say, "but I'm through being the fool. Obviously I'm meant to be alone, because women keep playing me for an idiot, and I keep accepting the part."

"You're not a fool," Jordy says. "But I didn't kiss Alexander."

I start to argue, but she holds up a hand.

"I didn't kiss him, *he* kissed me. What the hell was I supposed to do? Everything he said on that stage was news to me, and I was just as shocked as all of you. He pulled me into his performance without warning, and I didn't know how to get out of it without making it worse. Everyone was looking at me the same way you're looking at me now, and there was no way I could defend myself."

"And I suppose you think you're the true victim here?"

"No," she says, "I think Bernie is, and I think you, Bob, and Bec are. And I think this town is in real trouble if we don't shut this plan down before it starts."

"We need to stop the sale of the antique shop and hotel," Griffin pipes in. "Why, Mom?" he turns to Bernie. "Why didn't you talk to me first?"

We all look at Bernie. She appears more tired than the hour.

"I didn't want this to be your problem," she says quietly, her eyes on her hands. She looks up at him. "You have the restaurant to run, and that's enough. I knew if you offered to help, I wouldn't be able to say no, and I didn't want to put that on you. So I didn't tell you at all. I tried to fix it on my own, but the debt kept growing, and creditors were threatening to take the hotel. Then Mr. Winslow called, offering to give me more money than I'd seen in my life."

Bernie turns to Bec, taking her hands. "He told me how your family was in the same situation, and how much it's helped you to breathe easier. He said I couldn't talk with you about it because the details of your sale were confidential, but he assured me that it was the best choice I could make for myself, and for my son."

"No," Griffin cuts in, "the best choice would be you coming to me for help."

"But—"

"No, Mom, that's what family does. We stick together, and we figure out a solution together. You have friends in this town who would pitch in to help. We could have held fundraisers, or found other creative ways to raise funds. There's a lot that could have happened if you'd just spoken up. I mean, how long has this been going on?"

She looks back to her hands. "Close to a year," she says, "maybe longer. I've had to let go of staff and work more shifts than I have energy for. I had to take a loan out against it last year, and the antique shop was getting ready to default. Mr. Winslow came in at the perfect moment, because I was just about to lose everything to the bank."

"I'll bet he did," Jordy mutters. She catches my eye, and her gaze shifts away just as quickly.

"What do you know?" I ask. I'm still angry with her, but I realize I won't get anywhere if I don't at least listen.

"Not much," she says. "I know Alexander as much as any independent contractor would know their employer."

"Well enough to kiss, right? Well enough for him to buy you that dress you're wearing, and maybe more."

Her eyes flash. "I bought this damn dress," she spits out. "What he said up there was an outright lie, unless he thinks giving me a paycheck makes him my benefactor. But I earn my money by working hard."

"Yeah, by dating your rich boss to get a job."

As soon as the words leave my mouth, I regret them. What I said is no better than Alexander standing on that stage, telling everyone he bought her clothes. She narrows her eyes, placing her hands on the counter as if getting ready to leave.

"That was uncalled for," I offer. "I'm sorry."

She breathes in through her nose, lowering back on her seat. "Apology accepted," she says through her teeth. "But in case you have any doubt, let me shed light on the truth. I do not date for money, which should be abundantly clear by the fact that I ended things before he hired me. I never went out with him again, even though he's expressed interest numerous times. I have my own money, and I will never be dependent on any man, no matter how rich he is. Second, I thought

Alexander was a nice guy, but we had nothing in common. I wasn't about to become another accessory on his arm. Third, once he hired me, that put an immediate boundary between us. I do not date people I work with. Once I determined he was hiring me for my skill and not because he wanted me in the sack, I was glad to work for him. It's a job that could open many doors for me and help me get my business off the ground." She looks down then, studying her hands. "At least, that was the thought process before I found out all of…" she shakes her head.

"Jordy signed an NDA when she was hired," Griffin explains. "She doesn't know much, but what she does know is bound by this contract. If she violates it and Alexander finds out, he could come after Jordy's business."

"So, you're saving your ass while we all lose ours?" I ask, rolling my eyes.

"No, she's protecting her family and the business they all own, just like any of us would do for our own families."

Okay, fair. "Fine, then what do we do now?"

"You hire a lawyer," Jordy says. "This contract was drawn up rather quickly. There might be some things they overlooked—things we could work with to stop the sale."

"I know someone," Bob pipes in. "My cousin over in Collingstown. He owes me, so maybe he'll even take the case pro bono."

"Well, we can call tomorrow," Bec says, glancing at the clock on the wall. It's nearly one in the morning, and just hours from first feeding.

Everyone stands up, and I can sense the unasked question in the room. Will Jordy stay here? "I'm beat," I say. "Lock up on your way out."

Then I turn and leave everyone in my kitchen, letting Jordy figure out her living situation on her own.

28

Overstayed Welcome

Jordy

"Dear, stay at our place." Bec places a hand on my shoulder before I can pick up my bags. I refrain from brushing her off, even though I'm still angry with her. With all of them. I didn't ask for any of this by coming here. I wish I'd never come at all. It seems my life has been catapulted into one drama after another, from Alexander's bad business dealings to their family issues—and none of it is my doing.

But even still, I love Bec. Despite the way she turned her back on me—just like everyone else in this goddamn town—I love her. I can't forget all the ways she's been kind to me over the past few weeks, starting with giving me—a stranger—her daughter's room, and continuing with all the ways she cared for me. In many ways, she's been more of a mother to me than my own mom.

But then she took Alexander's word without caring about mine.

I don't hate Bec. I'm devastated.

"No, thank you." I feel her hand slip away, and I pick up my bags with one hand, my shoes in the other. By now, this dress I'm wearing feels like one huge joke, and there's no way I'm putting those stilettos back on. Not with this dirt road. Lord knows my feet will be black by the time I reach the airport.

"There's room at the hotel," Bernie says.

"No offense, Bernice, but I know Alexander is staying there, and I won't stay within a hundred yards of that man. As soon as I reach New York, I'm…"

I'm what? Because what do I have to go back to? I've been working for Alexander for most of the time I've lived in the City, hoping to make a name for myself. But so far, my only real connection is him. Without Alexander, I have nothing.

"It's late," Griffin says, taking my luggage from my hands and placing it in the backseat of my car.

"Alexander is on the top floor," Bernie says, "in the penthouse."

Griffin rolled his eyes, laughing. "That old room? You're still calling it the penthouse?" He turns to me. "That used to be my playroom when I was a kid because no one rented it out, then it became storage." He looks at his mom. "Even for that asshole, I can't believe you gave him that room."

She shrugs. "He insisted, and I felt bad about it before. But now, I'm not so sure." She looks at me. "I can place you in a modest room on the second floor. He won't even know you're there, and I'm not telling him. But it's much too late to leave. Besides, we need you."

"You don't need me," I say, though I'm softening. I'm exhausted. Maybe everything will feel easier with a good night's sleep. "Fine, one night. But in the morning, I'm headed to the airport, and I'm never coming back. You all can figure out this mess on your own. I didn't cause any of it, and I'm sure as hell not getting more involved than I already have."

"Fair," Bernie says.

I wake up the next morning with a feeling of heaviness and dread I cannot name. Yesterday's events wash over me as the sleep leaves my body, and I sigh heavily into the quiet of my room. I open my eyes, not yet ready to move and in serious need of some coffee. When I finally rise to sitting, I feel the weight of a thousand pounds on my shoulders.

Even though I'm not a part of Alexander's horrible plan to take over Lahoma, Ashton still hates me. I'm devastated for the town, and I wish with all my heart I could fix it. Now that the ink has dried, I'm not sure how. More than anything, I wish Ashton would look at me again the way he'd looked at me before.

Leave it to Alexander to ruin one more good thing.

I go to the bathroom, then look in the mirror when I'm done, grimacing at what I see—yesterday's makeup with black smudges under my puffy eyes, my hair all over the place, and my lips chapped from not enough water. I'm a wreck.

My phone vibrates on my bedside table, and I cross the room to see Nina's face on my screen. I think about ignoring it. But more than anything, I need a friend.

"Hello?"

"Oh, there you are, stranger. I was getting ready to send the brigade out." Nina's voice is perky for the morning. I imagine she's already had several cups of coffee, and I desperately need to catch up.

"It's been a crazy couple of weeks," I say, standing up to stretch. I look around the room for the coffee pot, but I'm interrupted by a knock at the door. "Hold on a sec, kay?"

I set the phone down and cross the room. Bernie is on the other side of the door, a wheeled tray in front of her. "Coffee and breakfast?" she asks, then rolls it into the room. She lifts the lid to the plate, revealing a simple meal of eggs, bacon, and toast with jam. It looks absolutely perfect.

Where was this woman weeks ago?

"Bernie, you're a lifesaver." I go for the coffee pot, but she waves me off so she can pour a cup for me. Then she sets everything up on a table next to the window.

"You can return the favor after breakfast," she says as she opens the curtains.

"I'm leaving after…"

"Tut tut," she interrupts. "You can leave later today, but we can't do this without you. Eat your breakfast, then meet me at the front desk when you're ready."

"But Alexander. I don't want to see him."

She thinks for a moment. "You're right, meet me at Charred. It's closed, so just knock on the door."

Once she's gone, I dive for my phone on the bed. "I'm sorry about that." I sit down at the table and rest the phone against the coffee pot while I eat.

"No worries. It really has been busy, hasn't it? Want to Facetime?"

"Sure," I say. "But you're going to have to watch me eat."

I switch the phone to video, and there's Nina. Then her eyes widen at the same time I realize how awful I look.

"Oh man, I'm sorry. I just woke up. I was so tired last night, I didn't even wash my face." I glance out the window, peering down at Timeless. There's a delivery truck outside, and I realize the watches have arrived. Alexander appears just then, emerging from the shop. I duck, even though he can't see me.

"What's going on? What's wrong?"

I straighten, feigning a laugh. "Sorry, I just thought I saw someone."

Nina's expression lets me know she's not fooled. "Jordy Gallo, you've barely talked to me for weeks. You look like death warmed over. You told whoever was in your room that you don't want to see Alexander, except that he's your boss and the whole reason you're in New York instead of here where your family is. Now you're acting like a scared little girl. The Jordy I know faces her fears head on. She doesn't hide behind curtains or fail to say what's bothering her. So tell me, what's going on? The truth."

I let out a breath, feeling the full weight of this past week pressing on my chest. I'm without an ally. Even if Bernie is being nice by letting me stay in the hotel, I don't have a friend here. More than anything, I need someone on my side—someone who knows all the good and bad parts of me and still loves me.

I need my family. Fuck this NDA.

"Alexander isn't who I thought he was," I say, sinking on to the bed against the pillows. I told her everything, starting with the decorating job and going on about the picketing, being blackballed by the whole town, then staying with the Felixes. I tell her briefly about Ashton, but it feels too sad to talk about him. I end with the party, which was sabotaged by Alexander's bombshell.

"I'd never even heard of a corporate town before this, but it's exactly what he's doing. He's going to strip this whole town of everything that makes it special, and I can't help feeling responsible."

"You're not, though. Jordy, you had no idea."

"I know." I move the eggs around on my plate. They've already grown cold, but I keep taking occasional bites, knowing they came from someone's farm here in town.

"Where are you, exactly?" she asks.

I swallow a bit more egg, then wrinkle my nose. "Uh, Lahoma Springs?"

"Wait, is that in California?"

I nod. "In Northern California," I say. "North of San Francisco."

"You've been in California all this time, and you didn't tell me?"

But she's not mad when she says it. In fact, she looks elated. "We're coming to see you," she says.

"No, Nina. You can't, you have the baby."

"Exactly, and she needs to meet her favorite cousin. Come on, tell me where you're staying and we'll hit the road this morning and be there by tonight."

I shake my head. "You're crazy, you know that? I should be driving to you."

She tilts her head. "Okay."

"Okay what?"

"Okay, you can drive to us. You can stay in one of the cabins that wasn't rented out this week. We'll have it ready for you by the time you get here. If you come early enough, you might even get some BBQ."

Barbecues at the Salt and Sea Ranch are some of the best food to be had. My mouth waters just thinking about it.

"Okay fine. I was going to go back to New York anyway, but there's not really a reason to rush, right?" I glance out the window again, and this time I see Bernie heading down the street to Charred. My heart lurches when I see Ashton's truck outside. "Listen, I have a meeting I need to attend. But once I'm done, I'll text you to let you know I'm on my way."

I manage to reach Charred without seeing any sign of Alexander. I'm more than nervous knowing that Ashton is inside, and that this is likely the last time I'll ever see him. I don't even know why I'm meeting everyone here. It's not like I can do much. Still, I press on, rapping my knuckles on the glass door while looking over my shoulder. If Alexander sees any glimpse of me now, it doesn't matter if I kept to the NDA, he'll likely assume I'm breaking it. As it is, he probably assumes that anyway, and I'm in danger of losing everything.

But it still won't be more than the Felixes lost, than Bernie lost, and what this town is facing if they don't stop the trend now.

Bob opens the door to let me in, nodding with a grunt as he lets me pass. I enter, hearing him lock the door behind me as I join the group already seated. Bec pats the seat next to her and squeezes my hand when I sit. Bernie nods her head in my direction from the space opposite me. Ashton keeps his head down, attending to Lottie in a highchair. Bob sits on the other side of Bec as Griffin makes his way in with coffees for all of us. He sets one down in front of me with a smile.

"Thanks for being here," he says.

There's another knock on the door, and I freeze, sure that it's Alexander.

"That's my cousin," Bob says, getting up again.

When he returns, an older man follows, sporting a large white mustache that extends like handlebars across his face, similar to Bob's. I can absolutely see the resemblance.

"Good morning, everyone," the gentleman says, placing a briefcase on the table. "When Bob told me what was happening, I headed straight here." He looks at Bob. "You should have called me sooner."

"Sorry, Clyve. Everything happened so fast, and Mr. Winslow said his lawyer could take care of everything."

"And that's what I think is going to work in our favor." He looks at all of us. "My name is Clyve Felix, and I am happily taking this case. Do you have the paperwork you signed with Mr. Winslow?"

Both Bob and Bernie nod, and each produce identical manilla envelopes, handing them to Clyve. Once in his possession, he turns to me. "Now I understand you signed an NDA that's keeping you from sharing anything," he says. I nod. "Would you happen to have a copy of that?"

"His secretary emailed a copy to me when I signed. I'll see if I can find it." I do a search and find it quickly, forwarding it to Clyve. He opens his computer and pulls it up, perusing it quickly.

"Yup, this is pretty standard. Any information you've learned after signing this is protected by law, unless it's to report illegal activity."

"I don't know much, anyway," I admit. "I don't work in Mr. Winslow's office."

"I think we've guessed correctly on what he has planned," Griffin says, looking at me.

I shrug, feeling like a fool for even being here. I can't say anything I do know, and it's not really that much anyway.

Clyve pushes his glasses back on the bridge of his nose, then leans in his chair. "Any conversations you had before this NDA was signed?"

I glance at Ashton, who still won't look at me. Sighing, I think back trying to recall anything notable. All I remember is an extremely dull date where I mostly tuned out, and then later when he offered me a job.

"I can't think of anything," I say. "I'm really sorry I can't be of more help."

"It's okay, dear. We're going to keep researching this to see if there are any cracks we can take advantage of." He nods at his card. "If you think of anything, even the most trivial thing, let me know, okay?"

The meeting disperses soon after, and I slowly get up to leave.

"Well, I guess this is goodbye," I say, looking at my hands.

"Oh sweetheart, this has been quite the rollercoaster ride, hasn't it?" Bec wraps an arm around me, and I lean into her. I'm trying my hardest not to cry, though I can feel the tears stinging my eyes.

"It was definitely not anything I planned for," I say. "I never thought I'd leave my job in the same week I completed my biggest job to date. I suppose I have some thinking to do on what my next steps will be."

"Well, there's always Lahoma Springs," Bernie says. "Griffin here will hire you on as a waitress."

"Mom, I think that's my choice," Griff says, but he winks at me. "I might make an exception for you though."

"Thanks, but no thanks," I laugh, though I don't really feel like laughing. I glance at Ashton. This time he's watching me, and I think I see something in his expression. Something like regret, or maybe just a question.

Or maybe I'm just projecting.

I offer him a small smile. He's still, and then he gives a slow nod.

"Thanks for helping," he says, though his eyes don't quite meet mine.

"I didn't do much."

"Still, you showed up. You didn't have to. If I were you, I'd have booked it out last night and never looked back, but you didn't do that."

I glance at Bernie, who gives a small shake of her head. But secrets only make things worse.

"I was ready to," I admit, turning back to him, "last night, when I was leaving your house. But Griffin and Bernie made me stay the night at the hotel, and Bernie talked me into coming this morning." I take a deep breath. "I'm serious when I say I want to help. Even though I'm leaving, I will if I can." I gather my purse, unsure of what to do next. Because what I really want to do is tell Ashton how meaningful it was to meet him. Instead, I lean down to Lottie's level, the other most important person I met here.

"You are one special little girl," I tell her, stroking my finger along her soft cheek. She grins, even as tears fill my eyes.

"Up?" She holds her arms toward me, and I look to Ashton. He hesitates and I start to stand.

"Go ahead," he says, placing a hand on my shoulder.

I unbuckle the belt and pick her up, not even minding that the banana on her hands is getting on my silk blouse. I'll probably smell like banana the whole drive to Sunset Bay, and I don't care.

"I think I'll miss you most of all," I whisper, hugging her close. She lays her little head on my shoulder, and beyond the banana, I smell the powder scent of her shampoo and feel the heat from her soft baby skin. This little girl has helped me work through one of my biggest fears. In a few hours, I'll meet my new baby cousin for the first time in person, and it's so much less scary because I've gotten to know Lottie first. I realize that even though I'm okay with never having children of my own, someday I might be able to love someone else's child the way I love Lottie.

"She's going to miss you too," Ashton says, standing close to me. His hand brushes the side of my hip, sending a sudden electric shock through me. "I think she wishes we had more time."

I look at him, taking in the gold of his eyes, the smoothness of his beautiful face, the crinkle in his forehead, and the slight twitch of his smile.

"Maybe in another lifetime," I say as I nod. Then I lift Lottie so I can kiss her on the cheek before handing her off. "Until then, right?"

I say one last goodbye, then I head out of the restaurant without looking back, making my way to the hotel so I can get my things and leave Lahoma Springs for good.

29

Not So Timeless

Ashton

I watch Jordy leave, feeling the loss of it rip through me like a silent shift in the earth. There's so much I want to say, *I'm sorry* being at the top of the list. I feel like the biggest tool by believing that asshole, Alexander Winslow, before ever talking with her first. Now, she's leaving. I'll never see her again.

I turn to Bec and realize she's been staring at me, and not just her—everyone is watching me.

"What?"

"What do you mean, *what?*" Bec says. "Are you going to go after her?"

I laugh, then shake my head. "Why would I? I royally messed up, and it's not like she seemed all that interested in talking things out. She's so ready to go back home, and trying to make something out of this would be ridiculous." But even as I say it, my heart is already chasing after her. I want to run to her, kiss her, tell her I was an idiot. Tell her I'm not ready to let her go, and I don't think I ever will be.

But who am I to stand in the way of her future? She's already had one guy jerk her around before dumping her for her cousin. I'm a small-town guy and she's a big city girl. Our worlds are too far apart to make sense, and I don't want to stand in her way.

Bec takes Lottie from my arms and gives me a gentle push. "I can see your mind working against you right now. You have that moody furrowed brow thing going on. Stop thinking so hard and go after her."

"But—"

"No buts," she says. "You're crazy about that girl, and you're only torturing yourself by not pursuing her. Go tell her how you feel, grovel if you have to. Do what it takes, but do not let her leave this town without knowing how much you care about her."

I glance at Griffin, seeking some kind of sign from my closest friend in this town. He nods then juts his chin towards the door.

"She's one of the good ones," he says. "And I'll personally kick your ass if you don't go after her."

I shake my head, but with a smile on my face. "I love you guys."

Then I run from Charred, ready to tell Jordy everything, and possibly win her back.

But what I see outside the restaurant makes me stop. There's Alexander, his back to me as he faces Jordy pressed against the wall of Timeless. At first, my heart sinks, believing

I'm catching a romantic moment between them. But then I notice the tightness of her body, how she's making herself small while he towers over her.

She's afraid.

I don't remember how I got there, but next thing I know, my hands are on the back of his jacket as I pull him off her. I have the element of surprise on my side, I also have the muscle to back it up. He might be taller than me, but I've spent more hours hoisting hay and lumber than any of his hours at the gym.

His face is furious as he whips around, but then relaxes into a political smile when he sees it's me.

"Mr. Elliot, what a surprise! You know, I'm glad I caught you. I realized that Mr. Felix missed a whole packet of papers to sign when we finalized the deal last month. I was going to drop by the farm on my way out of town, but maybe you can get him to meet me here."

"Are you okay?" I ask Jordy, ignoring him. She nods, moving to stand behind me.

"Mr. Elliot, I—" he starts, but I stop him with a glare.

"What were you telling Jordy?"

"Nothing." Confusion washes over his face. "Just employee, employer stuff. Nothing for you to worry about. So, about those papers?"

"You can talk with our lawyer about it," I say. His expression darkens, and he narrows his eyes.

"May I remind you that you came to us about this sale?" He smiles as he steps back and brushes off his coat. "And it was to your benefit. I paid more for this shop than it's worth, all to help your family keep the farm." He looks to Jordy. "It was a pleasure working with you. I'll have my secretary send you everything we owe you, minus a few items we didn't agree on."

Then he turns and walks away.

Jordy looks like she's going to cry. Her hands are trembling, and she shivers despite the warm morning. She starts to move away, but I take her into my arms. Her body stiffens, but then she relaxes, her shoulders shaking as she leans into me. I hold her, rubbing her back as she cries. I'll stay here all day if she needs me to.

She pushes back after a few moments, her nose red from crying, her eye makeup completely messed up, her face blotchy and fallen—and she's the most beautiful woman I know.

"What did he say?"

She shakes her head, then looks over her shoulder. I wrap an arm around her and guide her back to the hotel. She leads the way to her room, using her keycard to get inside. On the other side of the door, her luggage is stacked, her bed made. All she has to do is grab her luggage and go, leaving me forever.

Instead, she sits on the bed. I join her, taking her hand.

"He said he couldn't trust me. He thought we had a good partnership, and he was ready to tell everyone he knew to work with me. It's all I've been wanting since I moved to New York. I thought he could open doors for my business. I wanted to make a name for myself. Instead, he told me that if I didn't continue working with him here in Lahoma, he was going to ruin me. He said that after he was done with me, no one in the whole country would hire me."

She looks at me then, her mouth trembling. "So I told him to do his worst, because I wouldn't work for a fuckhead like him if my life depended on it." Then she buries her head in her hands, a sob racking through her.

I place my hand gently on her back, my heart breaking for her even as anger simmers just below the surface. This is her dream—something she's poured herself into, something she's damn good at—and because Alexander can't control her, he's trying to take it all away.

He'll walk away unscathed, no matter what. But she's the one left to deal with the fallout. He's using his power to make her pay for standing her ground, like she's nothing more than a piece in whatever game he's playing.

I can't stand it.

"That fucking asshole," I say through clenched teeth.

"It gets better. He's refusing to pay for any of the local items in Timeless. Rather than return them, he's taking it out of my contracted fee, which will basically leave me nothing. He's also cut off all business expenses, which means I have to return the rental car today and book my own flight home."

"Do you need money?" I ask.

She shakes her head. "No, I have it. It's just an inconvenience. I wasn't even going home yet, I was going to hold on to the rental car a few more days so I could visit my cousin in Southern California before I figure out what's next." She looks up, then nudges me with her body. "Listen to me. I'm crying over fixable problems. I guess I'm just tired. All I really want to do is curl up in a ball and sleep until I can forget all of this." She looks down at her hands. "I don't even know what to do next. I had all these plans…" She wipes at her eyes, then offers a watery smile. "And now everything's changed in a day."

Jordy stands, moving to peer out the window. I join her, looking down toward Timeless. Alexander is there, signing papers with a delivery person. Through the large windows of the shop, I can see dozens of balloons at the ceiling and flashes of light as the tech guy messes with visual effects. The official grand opening is tonight, and judging by the luxury cars lining the streets, Jordy is right—not one person in attendance will be local. Griffin even told me there was a party boat scheduled to dock this evening, with a huge crowd of people who'd made reservations at his restaurant. For now, this is the upside of whatever Alexander has planned. But give him enough time, and he'll probably get his clutches on Charred too.

I wrap an arm around Jordy's waist, and she leans into me. When she looks up, I press a kiss on her forehead. "I'm so sorry," I say, "I'm sorry about your job, that Alexander is such an asshole. I'm sorry that this town treated you like shit when you didn't do anything to deserve that. Most of all, I'm sorry that I doubted you for even a second, because you're the most incredible woman I've ever met. I wish we had more time because I think this could be something, and I'm sorry I'm saying this now, because you're leaving, and you have every right to never speak to me again."

She turns in my arms and traces a line over my face with her finger. Her eyes follow as she caresses my eyebrows, my cheeks, the bridge of my nose, my lips, then she tilts her head and kisses me, long and slow. Her hand wraps around the back of my neck, and I pull her closer at the waist. I want to devour her, to make up for one night of lost time, to make this goodbye count by tasting every inch of her body. But I restrain myself, knowing it's enough that she's in my arms.

This woman. I could lose myself completely to her.

She ends the kiss and touches her forehead to mine, our breath mingling in gasps. "What do we do now?" she whispers.

"I don't know."

She pulls away so she can look me in the eye. "What do you *want* to do?"

I see the hope in her eyes because it's mirrored in my heart, and I know I can't keep this inside. I have to tell her, even if my pride is screaming not to.

"I want to make this work," I say quietly. "I've never met anyone like you." I take a breath. "We've only just met, and somehow it feels like I've known you forever. The thought of saying goodbye…" My voice catches, "It's eating me alive."

I look into her eyes. "I don't want to say goodbye. Not today. Not ever. I want to make this work until the day it doesn't make sense anymore. But Jordy…" I swallow, heart pounding, "in my gut, I don't believe that day will ever come, because you are the person I've been looking for all my life. You're who I want to wake up to every morning and fall asleep with every night. You're the one I want to share my life with. Raise my daughter with. Build something new together."

I laugh softly, shaking my head. "I know I barely know you, but when I look at you, I see my past and my future tangled up together, and somehow it makes more sense than anything I've ever known." I take a shaky breath. "I want the chance to find out if this is real. Starting right now. Starting today."

I pause, my heart pounding so hard it takes my breath with it. Then she becomes my air—her mouth on mine, urgent and certain, matching every beat of what I feel.

"What are we doing?" she murmurs against my mouth, barely pausing before kissing me deeper. Her hands tug at my hair as she climbs on top of me.

"I think we're kissing," I laugh, though I'm at war in my body. There's nothing I want more than to rip her clothes off and show her exactly how much I missed her.

"No," she breathes, pulling herself away. "I mean, why are we so stupidly stubborn when we're obviously crazy about each other?"

"I don't know what you're talking about." An involuntary growl escapes my throat as I stand and turn, falling on top of her and the bed. She grins as my hands find the buttons on her jeans, which I quickly unfasten before tugging them over her hips. "Because I'm about to make you forget all your reasons you don't want me."

She laughs, throwing her head back as I continue pulling at her clothes. "I think you were the one who decided that."

"Bull shit," I say, taking my own pants off as she tears her shirt over her head. "You're obviously delusional."

"Way to gaslight me, Oregon. Oh!"

My mouth finds her slick cunt, and I slide my tongue across her before looking up with a grin.

"Do you want to argue? Or do you want to experience the best orgasm of your life?"

"If this is how you're going to win every argument, I think I'm going to spend this relationship being wrong."

Relationship. I love the way that sounds coming from her mouth.

"You and I both know you're much too stubborn for that," I say, then duck my head again so I can taste every drop of her.

"It takes one to know one. Fuck, Ashton!" She cries out, writhing against my mouth as I lap up every bit of her. My god, she's sweet. The milk and honey of her essence drips down my chin as I greedily devour her. She clutches at me, but then gently pushes, scooting herself away. "I need you inside me."

Agreed. Leaning across the bed, I grab my pants and reach for my wallet. But the condom I thought was in there is gone. Fuck.

"I'll finish you," I promise, dropping my pants before climbing on top of her. I run a finger along her sex, but she swats it away and tugs me against her.

"No," she says, her mouth claiming mine as she grips me. "You. I want you to fuck me."

"I don't have a—"

"I was tested months ago, and haven't been with anyone but you since. I'm safe," she breathes against me, "and I can't get pregnant. Please don't stop."

So I don't. I slip inside her as if her body has been made to fit mine, rocking against her as my hands tangle in her hair, kissing her like my life depends on it—and fuck me, it feels that way. The relief I experience just being inside her, as if I've been waiting my whole life for this. For her. I know right then that if this isn't love, the real thing is going to explode my whole world, because I have never felt so much as I do just being inside Jordy Gallo.

We make love most of the morning, as if the rest of the world doesn't exist. I take my time, running my hands over her skin and feeling the trail of goosebumps left in their wake. I taste every inch of her like she's my personal nectar. I run my hands over her breasts, watching her nipples pebble into taut peaks. Then I taste each delicate bud, my tongue teasing her while she arches her back. When I get close to completion, I pull out and replace my cock with my hand, feeling her juices run over me while I pump her to orgasm. If the walls are thin, we don't care. She cries out my name as I make her come again and again, and then moans as I clamp down on her, drinking her in while she flows into my mouth.

I will never get enough of her.

"Please," she begs, and I enter her one last time, thrusting as she grips my hips, driving me deeper inside her. I can feel her clench around me, and I swell in response. We come together, our bodies slick with heat and sweat as we move as one.

I slow, her body melting against me as I draw her close to me. Having her in my arms feels like I'm holding the whole world. I know I can't let her go. Not again. Not ever.

"I'm so crazy about you," I whisper, kissing her salty forehead. She grins against me, then looks up. Her hair is wild, and she looks every bit like a piece of art. I want to sit and stare at her for hours.

"I'm pretty crazy about you too."

"Do you have to go?" I ask. She scrunches up beside me.

"I don't have to," she says, "but Nina is expecting me, and it's been long enough."

I realize the importance of this. "How are you feeling?"

She runs a lazy hand over my chest. "Nervous," she says, "and excited. I know it will be a little awkward being that this is Brayden's baby, and well…" She trails off, but I know what she means. This will be like seeing her own child she could have had with Brayden. I squeeze her against me, and she kisses my chest then looks at me. "I think I'm ready, though. I know I'm going to love this little girl so much."

"I know you will too." I sit up, only because I know I could stay in this bed forever with her. But if she still needs to work out transportation and get to Southern California at a decent time, she needs to start moving now. I don't even know where this leaves us, but we have time to figure that out. "Wait, what if you borrowed my truck?"

She shakes her head, giving me a curious smile. "I can't do that, silly. You need it for work."

"I can use Bob's," I point out, "or anyone else's in town. Besides, this gives you a reason to come back to me."

"Ugh, I can't believe I have to leave you right after we made up. It's so unfair."

I grin, then nod. "It's all a part of the plan," I say, and she laughs, throwing herself in my arms.

"What, to make you irresistible?"

"Exactly."

She pulls away then, looking at me with a serious expression. "Come with me."

I gape at her. "What? No, you don't want that. This is your trip to see your family. I'll just be in the way."

"You'd never be in the way. Besides, you're the reason I can even do this—you and Lottie. Before I met you, I wasn't even able to look at young kids because it hurt so much. But getting to know Lottie helped me heal."

"I can't leave her, though. I mean, Bec would totally watch her, but I don't want to leave her that long."

"I don't want you to leave her, either. Bring her with us. I want both of you to come." She caresses the side of my face, her thumb stroking my jaw. "Please come with me, I don't want to do this without you."

And honestly? I don't want her to either. "Fine," I say, "but we're stocking up on road snacks, and I don't want to hear anything about how unhealthy they are."

30

Salt & Sea Ranch

Jordy

Traveling with Ashton and Lottie feels like the most natural thing in the world. Lottie has commandeered the back seat, her little socked feet swinging while she plays with her stuffies. When she gets fussy, Ashton hums a country song under his breath until she calms down—or we pull over at the nearest rest stop so she can stretch her legs and burn some energy.

Ashton insists on driving the whole time, one hand draped casually over the steering wheel, the other occasionally claiming my thigh or playing with my fingers. Every now and then I feel his eyes on the side of my face, just like I keep sneaking glances at him. I can't believe we're doing this—just traveling hundreds of miles together like we're a family.

I like it. I more than like it.

He packed snacks like we were heading across the country instead of just a few hours down the West Coast. A whole tote back is stuffed with every craving imaginable—Pringles, Chips Ahoy, beef jerky, and a Costco-sized canister of M&Ms. I mix the latter with Chex Mix in a Ziploc bag and call it gourmet.

We have some healthier options too—grapes, string cheese, baby carrots—but let's be honest: this is not the time for restraint. There's something sacred about road trip snacks, and I intend to honor the tradition.

Nina was thrilled when I called to ask if I could bring Ashton and Lottie along. She promised to have a crib set up in the cabin and said she'd save us a plate of BBQ if we got in past dinner—and we would. It was already past noon by the time we packed up Ashton and Lottie and returned the rental car. We probably wouldn't reach the ranch until close to eight.

"My parents live here," I say quietly as we pass a vibrant *Welcome to Santa Barbara* sign. The words slip out before I can stop them, and just like that, my hands are clammy and my stomach twists into nervous origami. I haven't seen my mom in ages. The distance has been, well, peaceful. Her disapproval hits softer over the phone, and I've stopped bending myself into knots to earn her approval. Still, driving through her zip code feels like brushing up against a forgotten bruise.

Ashton glances at me and takes my hand. "You okay?"

I look to him and smile. "Yeah," I say. I like that his expression tells me he doesn't believe me, like he knows me better than I know myself. "My family is just complicated," I say.

"I know the feeling." He gives me a little wink, and I squeeze his hand. I suddenly feel bad for even wanting to complain about my mom when he had it so much worse.

"We had such different upbringings," I say. "I know I was lucky to be raised the way I was."

"You still have scars," he says. He offers me a small smile. "We're products of our past, no matter what. We just get to decide how to move forward." He laughs, then wrinkles his nose. "I'm sure that someday Lottie will be crying to some guy about how awful her upbringing was."

"I doubt it," I laugh. "That girl thinks you hung the moon."

"Only because I told her I did," he teases.

I look at him sideways. "Yeah, that," I laugh. "Not because she's so well loved and safe."

Then I rest my head against the window, watching the ocean and the setting sun pass us by—a fading thread of wistfulness in my heart. "She's lucky to have you."

We pulled into the Salt & Sea Ranch about twenty minutes earlier than expected, even with so many rest breaks. Lottie is completely passed out in the back, and I hate to wake her. When I do, she reaches for me, snuggling her sweaty head into the crook of my neck in a way that makes my heart melt.

"She's here!" Nina bounces down the steps, her blue hair flying behind her as she runs full throttle at me.

"Wait," I laugh, and Nina's eyes fall on the precious cargo in my arms. She keeps herself from throwing her arms around me, clasping them at her chest instead. "Oh, she's so sweet," she coos, slowing to a stop in front of me. She grins then kisses me on the cheek. "Oh Jordy, I can't believe you're here!"

Her eyes have tears in them, and I feel my own well up. Now that she's in front of me, I realize I've missed her terribly. Here's my best friend since birth, practically a sister, and she's absolutely glowing.

"You look so beautiful," I say, then finger a lock of her blue hair. Nina never wears her hair natural, opting for brighter colors depending on her mood. It's something that drives both our mothers crazy, but I've always loved it. With my dark hair, I could never pull off something so wild without completely ruining my hair with bleach. But Nina is the fairer of us, with her pale skin and natural blonde hair. "I think this color might be my favorite, it really draws out your skin tone."

She blushes, giving me an *aw shucks* wave of her hand.

"And these dark shadows under the eyes from sleepless nights really do wonders for the complexion," she jokes. But if she's not getting any sleep, it doesn't show. Her face is brilliant. She's so obviously happy, just like she was the last time I saw her on her wedding day.

"You must be Ashton," she says, then gives me a side glance. Her eyes widen, and that cousin telepathy kicks in. *Well done*, she seems to say, her eyebrows raising with a wicked grin.

Behind her, Brayden stands on the steps, a bundle in his arms. Little June peeks out, her eyes wide from the lights of the bonfire happening in the center of the courtyard and the stringed lights draped over the yard from the house to the trees surrounding the property. Nina and Ashton are making small talk, but I can't tear my eyes away.

It's strange seeing him this way. Strange, but it also makes sense. He always wanted to be a father, and now he's holding this sweet little girl in his arms, like she's the most precious thing in the world. I feel my heart melt, even as it breaks a little. I don't want Brayden anymore. I'm not sure I ever did. But for a moment, I feel the pangs of a life I almost had before it was ripped away from both of us. It doesn't matter that we got pregnant on accident, or even the fact that I never wanted kids. When I was pregnant, and when Brayden moved heaven and earth to make sure I had everything I needed, I eventually allowed myself to look to the future—to envision myself as a mother. I let myself love our own baby girl before we met her. It didn't even occur to me that we'd lose her, and when we did, it wasn't only our daughter who died, but every single dream we had for her and our lives together.

Seeing Brayden hold his daughter now makes me happy, but it also makes me feel very, very sad.

Ashton touches my arm, letting his hand linger as I turn to him. The question in his eyes is unmistakable. *You okay?*

I nod, offering a smile even as my eyes sting with tears I refuse to let fall. His smile back to me speaks volumes. *I got you. I'm here. I understand.* His hand finds mine, and he squeezes it before letting go.

"Here, let me take her," he says, slipping Lottie from my arms. "You want to say hello?"

I nod again, turning back to Brayden. It's like a magnetic pull as soon as my eyes find June again.

"Hi," I breathe when I reach them. I look up at Brayden, then feel my tears spill over as soon as our eyes meet. I do everything I can to not fall apart, even though this feels like both the heaviest weight and the biggest relief.

"I'm sorry," I say, wiping my tears as I force a laugh. "I'm…" I trail off, not sure what to say. She's so precious. So tiny, even at nine months. Like a little doll.

"I know," he says, reaching over to squeeze my shoulder. At this, my face crumples. I can't help thinking of our daughter. Violet. The baby I didn't want, and then mourned in private when we lost her. She was only two pounds. They'd let me hold her, which was both comforting and traumatic at the same time. Every time I see a baby, I think of Violet—her unnatural color, the way she lay limp in my arms, the tiny features of her face, her eyes squeezed shut. It makes me turn away, haunted by the image of my daughter seared in my mind.

I think of Violet now as I stare at Juniper. I imagine she would have looked like June at this age, with her pink coloring and easy smile, with Brayden's wide eyes and narrow nose, and my grandmother's swollen lips—the same ones Nina and I inherited.

"Would you like to hold her?"

I don't reach out right away. "Was it hard?" I ask him, my voice trembling. His own lip quivers, even as he smiles.

"Yes," he whispers, "and no. I fell in love with Junie the moment I saw her, and even though I know she's not Violet, I can't help but feel like our daughter gets to live on through her."

I nod, reaching out to touch June's little hands. She grips my finger, then tries to bring it to her mouth, which makes Brayden and I both laugh as I pull my hand away.

"I'm afraid she's in a phase where she needs to bite everything," he says. Then he lifts her toward me again. Even though my heart is pounding, even though I'm fighting the impulse to turn away, even though I'm scared shitless ... I open and let him place June in my arms.

And oh god...

It's like my body remembers before my mind. My arms have been aching for this, for the weight of a baby, for the second chance I thought I'd never get.

After we lost Violet, I was desperate to hold a baby again. I didn't want to admit it—didn't know what to do with that craving—but I needed that closeness like I needed air. The ache dulled over time, or maybe I just learned to live around it. But holding June now, I realize that yearning never truly went away.

It had just been waiting for this moment.

I look up at Brayden and smile, tears blurring my vision again. "Thank you."

He returns the smile and gently squeezes my shoulder as we turn to walk down to Nina and Ashton.

Lottie is so tuckered out, we put her to bed in our cabin not long after we arrive. Nina thought of everything—including a baby monitor—so Ashton and I could enjoy some BBQ and a beer by the bonfire while Lottie slept peacefully in the cabin, and June dozed in Brayden's arms.

The bonfire crackles as we sit in its glow, accompanied by the sound of cicadas off in the distance. Nina and I talk into the night, quickly forgetting about our men as we fall into conversation like no time has passed. The distance between us over the past year has mostly been my fault, but she doesn't hold it against me. It feels easy again—natural—as we laugh about our ridiculous mothers and swap stories about her life on the ranch and mine in New York.

At one point, Nina leans in, her voice dipping slightly. "So, get this … my mom actually sent me a full Jillian Michaels DVD set just weeks after I gave birth."

I wince. "Oof. Seriously?"

She nods, her expression darkening. "It's like she can't get over the fact that I'll always have curves, like the only acceptable version of me is the one who's trying to be thinner."

"Or one who hates bread," I say, lifting my roll in solidarity, then taking a dramatic bite.

Nina bursts out laughing. "And here I thought I was going to be the only descendant of Nanna Dot who still believes in the magic of carbs."

"A few weeks ago, you would have been right," I say with a grin. "But then this guy introduced me to his irresistible pancakes and crepes and every cereal you could ever want."

I glance over at Ashton, who's deep in conversation with Brayden, his hands gesturing animatedly about something—probably farming or cattle, or whatever these ranch men bond over. It strikes me how *normal* all of this feels. The fire crackling, my cousin beside me, my ex across from me, and Ashton … just fitting into it all like he's always been here.

In this moment, I know. I don't want to lose him. Not now. Not ever. No matter what comes next, I'm all in.

Nina must've noticed the look on my face, because she nudges me with her elbow. "So, a cowboy, huh?"

I duck my head, then give her a shy smile.

"What can I say," I laugh, then glance at both our cowboys, then back at her. "Obviously I have a type."

She quirks her head, giving me a curious look. "But do you?"

She stops there, but I know what she means. When I was with Brayden, I hated farm life. He was always out in the field fixing something, sweating up a storm, and coming back in the house dirty as sin.

And those damn horse conventions … he'd drag me along as if it were some exotic vacation, but it was just boring seminars filled with guys who couldn't talk about anything but horses and ranching.

It's not like Ashton is a different kind of rancher. He loves the farm. It's his whole entire life.

Except this time, I want to be a part of it. I've loved our time together at the ranch. I love visiting the animals, the smell of hay, the way everything is homegrown. Even that Lahoma Aroma has grown on me.

The way Ashton smells when he comes in from the field? I can't get enough of it.

"What's different?" Nina prompts.

My eyes land on Ashton. He's deep in conversation, but he must feel my eyes on him because he glances at me. His eyes crinkle in the corners, and he gets that ridiculously charming crease in his cheek before offering me a wink. I feel warm all over, and I bite my lip, trying to hold back my grin and failing.

"Everything," I murmur.

She whistles low, and I turn to her, fully grinning now. "I mean, come on," I say, "he's fricking gorgeous and does all the right things." I raise an eyebrow, and she laughs.

"Well, that's a relief," she teases. Then she looks at our men too. "I'd say we both found our perfect match."

I laugh, shaking my head as I take another sip of my beer. It feels good to be around her again. She knows my history— even the messy, braided parts. Nina has always been the kind of person who doesn't have to ask how I'm doing, she just knows. Sitting here with her now, I remember exactly why we've always been so close, and why I ache for this kind of closeness again.

"And what about this Alexander guy? Any more news on him?" Nina asks.

"Not really," I say, then take another pull of my beer. "Bob brought in his cousin Clyve, a lawyer, to dig up what he can and try to get us out of contract. That was how we left it this morning, and that's all we know."

"God, I remember you telling me about this guy way back when. You know, when you went on that date with him."

"Oh yeah," Ashton pipes in, leaving his conversation with Brayden for ours. "Tell us about it. How did Jordy decide to go out with a tool like that?"

I smack him and he ducks, laughing as he guards his beer to keep it from spilling.

"I have no idea," Nina says. "Thankfully it was a one and done. Remember when he was bragging to you about hacking people's emails, and how weird that was?"

I look at her curiously. "No, I don't remember that."

"How could you forget? That was like your biggest red flag. He bragged about how he knew this guy who hacked into the emails of several large banks, and he'd alert him whenever he discovered someone in obvious financial trouble."

Slowly, the conversation starts to come back to me.

"I can't believe I forgot that! I must have mentally blocked that out."

"Well, he offered you the job of a lifetime," Nina says. "It was kind of the answer to all your dreams. He made a lot of promises, and sometimes you get a little blinded when you're on a mission."

"What? I do not."

Nina quirks her head at me. "Uh, the time you redecorated my entire house without checking with me first. Or the time you were planning your own…" She glances at Ashton, then at Brayden, "Uh, never mind."

"My wedding?" I laugh. I'd pretty much planned everything without even checking with Brayden at all, which kind of proves Nina's point. "Okay fine, that's fair. But this is actually some serious information." I look at Ashton. "This is something I learned before I signed that NDA, which means it's fair game."

"You're still looking into all the sale contracts too. Can I ask Mac to help, as well?"

Mac Dermot is Sunset Bay's best and hottest real estate broker, who's also married to Nina's best friend and former roommate, Maren Huerta—a big shot musician. Seriously. You can't turn on the radio without hearing her.

And you can't pass through Sunset Bay without seeing Mac's sexy face on the billboards.

"It couldn't hurt," I say. "We could use everyone and everything we can to take Lahoma Springs out of Alexander's hands."

That night, Ashton and I settle into bed together, exhausted but thoroughly happy. I haven't felt this complete in ages, and being here makes me realize that California never stopped feeling like home to me. Maybe I just needed a break from it to come to my senses. New York will always be special to me. It's the place where I finished my healing, and where I found myself after something cracked my joy. But now, I feel full, like the circle is complete. It makes me think that this could be a chance for something new in my life. Maybe losing my career is the opportunity I need to find my life.

We fall asleep in each other's arms and when we wake, I'm still against him, his arm wrapped around me and my legs entwined with his. Lottie's awake, and we bring her to bed with us, cuddling with each other as if we're a family. It feels like a family. I can see myself doing this for the rest of my life, being with Ashton and watching Lottie grew older.

This is what it feels like to be a complete unit. Nothing feels more important than this.

31

The People's Place

Jordy

We spend the next few days at the ranch, just enjoying each other's company. Nina threatens to hold a family dinner, like the ones she's been holding over the past year as a way to heal her rift with her mom. I appreciate the gesture, but tell her that if she invites my mom to the ranch, I'm going to redecorate her home in dark gray and black.

My cousin is not one who enjoys a muted palate. From her electric blue hair to her wildly vibrant clothes, Nina is an explosion of color—and my threat is enough to keep our moms out of this private party.

Besides, my mom and I are fine. She's a pain in my ass, and I can't tell her anything I don't want used against me. And sure, I'll probably hyperventilate again when we drive back up through Santa Barbara—but this is how it always is, and always will be. I've grown to accept it, and that is as good as it's going to get.

It's also good to be around Brayden, seeing him as Nina's husband and Juniper's dad. Even though I've been over him for a long time ago, there's still this part of me that stings at the fact he chose my cousin over me. It has this bitter taste of rejection that sours my mood every now and then.

But watching them together now, it's clear they have something we never did. Seeing him with his daughter heals something in me. Yes, there's a dull ache surrounding my heart—I realize it will always be there—but the way he looks at June, the way both he and Nina love that little girl … it's like our story didn't end in vain. It simply opened the door for a better one.

And not just his story. Mine too.

I knew this trip would be healing no matter what, but it's so much better having Ashton with me. There's this quiet way about him. I just have to look at him, and it's like he knows what I'm thinking. I love that he understands all the complicated feelings I've brought with me on this trip—from my trauma around babies to my broken engagement—and he keeps checking in to make sure I'm okay. Sometimes, it's just a touch of a hand and a look asking, *do you need a minute?* If he's not next to me, he's always nearby, catching my eye to gauge how I'm doing. Even when he's busy with Lottie, I know he's very aware of me.

I love the feel of his protection, how in tune he is with my emotions.

"I can't believe you have to go," Nina moans. The boys are busy loading up the truck while the two of us hold our girls. Lottie clings to me, fighting sleep as she rests against my chest. We prolonged naptime for as long as we could, hoping she'd fall asleep as soon as we hit the road. Judging by her quietness, it's a safe bet she will.

"I know. It feels like I just got here."

"Any thoughts on what happens next?" Nina glances at Ashton, then back at me.

It's a loaded question. I have a lot of thoughts—about Ashton. About New York. About Lahoma. About where I am, and where I want to be.

But I can't say any of them out loud. Not yet.

"Not quite," I say. "For now, I'm just taking it a day at a time."

She leans forward to kiss my cheek, then takes my free hand in hers. "Well, keep me posted, okay? And don't be a stranger, please? You haven't even left yet, and I already miss you. I don't want to go weeks without talking to you."

"Careful," I say, squeezing her hand, "I might just call you every day, and spam you photos of this little one."

Nina raises an eyebrow. "That sounds like a decision," she says, her eyes narrowing with a smile.

I just shrug, though I'm biting back my own smile.

"I have a lot of photos on my phone."

We reach Lahoma Springs by dinnertime. Bec and Bob texted now and then while we were away, but it was brief little updates, nothing significant. When we see Bec beaming from the front porch as we pull in, I realize she's been holding back.

"Mac and Clyve found the crack," she says, jumping up and down as we get out of the truck. We talked to Mac on the phone while in Sunset Bay, and connected him with Clyve. The two of them had been working round the clock for the past few days, and apparently found some kind of breakthrough.

Over dinner, she fills us in completely. The property came with a concession that any new buyer had to be from Lahoma Springs.

"But Alexander is from Lahoma," I say. Bec shakes her head.

"He claimed he was, but he's not. He must have known about the restriction and pretended to live here. But he grew up in Wisconsin…" she pauses, then gives us a meaningful look. "…in a town called Maisieville."

I perk up at this. "That corporate town?" I glance at Ashton. "Are you kidding?"

"I wonder if he was involved in that," Ashton says. "If he wasn't involved, he was at least inspired by it."

"Maybe his family was one of the ones who were pushed out," I muse. "But even if that's not enough, the email hacking will do it. Did Clyve figure anything else out?"

Bec nods. "A private investigator uncovered a whole hacking ring that's been going on, and Alexander's money is all over it. He's in a lot of trouble right now. He was forced to release Bernie's businesses, but that's not even the best part." She turns to Ashton. "We got The Till back!"

"What? How?" Ashton shakes his head. "We took the money, that sale was final."

"It wasn't though," she says, beaming. "There was a clause that said no criminal activity could be tied to any party within ninety days of the sale. With the hacking ring exposed, that clause kicked in, and since Bob never signed the final execution documents, we were able to back out." She's grinning, her eyes shining like I've never seen before. "Of course, we had to give all the money back, plus pay for all the improvements. So we still owe a fortune, but we can figure it out."

In this moment, I dread all the grand plans I'd made for that shop. A fortune is an understatement.

But I also know where she can get the money.

"What you need are investors." I give Ashton a side glance. "At least, one person who'd be willing to provide an advance."

Ashton's eyes widen, and he shakes his head. "Oh, hell no. You're not doing this."

"I lost my job this week," I say, "and I need something that's going to make me money. So what if I invested in The Till?"

"Jordy, come on. You and I both know that shop won't be able to pay you back that kind of money."

"You don't know that," I say, even though I'm aware of the risk I'm taking. This is a small town. I'm not going to make a huge name for myself or become wealthy from putting my money into this shop.

But looking around this room, at Bec and Bob with their arms around each other, at Lottie in Ashton's arms—at the conflicted look on Ashton's handsome face…

This is so much more important. This means more than seeing my name on a billboard or becoming some fancy designer. I realize I want this more than anything.

"You don't have to do this," Ashton says, reaching forward to touch my arm.

"I know I don't," I say, sliding my hand into his. "But I want to. My grandmother's money is just sitting in a bank account, waiting for an opportunity like this. I've been banking it for a while, kind of as a security fund in case I couldn't grow my business. But I'd always hoped I could do something important with it. I feel like this is it."

"But—"

"Kids, let's talk about options in the morning," Bob interrupts, but he and Bec are grinning at each other. "Right now, dinner is getting cold, and I'm hungry. There's plenty of time to talk business tomorrow."

Ashton and I settle in bed once Lottie is asleep. We're exhausted from the drive, but also buzzing from all the new information that emerged over dinner. It's hard not to feel excited about all of this.

"I can't have you tie up your money in our family business," he says. "It's not fair. It's not a money maker; it never has been."

"I know," I say. "And yes, you can. I'm partially offering this to help you guys out. But I'm also doing this for me too. I love Lahoma Springs, and I love being here with you. No matter what happens, I want to be a part of this town, and that could be by investing in The Till."

He sits up, looking down at me. "What are you saying? Are you—"

"Staying? Yes. I think I could probably rent a room from Bernie until I find someplace—"

He tackles me before I can finish my thought.

"You will do no such thing, young lady," he growls, climbing on top of me and securing my wrists in his hand above my head.

I squirm underneath him, laughing as he pokes my side with his free hand.

"Are you asking me to move in with you?"

He leans down, brushing his mouth across mine.

"Darling, you already live here. We just need to get your stuff here, and probably build an addition on to this house for all your clothes."

"Hell, I'm ready to just let all of it go and start over." It's true. There's nothing in my apartment I'd miss. Well, maybe my little black Chanel dress, or my Louis Vuitton handbag … and then there's my Alexander McQueen gown. "Okay, maybe I could clear it out and just sell what I don't want. You know, as part of the investment."

He laughs lightly, moving to the side of me. His hand runs over my bare stomach, light strokes that send chills all over my body. "If you did this," he says, "I'd want it to be *our* store."

"Okay," I say slowly.

"And I would want to rename it."

I turn to face him. "What would you want to call it?"

"You pick."

I think about it for a moment. In the early days of being here, I'd researched a bit about Lahoma Springs, and I'd learned that Lahoma is not just the name of Bernie's family who founded this town, but is also the Choctaw word for "The People." It seems such a fitting name, since the townspeople of Lahoma Springs are a bonded community. The people are who make this town what it is. You can't separate the two.

"What if we call it 'The People's Place?'" I ask, then explain what I'd discovered about the name of Lahoma. "We could continue what Sasha started," I continue. "Make it a collective of businesses, plus a kind of hub for people passing through to learn more about our town. We could help promote the other businesses in a way, just by helping tourists and visitors find where they want to go." I smile, even more when I see Ashton's face light up in the dark. "What do you think?"

Ashton kisses the tip of my nose. "I think that's a brilliant idea." Then he kisses my lips, softly, sweetly. "My god, I'm crazy about you." He grins against my mouth, then leans back to look at me. "Do you realize we get to see each other every single day of our lives."

I squeal as he wraps his arms around me, pulling me into him.

"Keep doing that, Oregon, and I'll give you a preview of what every night will look like with me as your roommate."

His laugh is low and rumbling, and his hands wander over my body, finding the space between my legs.

"Roommate, huh?" He swipes a finger across my center, and I gasp out a breath. "I think I'm getting sweet end of this deal." He dips one finger in, then another, biting his lip as he watches my expression.

"Fuck, Ashton." I close my eyes, and he stills his hand.

"Eyes on me, roomie," he murmurs and I laugh, which only makes me clench tighter around him. I lock my gaze on him, my breath coming out in shallow pants as his thumb runs over my clit, his fingers picking up speed until I can't hold back any longer. I try to keep my eyes on him, but the pressure is too great. My body completely on fire, his hand moves inside me until I finally explode.

He knows my body so well, he could play me like a piano. I'm lost in the intensity, but keenly aware how he tailors his movement to match my needs, slowing in a way that prolongs every sensation until it feels like a long strand of electricity.

"Welcome back," he says, when I finally find his gaze again. "Don't get too relaxed, because I'm not done with you yet."

My hand wraps around the length of his cock, and he sucks in a sharp breath.

"Don't I get a turn?" I ask, grinning at him as I maneuver my way on top. He grabs my hips, and I know all it will take is one movement and I'll be on my back again. But he just grips me.

"What exactly do you have in mind?"

I don't tell him. Instead, I kiss his mouth, feeling ravenous by the shape of his full lips against mine. Then I drag my mouth down his neck to the closely cropped hair that sprays across his chest. I let my tongue travel along every curve of his abdomen, the hills and trenches of his smooth muscles, down to the dark trail that leads to his cock.

I lick him base to tip, then lower my mouth over his thick head, reveling in the way he groans at my touch—and my god, does he feel good. I fuck him slowly with my mouth,

332 — Crissi Langwell

sliding up and down and offering the tiniest tease of teeth just to keep him alert. Every time I do, he bucks his hips, showing me how he likes a little bit of pain with his pleasure. That's good. I have plenty more of that to give him. Years worth.

I want to taste him, but he has other ideas. His hands grip me under my arms, pulling me up until he lands on my mouth, my head against the pillow. It's so quick, even the way his hands secure my wrists, his body holding me down, every part of me is secure as he clenches his thighs to hold me in place.

"You're mine," he growls against me, and fuck, I believe him.

"I'm yours," I whimper, feeling his cock nudging at my entrance. He stills, looking down at me. His eyes hold a mixture of defiance and vulnerability. I realize his statement wasn't just a command, but a question. A need for reassurance.

I loosen one hand from his grip, and he doesn't fight me. Then I place it on his cheek.

"I'm yours," I repeat softly. I run my thumb over his lip, feeling the flick of his tongue against my skin. "I'm not going anywhere. This is it, this is all I want. If you'll have me, I'm here to stay."

He sighs out a breath, then he leans down to kiss me. Gently. Tenderly. He pauses just long enough to look me over, his eyes traveling all over me as if to confirm my words are true.

And they are. I've never felt as complete as I have these past few weeks with him. I've never known a place like Lahoma that felt so much like home. If I'm being honest, I'm already in love. With him. With Lottie. With this whole damn town.

I hesitate for a moment, the words pushing against my lips. The feelings inside me are so intense, especially now that I know I'm staying here in Lahoma. Staying with him.

But I'm scared to say them. I've had enough rejection to last a lifetime. Maybe I'll just wait a few weeks more, maybe a few months.

"What are you thinking?" He slows, his hips still rocking against me. But he pushes up to see my face. "I can see your wheels turning. What's going on?"

I shake my head, but the need to tell him is so great. "I love…" I slam my mouth shut, then my eyes, then my whole body.

He stops completely. His hand brushes over my cheek, then to my eyelashes where he catches my tears. I feel the warmth of his breath, and then the soft caress of his lips.

"I love you, Jordan Gallo. I think I loved you the moment you tripped into this town and fell into my heart. I love every part of you. The good. The complicated. The mess. I love all of it, and I love that you love me."

I open my eyes, searching his. "I couldn't even get the words out," I say, feeling like a complete failure. He shakes his head, brushing my hair from my face.

"Then tell me, silly," he says. His smile is so beautiful. His eyes the color of warm honey as he watches me. Everything about him…

"I love you," I whisper.

And his mouth crashes onto mine, claiming me as he wraps his arms even tighter around me. I exhale as he pushes deeper inside me, and I match the rhythm of his hips, my hand memorizing the way his muscles ripple as he moves.

I love you.

He squeezes his arms against mine, caging me in as his movements increase. Something about it makes me feel so secure, completely taken. I feel the beginnings of the orgasms start at the top of my head, travel down my center, then hit my core like a damn eruption. I cry out, clutching him at the sheer intensity of it all. When we're through, we collapse together, completely spent. He remains inside me as he strokes my body.

"I love you, Jordy," he whispers, feathering sweet kisses along my sweaty brow as I come down.

"I love you, Ashton," I murmur, my eyes already growing heavy. I try to stay awake, try to count every one of his breaths as my heart expands within the embrace of the man I love. The man I want to be with forever.

But eventually, my body gives out to exhaustion and sleep finally takes me, safe in his arms.

Epilogue

Jordy

Reader, I married him.

I know. This is so not like me. But when you know, you know.

It was just a small ceremony—Bob, Bec, and Lottie of course, my parents, Nina, Brayden, and Junie, Griffin and Bernie…

And the whole damn town.

I guess when anything happens around here, you can't leave anyone out. Everything in this town is everyone else's business.

And I love it.

Married life is nothing like I imagined. I always thought marriage was something that would hold me back, but that was back when I was preparing to marry the wrong person. Things with Ashton are easy and intense. We go hard, from the way we communicate about everything, to how we work together on the farm and at the shop, to how we fall into bed every night, worshipping each other's bodies until sleep wins. Sure, we have our moments; both of us are strong-willed individuals who are dead set on getting our ways. But god, the make-up sex makes it all worth it. Sometimes I think we fight just so we can fuck the aggression out of each other.

Basically, we make a perfect team.

I spend most of my days with Bec at the People's Place. I invested just like I promised, but not as much as I'd originally planned. The town pulled together to help the Felixes get back on their feet, and the bank allowed them a low interest loan to make up a portion of it. I tried to talk them out of the loan, but they wouldn't have it.

"She was our daughter," Bob explained. "It's our debt to repay."

He and Bec finally went public with the reason they needed to sell, knowing they couldn't protect Sasha's reputation any longer. In any other town, it would have been nobody's business, but in Lahoma, we're family—and family helps each other out.

The town helped Bernie too. Through a few generous investments, Bernie was able to pay off her outstanding debts, and even had enough left over to spruce up the place.

As her designer, I'm proud to say that Bernie not only let me chuck the outdated orange and purple furniture, but redesign the place with a sleek modern look—lots of black and gray with some silver and a few colorful accent pieces. Nina would have hated it. But I love it.

More importantly, Bernie loved it. So did many of the surrounding businesses. I became the official designer of

Lahoma Springs. Anytime there's a need for a redesign, I'm called upon to work my magic. I once thought my dream was to have my name in lights in New York City, to be known by every business in that big city as the one person to make their vision come true. But I learned that being known in this small town is much closer to the core of my heart. Lahoma Springs is my home, and every fiber of my being loves this town. To be the trusted name among the businesses here is a dream come true, and one I can live with all my life.

The People's Place has become the true hub of the city, just like I envisioned it to be. I love that we're a collective for small business owners, just like Sasha had dreamed up back when she ran the store. I have a soft space in my heart for that girl, even though I don't know her, and even though I can't understand why she'd steal from her parents or leave her daughter. She had a vision that included everyone in this town, and I'm happy to continue the dream.

More than that, she helped create brilliant, beautiful, incredible Lottie—the true keeper of my heart. I love Ashton, but I'm crazy in love with his daughter. I want to do everything with her, and I do when I can help it. She comes to work with me in the summers, and I cried when I had to finally let her go to preschool. I took over her bath times, and Ashton and I share the bedtime routine.

I may not be her mommy, but I'm Jor-Ma, as she likes to call me. It came from one time when Ashton said it as a joke, and it kind of stuck.

"Jor-Ma, can we make cookies again?"

It's been almost two years since I made Lahoma Springs my home. Lottie's four, and it's like a light bulb went off in her. I noticed it first as she neared her third birthday—the way her words became clearer and how she started to have a preference for how I did her hair. She likes my tight braids the best, which is ironic since I only learned how to braid two years ago.

Now at four, she's like my little friend. I think she likes having another girl in the house. I find her sometimes touching my clothes or trying on my shoes, sometimes even testing out my lipsticks. I never stop her from any of it. I recall my own mom getting mad at me when I experimented with her makeup. I'd longed to have someone teach me these things, but ended up learning on my own from fashion magazines and friends.

I'll be here to teach Lottie when she's ready. For now, I let curiosity be her guide.

"What kind of cookies do you want to make?" I ask, closing my laptop to give her my full attention. We just returned from the pickup line at school. Her backpack is strewn across the living room, right under four original paintings by my good friend, Grace, plus a super sloppy painting of a jellyfish that neither Ashton nor I can bear to part with. It holds the threads of our beginnings, as silly as the image is.

Lottie tilts her head, pausing from the papers in front of her—pretend homework, we call it, since preschool doesn't give real homework. But she likes to practice her letters all the time. This girl is so dang smart.

"Chocolate chip?" she asks, then grins when I nod.

"Of course, love. Want to get out the butter and eggs while I find the dry ingredients?"

Lottie scrambles off the couch and opens the fridge to start digging. I laugh, then rummage through the pantry to find the rest of the things we need. In one cabinet, I find a big box of forgotten Cheerios, pulling them out with a smile.

"Remember Zowies?" I ask her. She looks confused for a second, then laughs a little when she sees the cereal box.

"That's Cheerios," she corrects me. I smile, but feel a little sad as I put them away. My little girl is growing so fast.

I get the stand mixer out and let her drop in the butter. Ashton walks in as I turn on the mixer. I look up to find him covered in dirt, head to toe.

"The pigs," he groans as an explanation. We just got a new herd a few weeks ago, and these guys are definitely unruly. Ashton comes in for a kiss, and I screech as I jump out of the way.

"Dad, kiss me too!" Lottie cries, but I bar his way.

"No way, Jose. She's making cookies and your dirt is not included."

He swats my butt, then sneaks in a kiss anyway. "I love you, Jor," he murmurs, and shoots me a wicked look. I turn to complete mush. This will never, ever get old.

"I love you, stinky," I say. But he doesn't stink. Okay, maybe there's a bit of Lahoma Aroma on him. But goddamn, he's all man, and I can't help inhaling the sweat off his skin.

"Later," he whispers, then winks as a promise. "Save a cookie for me." Then he scoots off to the shower.

Lottie and I finish mixing the ingredients, then spoon quarter cup cookies onto the baking sheet before sliding the pan into the pre-heated oven.

"Did I tell you what my friend Tobin said to me today?" she asks. I sit in the chair next to her, licking one of the batter paddles as I hand her the other.

"No, what did he say?"

"He said that girls come from Jupiter to get more stupider." She pouts. "But we didn't come from Jupiter, we came from Earth. So who's the stupid person?"

I laugh. I have a feeling Tobin has a puppy love crush on Lottie, because he's always teasing her. It reminds me of Ashton, who loves to tease me just so he can get a rise out of me.

Of course, I'm not about to tell Lottie this, because no little girl should think bad behavior is attractive, as I also tell Ashton whenever he's wicked—well, most of the time, that is.

"Sounds like Tobin needs a few more years of preschool," I say, laughing as she breaks into a grin. There's a knock at the door then, and I look at Lottie. "Were you expecting anyone?" I tease.

"No!" she laughs, and she follows me to the door.

Truth is, it could be anyone. People show up here all the time, so a knock on the door isn't anything new. But this time it is, because I don't know the person on the other side.

"Can I help you?" I ask. She's shorter than me, with deep red, unruly hair and a spray of freckles across her pale skin. Dark tattoos line her arms, large tiger's eye gauges in her ears, and a bull ring adorns her nose. Her jeans have rips in the thighs, revealing even more tattoos. For a moment, I wonder if she's too rough to be around Lottie, though I also note the nervous expression on her face. Even more, I note those familiar wide eyes looking back at me, the same ones on Lottie's face now. I notice the slightly older version of someone I've seen before in a picture at Bec and Bob's house.

"Oh," I say, taking a step back.

"Honey, who's at the door?"

I turn in time to see Ashton round the corner in nothing but a towel, and then the shocked expression that takes over his face.

"Sasha."

Lahoma Springs Character List

Main Characters
- Jordy Gallo
- Ashton Elliot
- Lottie Elliot (Ashton's and Sasha's daughter)
- Bec Felix (Sasha's mom)
- Bob Felix (Sasha's dad)

Side Characters
- Sasha Felix (Ashton's ex, Lottie's mom)
- Bernie Lahoma (Part of founding family, owner of many local businesses)
- Griffin Lahoma (Bernie's son, friend of Ashton, part owner of Charred)
- Grace Dalton (Local artist, friend of Jordy, works at Lock & Key)
- Michael James (Owner of Leaf, friend of Jordy)

Just a Mention
- Mabel (Grace's sister, works at Lock & Key)
- Grayston (Mabel's oldest son)
- Alex (Mabel's middle daughter)
- Logan (Mabel's youngest son)

Not Worth Mentioning
Alexander Winslow

Before You Go...

It means the world to me that you made it to the end of this book. If Jordy and Ashton's story moved you in any way, I'd be so thankful if you'd leave a review.

Every single review—short or long—helps this story reach other readers who might need it. Thank you for being here, and for supporting my words.

You can leave your review wherever you purchased the book.

And if you're not quite ready to leave Lahoma Springs, Sasha's story is coming soon. Stay tuned for *The Lost Lovers Club*. Sign up for my newsletter to keep posted: crissilangwell.com/subscribe

Author's Note & Acknowledgements

When I was twenty-two years old, I became pregnant with my third child. At the time, I already had my hands full—two young kids, one still in diapers—and very little support from my then-husband. So when I found out I was pregnant again, completely unplanned, I spiraled into mourning ... while my husband celebrated.

It wasn't until month five that I began to soften to the idea of having another baby—a son. I let myself imagine a future with him. I bought a new crib, a rocking chair, little toys, tiny clothes. I started building a space for him, both in my home and in my heart.

And then, in my seventh month, he went still.

Losing my son came with a storm of complicated emotions. I was overwhelmed with grief for a child I never got to meet. My arms physically ached to hold a baby. I went to a very dark place. And my already fragile marriage didn't survive it.

But what hurt even more was the guilt. I couldn't talk about it—especially the part where, after the loss, I felt a flicker of relief. I hadn't initially wanted another baby, and I feared that somehow my reluctance had caused this. That I'd wished him away.

Now, looking back at my twenty-two-year-old self, I feel so much compassion. I was exhausted. I was unsupported. I was human. That small sense of relief didn't mean I didn't love my son—it meant I was completely depleted.

Writing *The Jilted Lovers Club* gave me space to process those emotions—grief, guilt, even relief. Through Jordy, I explored the way loss lingers, how it can reshape us, how we try to hide it so we don't scare anyone off. Writing her story was cathartic. And somewhere along the way, I fell in love with this flawed, complicated, beautiful character.

It's estimated that 1 in 4 pregnancies ends in miscarriage or stillbirth. When I lost my son, I thought I was alone. But if this is your story too, please hear me when I say: you are not alone.

Your loss wasn't "meant to be." It wasn't divine will or part of some bigger plan. It was unfair. It was heartbreaking. And whatever you're feeling—grief, numbness, guilt, anger, confusion, and even relief—is valid.

More than anything, I want you to know you don't have to carry this by yourself.

Here are a few places where you can find support:

- www.pregnancyloss.org
- www.emptyarmsbereavement.org
- postpartum.net/get-help/loss-grief-in-pregnancy-postpartum
- www.marchofdimes.org/find-support/topics/miscarriage-loss-and-grief
- www.rachelsgift.org/infant-loss-support-groups

Thank You

You could say the *Lahoma Springs* series is my love letter to my hometown of Petaluma … and you'd be absolutely right.

So much of Petaluma made its way into these pages—and it will continue to appear in the books to come. From the architecture and the quirky co-op shops to the sense of camaraderie between neighboring businesses, the spirit of my town is everywhere in *The Jilted Lovers Club*.

Charred, The Till, Hotel Lahoma, Lock & Key—they're all inspired by real places I know and love, even if their names have changed in the telling. Writing this story felt like walking the familiar streets of home with a fresh pair of eyes.

So my first thank-you goes to Petaluma—for letting me borrow your small-town charm and sprinkle it through the pages of this story. I can't wait to continue your story in the rest of the books in this series.

Another little love note goes to Charlotte Brontë, whose *Jane Eyre* remains one of my favorite novels. Her iconic line— "Reader, I married him"—felt like the perfect way to end this story, a nod to strong women, enduring love, and the kind of bold declarations that give me chills.

The Jilted Lovers Club wouldn't be possible without the love and support of a few very special people.

To my first readers—my dear friend Helga Breyfogle, my daughter Summer McLerran, and my husband Shawn Langwell—thank you for reading the early, clumsy drafts of this story and helping me smooth out the rough edges. Your feedback and encouragement mean the world to me.

To my favorite editor in the whole world, Sarah Villanueva—what book number is this??? I feel so lucky to have you in my corner. It's wild to think we met in the Tarryn Fisher PLN group, and all these years later, we're still creating magic together. I'm forever grateful for your brilliance and the heart you pour into every single one of my books.

To the amazing crew at The Author Agency, especially Shauna and Becca—your guidance and support with promotion have transformed my author career. I truly can't thank you enough.

To every reader who's picked up my book and loved it, shared it with a friend, left a review, or reached out to say it meant something to them—thank you. I may not be a household name, but I write with everything I've got. Your support keeps me going, especially when the journey gets hard. I'll never stop being grateful that you took a chance on me and my stories.

To my grown-up kids—Summer, Lucas, and Andrew—watching you become the incredible adults you are is one of the greatest joys of my life. I love every moment I get to spend with you as you build lives of your own. I'm so proud of you, always.

And finally, to my husband, Shawn—words will never be enough. You've shown me what real romance looks like, and what it feels like to be truly cherished. Thank you for loving me so well. I love you bigger than the sky.

Books by Crissi Langwell

ROMANCE

The Jilted Lovers Club ~ Lahoma Springs 1

The Lost Lovers Club ~ Lahoma Springs 2 *(Coming in 2026)*

Masquerade Mistake ~ Sunset Bay 1

Naked Coffee Guy ~ Sunset Bay 2

Savior Complex ~ Sunset Bay 3

For the Birds

Numbered

OTHER BOOKS BY CRISSI LANGWELL

Loving the Wind: The Story of Tiger Lily & Peter Pan

The Road to Hope ~ Hope Series 1

Hope at the Crossroads ~ Hope Series 2

Hope for the Broken Girl ~ Hope Series 3

A Symphony of Cicadas ~ Forever After 1

Forever Thirteen ~ Forever After 2

www.crissilangwell.com

Sign up for Crissi Langwell's romance newsletter:
crissilangwell.com/subscribe

About the Author

Crissi Langwell is a romance author who writes heartfelt stories filled with humor, emotion, and a heavy dose of angst. She has been publishing books for over a decade, including her steamy *Sunset Bay* romance series, and now her *Lahoma Springs* series. She has a heart for the struggling writer, and shares "Love Letters to Writers" at crissi.substack.com.

When she's not writing, Crissi stays busy as president of Redwood Writers, her local branch of the California Writers Club. She lives in Northern California with her writerly husband Shawn, Maine Coon cat Cleo, and a chair of laundry she swears she'll fold any day now.

Find her at crissilangwell.com.